SHADOWMAKER

SHADOWMAKER

Roy Lewis

Constable • London

Constable & Robinson Ltd
3 The Lanchesters
162 Fulham Palace Road
London W6 9ER
www.constablerobinson.com

First published in the UK by Constable,
an imprint of Constable & Robinson, 2009

A copy of the British Library Cataloguing in Publication
Data is available from the British Library

ISBN: 978-1-84901-007-8

Printed and bound in the EU

PEFC
PEFC/16-33-111
CATG-PEFC-052
www.pefc.org

Prologue

1968

She emerged into the harsh sunlight, hesitated at the exit door of the Concorde and looked about her, a tall, long-legged, deep-bosomed young woman with a wide red mouth, a confident air and a stunning, voluptuous figure, displayed to advantage in a cream-coloured, close-fitting sheath dress. As she stood there, casually, she slipped on a pair of dark sunglasses, tossing back her long blonde hair. She remained at the exit door for several seconds, posing elegantly, provocatively. Only when she caught sight of the black Mercedes with the smoked windows moving almost silently towards her across the airstrip did she begin to move slowly down the steps to the hot tarmac.

The Mercedes purred to a stop at the foot of the steps. The slim, elegantly suited man who emerged from the back seat of the car moved forward to greet her. He looked at her with open approval. When she reached the foot of the steps and hesitated he stood before her; he inclined his head in a slight bow. His voice was strong, his tone confident.

'Miss Christine? My name is Mohamed Mehti. I trust your journey from Paris was a pleasant one. I am here to welcome you. I am employed in the Ministry of the Court. A room at the hotel awaits you.'

He stepped to one side and made an extravagant, sweeping gesture towards the back seat of the Mercedes. Christine paused, looked him over. He was perhaps thirty

1

years of age, six feet in height, swarthy of feature; his dark, curly hair was swept back, carefully groomed. He wore reflective-lensed sunglasses, and was dressed in an immaculately cut light grey suit. His expensive shoes were highly polished; the lean hand that was extended to her was carefully manicured, heavily ringed. The expensive gold watch flashed in the sunlight. There was a certain arrogance in his thin-lipped smile: he was handsome, and he knew it. He was impressed by her, and he clearly expected her to be equally admiring of his appearance. Coolly, she ignored the extended hand and stepped past him, slipped into the back seat of the car. The uniformed chauffeur glanced at her in the mirror as she took her seat, caught her eye, and immediately looked away. He knew his place.

She suspected Mohamed Mehti did not, as he opened the other door to the back seat and made to slide in beside her. She placed one hand on the cool leather, raised her other in an admonitory gesture. She had been well instructed by Madame Arlene herself and she knew the warning signs. 'I think it would be better if you travelled in the front seat, beside the driver. It has been a long journey, and I am tired.'

He hesitated, then smiled. His teeth were very even and white. He nodded, inclining his handsome head in a knowing acquiescence, and without a word closed the door with a firm click. He joined the chauffeur in the front seat. Nothing further was said as they travelled swiftly along the highway from the airport to the city.

They did not check in at the hotel but swept through the lobby, Mehti leading the way past the desk clerks, and they ascended in the lift to the top floor, where he showed her to her penthouse suite. At the entrance to the suite he bowed slightly, smiling. 'I am responsible for your security. If there is anything you require, anything at all, you need only ask. I will be staying in the suite next door. A simple call . . .'

He removed his sunglasses, held her glance; there was a

clear appraisal in his dark eyes, linked with open admiration and an unspoken challenge.

When he left her, after taking her hand, holding it just a little too long in a farewell handshake, she wandered around the suite, enjoying its luxurious furnishings, the magnificent bathroom and the stunning view of the city from the large windows. She poured herself a gin and tonic from the elegant glass-fronted drinks cabinet, then rang room service and ordered a meal to be sent to her room in two hours' time. She sat down on the deep, plush settee and drank her gin slowly, relaxing. When it was finished she rose, and stripped off slowly, in front of the full-length mirror. She watched herself as she did so, acting as though the man who had arranged her visit was already there in front of her, teasing him, running soft hands over the smooth swell of her breasts and belly, the long soft skin of her inner thighs. She shook loose her long blonde hair, extended her arms, practised her smile . . .

When she was in the shower, feeling the cool water caress her glowing skin, her thoughts slipped to the man who had met her at the airport. Mohamed Mehti. He would take careful handling: she knew men, and she knew he could cause trouble. She had read the admiration in his eyes, but she had been warned by Madame Arlene: the man she would be meeting would want her untouched by hands of his own countrymen. The hotel staff at the Hilton would all be aware of exactly why she was there. Eyes would be watching; gossip would be rife; if she allowed herself to be seduced, the hotel staff would know about it, a report would be made and she would be out on the next plane . . .

She emerged from the cool shower and after she had dried herself she slipped into a silk gown that had been placed ready for her on the smooth sheets of the bed. She poured herself another gin and tonic. The sun was low in the sky, casting a golden glow over the city, outlining the tall modern buildings towering their affluent way to the sky, screening the noisy, crowded streets where poverty lurked and resentment grew. She became aware of the distant voice of the muezzin, calling the faithful to prayer.

There was a discreet tap on the door. Assuming it was room service, Christine walked barefooted across the deep pile carpet and opened the door. It was Mohamed Mehti. He stood there, a confident smile on his full lips. His glance travelled over her, dwelling on the curve of her breasts under the silk gown. 'Miss Christine . . . I trust everything is arranged to your satisfaction.'

'It is.'

He arched a confident eyebrow. 'I thought you might wish to have some company on your first evening.'

One hand on the door, he allowed his glance to slide again over her body under the thin fabric of the silk gown. Christine looked him up and down with a studied insolence. 'I am happy to be alone,' she said slowly.

He was not easily dissuaded. He put a hand on her arm, caressing the silk of the sleeve lightly with slim, predatory fingers. His fingers slipped upwards to the soft base of her neck. 'Such beauty should not remain without admiration, even for an hour,' he said, and stepped forward.

She put a firm hand on his chest. He stood still, raising his eyebrows in question. 'Madame Arlene –' he began.

'Madame Arlene has made the position very clear to me,' she interrupted coldly. 'Now, if you will excuse me, I wish to remain alone.'

'But you should eat,' he suggested in protest.

'Alone in my own room,' she replied.

He smiled, mockingly. 'It could be a long wait.'

She knew he was not referring to the room service. He stepped back reluctantly as she closed the door firmly in his face.

But he was right. It was a long, boring wait. She could make no complaint about her surroundings: they were luxurious in the extreme. The clothing that had been supplied to her was expensive; the Paris high couturiers had been instructed to make available all the most appropriate wardrobe for the occasion. The food sent to her room during the next few days was prepared by the best chefs in the hotel. The service was impeccable: discreet, polite, self-effacing. But she could not leave the confines of her room.

And there was Mehti, constantly hovering.

He was certainly insistent. Each time she refused him it was as though she became even more desirable to him, and he was clearly enamoured of her. But Madame Arlene ran the most prestigious and exclusive call-girl business in Paris, and she had warned that a false step from Christine now could cause problems, not only for Christine and her well-paid activity, but for the reputation of the cat house itself.

It was not that she was not tempted. As the long days passed, and she sat in her room watching television, listening to music, eating and drinking as she willed, Mehti tapped on her door, or rang her at least four times each day. His persistence in other circumstances might have paid off, for she found him attractive, she was alone, and she had the feeling that his lust for her was growing with each refusal. But she held out: the fort was not to be stormed.

There were few books available, but there was a selection of expensive magazines. There was also an island brochure: she read that the hotel was located on a low, sandy spit overlooking the Strait of Hormuz, south-east of the Persian Gulf. The brochure told of the island's history: formerly it had been a pirate base for men living off the vast fortunes of gold and pearls looted off passing ships, but it had been transformed after the British fleet had cleared the seas of piracy in the 1850s. Later, when the pearling industry collapsed, the island had fallen into a slow decline, somnolent under the hot sun. Until, finally, the Pahlavi family had decided to develop it. A palace was built on the beach; royal family members, courtiers, even horses were shuttled in for weekends. Inevitably, the building of the palace was followed by other mansions as the island became a winter playground for the rich, European jet-setters and Arab gamblers. Serviced by women like herself.

On the fifth day Mehti came as usual to her door but when she opened it to him his attitude seemed to have changed: his sharp-suited bearing was stiff, his speech formal. There was no smile in his eyes. 'Miss Christine, you are to get ready. We leave in two hours.'

She did not keep him waiting. When they came out of the cool, air-conditioned hotel lobby into the glare of the hot sunshine the black, smoky-windowed Mercedes was waiting at the steps. They drove out of the immaculately manicured grounds, past the sprawling cluster of hotels, the casino and the golf courses to the north of the island, and the remote area where further building development had been forbidden. Almost an hour later, she caught sight of the palace, gleaming against the startling blue background of the sea and the gold of the sparkling sands. The Mercedes swept past the blinding white walls and sharply gabled blue roofs and through the Moorish-style gateway, flanked by armed guards in green uniform. Mehti remained silent, stiffly punctilious in the front seat as they turned into the grassed garden area, bright in the sunlight. Around them high white walls gleamed in the sun: the car crunched over a gravelled drive leading to the west side of the palace where cool fountains played in the courtyard. Mehti handed Christine from the car, as the chauffeur stared straight ahead; Mehti led the way to the steps of shining marble.

The reception hall beyond was vast, cool and opulent. Mehti hung back as Christine was welcomed by a plump, bald-headed flunkey, somewhat overdressed with a profusion of gold braid on his blue uniform. He bowed, portentously introduced himself as the Grand Chamberlain, then with a sweeping gesture of the hand led her past several guards: dark-suited, grim-visaged, burly, with blank, uniform sunglasses, they stood near the doors, hands clasped in front of them, motionless, impassive, but watchful. The Grand Chamberlain showed her into a wide room with wall-to-ceiling windows, at one side looking out over a cool-fountained inner courtyard, at the other open to the beach, granting long views over the sparkling blue of the

6

sea. A table ran the length of the room, laden with exotic foods. At its centre stood a bottle of Chivas Regal and two cut-glass tumblers. The Chamberlain withdrew and she was left alone.

She waited there for several hours. She stared at the views, wandered through the various rooms leading off to the right: the first was an opulently furnished bedroom with a glass wall overlooking the swimming pool; there were five other rooms, equally furnished with style and expensive taste. She explored the rooms, running her hands over silken drapes, polished tables, marble-tiled walls. She inhaled the varied fragrances of each of the five luxurious bathrooms, all with adjoining dressing rooms. In one she found a wardrobe where brand-new dresses hung; she noted they were all in her size. The adjoining room held a magnificently draped king-sized bed, hung with damask, satin-sheeted; the carpet was white, deep, sensuous to the touch. On the walls were hung paintings: Picasso, Miro, Dali. She smiled to herself: Madame Arlene had warned her of what to expect but she had not been able to explain just how opulent, how lavish Christine's new surroundings were to be . . . if only for a few days.

She returned to the main room; she picked at the exotic dishes laid out for her delectation; she drank several glasses of Chivas Regal. The time dragged past as she played a little music. Bored, she switched off the hi-fi and took some more whisky, stood leaning in the window, stared out at the shining sea as the sun glinted lower in the sky.

She was more than a little light-headed when the doors finally opened and her client entered the room. He stood there for a few moments, silently staring at her, tall, lean, tautly nervous, dark-eyed, immaculately suited.

From the wardrobe in the bedroom she had chosen a figure-hugging, backless black dress, with a low cleavage. Her long blonde hair hung loosely about her tanned shoulders. She had decided against the use of any of the luxurious silken underwear that had been provided: underneath the gown she was naked. Madame Arlene had

7

advised her she would be expected to curtsey and had indeed given her some training in the art, not least to allow her to offer full advantage of her cleavage to the man who had enlisted her services. Now, she spread her bare, slim arms, sank to a curtsey, then wobbled a little as the Chivas Regal inevitably took its effect. Suddenly staggering, she pitched sideways, catastrophically, falling to the thick carpet and rolling over.

She placed her hands on the carpet and knelt there, looking up at the hawk-faced, handsome, now broadly smiling man gazing down upon her.

'*Merde, merde, oh merde,*' she muttered.

He laughed, came forward, extended his hand. 'It is of no consequence,' he said in perfect English. Then, in French, '*N'importe pas.*'

He raised her to her feet: his hands were lean, strong, immaculately manicured. She stared at him for several seconds, holding his amused glance, then she recovered herself, turned away, poured him a glass of Chivas Regal, as Madame Arlene had instructed. He accepted it gravely and saluted her with the glass, before walking around her, staring at her voluptuous curves, the swell of her breasts, the redness of her wide mouth. Satisfaction glowed in his dark, deep-set eyes.

'Perhaps we should dance,' he suggested, after sipping at his drink.

He walked across to the hi-fi against the far wall, turned it on, set down his glass and extended an imperious hand. She put down her glass and moved into his arms, a little drunkenly. They danced, a slow, sensuous tango. 'Jealousy'. He held her close, as the music surged around them, and her body moulded into his as they followed the steps together. He was a good dancer, and she responded sinuously to his movements, her thighs riding against his when they came close, her eyes never leaving his intense features.

The dance stirred her. She became aware of the movement of his body, she felt secret fluids flowing in her and her eyes widened. She broke away from him, went back to her Chivas Regal, drained the glass. She faced him squarely as he stood watching her in silence, and then she heard him laugh loudly as she extended a hand and said not what Madame Arlene had taught her to say, but what she suddenly felt to be more appropriate for the moment.

'*Allons-y.*'

He allowed himself to be led to the bedroom. She closed the door behind her, looked at him provocatively over her left shoulder. She smiled, slowly, and unzipped her dress. It fell to the floor and she stood facing him, chin held high, proudly, completely naked. She stared at him silently, as his glance swept over the swell of her breasts, her flat stomach, the long smooth curve of her thighs. His glance lingered on her body and after a short silence broken only by his harsh, quickening breathing she smiled again, extended her arms wide, lifting her breasts, throwing back her head to expose the graceful line of her throat. She gestured towards the bed.

'*Alors, baisons!*'

She heard later that since her client had spent two hours longer with her than had been intended, there had been an angry family scene on his return to the larger palace at the north beach of the island of Kish. But he came to Christine again that weekend, and indeed was so pleased that he insisted that she extended her stay. Christine had no objection. As she explained in her telephone call to Madame Arlene: 'I find him to be a nice, kind, gentle man, with immense dignity. And his passion seems real. There is also something almost child-like in the way he likes to play games, like catch as catch can in the bedroom – before we end up in the sack. And I make him laugh a lot. Northern humour, I suppose ... Yet he seems a very sad man, somehow.'

She stayed at the Hilton for three months. Twice each week she was conveyed to the villa in Kish. They followed a pattern: they danced, they made love, they talked long about politics and monarchy and the needs of the people, the land reforms he was instituting. But back at the hotel she felt caged – and under a constant pressure. Mohamed

Mehti resumed his persistent attempts to seduce her. He tapped on her bedroom door late at night; he rang her in the early hours, as dawn brightened the sky. He whispered to her, his voice low and suggestive; there were words of love, sexual innuendo, promises of devotion. In the long, claustrophobic days she was severely tempted, but she held out doggedly, in spite of his persuasive words, and his own attractive appearance.

She was now allowed to go down to the hotel pool occasionally, with a uniformed guard in close attendance. The only man who was permitted to visit her at her suite was Mohamed Mehti, the man from the Ministry. He continued in his attempts to sleep with her, asking her to dine with him in his suite, once appearing at her door straight from the shower, his dark skin glistening damply, black hair curling, his dressing gown gaping open, his desire obvious. 'No one will know,' he insisted, pleading. 'I promise you, no one will know!'

And when she visited the pool there were other propositions from American businessmen in the hotel: some offered her thousands of dollars. And as she heard rumours in the city, talk of rebellion, distant clamour, she reflected upon her client's real needs. There were times at the island palace when he did not seem to want sex: he would talk to her, telling her of his problems, his philosophy, his political desires for his country. She came to realize that she provided him with a release from the strains of government and the obsequious servility that he himself demanded from his courtiers. He wanted sex, certainly, but he also desired relaxation and companionship.

And then, one day, abruptly, it was over.

Mohamed Mehti tapped on her door. He stood there, staring at her seriously, for once making no attempt to enter. 'You must make yourself ready,' he said quietly. 'Your plane will be leaving in two hours.'

She stared at him, uncomprehending. 'What's happened?'

Mehti hesitated, then shrugged. 'His Highness has left the country.'

'I don't understand. Where has he gone?'

Mehti frowned slightly, as though the question was an irrelevance. 'It is of no consequence. Your time with him is over. But if you desire to know ... he has gone to Contadora.'

She had no idea where the place might be. But there was no point asking. She had never been under any illusions about her situation. She turned away, to concentrate on getting her things together.

Mohamed Mehti watched her, on this occasion making no attempt to leave the room.

'You will never see him, again. Will that be important to you?' he asked quietly.

She shook her head, long blonde hair falling over her eyes. 'No. It was simply a business arrangement.'

There was a short silence. Then in a muffled, sober tone he said, 'Mine will not be a matter merely of business.'

She turned away from her packing to stare at him. She realized he was serious. 'What are you saying?' she asked.

'You will never again see the King of Kings, but you will see me again. I am owed some two million US dollars ... for certain services. I shall be going to Contadora. I will be paid ... one way or another. And then, when my affairs are settled, I shall seek to join you.'

Her tongue flicked over her full, red lips, and she frowned in puzzlement. 'I'm going back to Paris. To Madame Arlene. I cannot afford simply to sit around and wait for you to —'

'You will no longer need Madame Arlene.' He extended his hand. He opened his palm, and she saw nestling there an enormous jewel. 'I want you to take this. As an earnest of good faith, and to persuade you that I will come to you. Sell this, and you will be wealthy. And when I come to you we will have all the riches we might ever desire ... '

She flew out of Tehran two hours later, the jewel with her. She never worked for Madame Arlene again.

And within the year Mohamed Mehti came to claim what he had bought.

11

Chapter One

1

Karen Stannard had made a few changes to the office of the Chief Executive, of course. The previous austere appearance of the room had been softened: there were new curtains at the windows, a carpet in a lighter shade had been laid, and the heavy, scarred desk that Powell-Frinton had used for the duration of his lengthy service had been replaced by a sleeker model, curved, highly polished with an inlaid leather surface. The room had been redecorated also: the walls had been repainted in a light cream, there were some modernist prints on display in place of the sombre Turner copies Powell-Frinton had favoured, and the lighting units had been replaced in the ceiling. The result was a combination of efficiency and femininity. Karen Stannard had clearly wanted to make a break with the past, and highlight her intentions. Powell-Frinton had never countenanced flowers on the side table. Karen noticed the frown on Arnold Landon's face as he glanced at them, and she smiled.

'A woman's touch. Sit down, Arnold. Here, beside me. I think we can keep this interview fairly informal. It's why I'm holding it here in my office, rather than the interview room.'

She was wearing a cream shirt under a dark formal business jacket; her skirt was fashionably short and when she seated herself in one of the three armchairs ranged in the corner of the room, away from her desk, her long legs, stretched out in front of her, were appropriately displayed.

Arnold sat down beside her: he glanced at her legs, instinctively. She would expect it, of course: she had never been slow in taking full advantage of her appearance.

'This shouldn't take long,' she advised Arnold cheerfully, glancing at her watch. 'I've already told my secretary to send in the candidate, as soon as he's finished his coffee.' She smiled winningly at Arnold, confident, happy, in control. He made no reply, and stared at the papers he held in his hands, the curriculum vitae of the man they were awaiting. They sat there silently for a little while, each keeping their own counsel on the way in which things had turned out.

A few minutes later, the candidate entered the room.

He was about six feet in height, forty years of age according to the papers he had submitted, which also declared he was of American-German origin. His features were hawkish; dark eyebrows seemed to be clenched in an habitual frown of concentration, and his dark, thinning hair was swept back, closely trimmed to the ears, greying at the temples. He wore a charcoal pinstriped suit, formal tie, white shirt; his gaze was penetrating: he looked them over as though it was he who was running the interview. His air of confidence was slightly irritating to Arnold; the man puzzled him in some indefinable way. His emotional hackles, already irritated by recent events, were rising, but Karen's attitude seemed to be at variance with his own. She extended a hand, waved the candidate to a seat. She glanced down at her notes, looked up and smiled. 'Mr Karl Spedding.'

'That's right.' His tone was cool; his tone well modulated; his English was precise with a slight American accent and his voice carried a deep impressive timbre.

'We've now had the opportunity to interview the other candidates for the post vacated by Miss Portia Tyrell,' Karen continued. 'Before we make a final choice, I thought it would be appropriate for you to meet Mr Landon. The successful candidate will report to Mr Landon in his capacity as Acting Head of the Department of Museums and Antiquities.'

Spedding turned his glance towards Arnold: there was a hint of calculation in his eyes. 'It would seem there have been several changes in the department lately,' he murmured.

Too many, from Arnold's point of view. Somehow, the events of recent months had led to significant changes that could not have been foreseen: Portia's betrayal by the Chinese-American man she had fallen in love with, so disastrously, had caused her to lose confidence in herself, determine her to make a new beginning professionally; Karen Stannard's own experience in the wake of the Dragon Head affair had left her equally unsettled. Karen herself had talked of leaving the service entirely, perhaps seeking a research post at the University of York, until conversations with their political masters had persuaded her that she should attempt to succeed to Powell-Frinton's position as Chief Executive, when it was announced that he would not be returning to his office. So it was Portia Tyrell who had gone to York, and Karen who had remained.

Arnold had gone to see Powell-Frinton at his home, in the last days before the cancer that was eating away at his bowels had finally taken his life. As he lay there in his bed, Powell-Frinton had stared at Arnold, eyes deep-set in the gauntness of his wasted features, as though weighing him up. His voice was weak, the rustle of dry leaves in the room. 'I believe Miss Stannard will be applying for the post I am vacating, Arnold.'

'I'm not certain, but it would seem so,' Arnold had replied uncomfortably. He had never been close to Powell-Frinton: the Chief Executive had retained throughout his long tenure a lawyer's remoteness, maintaining a formal distance between himself and the other senior officers in the authority. Now, it seemed odd that Powell-Frinton should wish to discuss the future of the position he had held for so many years.

'I think she'll want the job,' Powell-Frinton asserted wearily. 'I think also she has the qualities to make a good Chief Executive. Certainly, most of the councillors think so.'

Particularly the ones who were aware of her physical attractions, Arnold thought to himself. As though the suggestion was communicated to the dying Chief Executive, Powell-Frinton permitted a ghost of a smile to touch his lips. Oddly enough, Arnold could not recall ever seeing Powell-Frinton smile before. A controlled, private man who nevertheless had seemed to betray a certain liking for Arnold, over the years, he had nevertheless never seemed to express pleasure in his work. But there had been occasions when he had overruled the head of department, protecting Arnold from decisions that were dictated by malice, or jealousy.

'If she does become Chief Executive,' Powell-Frinton asked, coughing slightly, 'what will you do?'

'About what?' Arnold asked, guardedly.

'The vacancy she will leave as Head of the Department of Museums and Antiquities.'

Arnold sighed. 'I've never wanted the post.'

Powell-Frinton had nodded weakly; Arnold thought he detected a light chuckle deep in the man's throat. The retired Chief Executive shifted slightly in his bed, and a spasm of pain crossed his wasted features. 'Yes, I've been well aware of your reluctance to take the position. I've never quite understood it. It's not that you're afraid of responsibility, I'm sure . . .'

It was difficult to explain. Powell-Frinton was right: it was not the thought of added responsibility. In some ways the opportunity to put his own stamp upon the department was an attractive one; it would have enabled him to reorganize priorities, change the focus of direction towards what he considered more worthwhile projects. But on the downside there was the prospect of interminable meetings with local councillors, with committee involvement looming larger in his life, and the consequent lowering of activity in the field. And it was that loss of fieldwork which basically had deterred Arnold in the past. It was the passion that his father had endowed in him, all those years

15

ago when they had walked the Yorkshire moors, a delight in the past, an excitement at the discovery of the remains of ancient human activities. It was what he enjoyed, what he was good at. It was the open-air life on the fells and the sea-coast; it was the opportunity to feel the closeness of other, long-dead lives; the chance to experience an unmatched adrenalin rush that had brought him wonder and amazement, the richness of discovery, such as his unearthing of the *Kvernbiter* Viking sword, and the mythical *sudarium* of Christ. Chances such as those would be fewer, possibly non-existent, if he were to become Head of the Department of Museums and Antiquities. It was for these reasons that he had persuaded himself on two previous occasions that he did not want the job.

When he left Powell-Frinton's side that last time he was still of the same opinion. In spite of the former Chief Executive's warning.

Powell-Frinton had fixed him with clear eyes. 'You've now worked for two heads: the first was an incompetent fool, the second a woman with a forceful personality with whom you often failed to see eye to eye. Do you want to take the chance of once more finding yourself being led down roads you do not wish to travel?'

It was a consideration Arnold had not really taken into account. It was surprising to him that Powell-Frinton had taken the trouble to make the observation, demonstrating concern for Arnold's future. It led him to realize that he had long underestimated Powell-Frinton's warmer, if carefully concealed, human qualities.

But in the event, there was little Arnold could do about it: he was not really master of his fate.

It was the Leader of the Council who approached him. Councillor Raby was a self-important political wheeler-dealer who had made a fortune in scrap-dealing and now had the opportunity to indulge his power fantasies in local political circles. He had obtruded his paunch into Arnold's office, sat down without invitation, breathed a gusty sigh as he glanced around him with a proprietorial air as though surveying a kingdom of his personal making, and announced, 'We've decided to go ahead with the appointment of Karen Stannard to succeed Powell-Frinton. Without advertisement: no need to trawl for a better candidate. She'll suit us to a T. Besides, if we weren't to offer her the post, I've no doubt she'd be off like a shot.' He had leered at Arnold, confidentially, man to man. 'And why would we want to lose such glamour in this drab political world of ours? She can do us a lot of good, outside this authority.' His lips were fleshy, glistening. He winked suddenly, disconcertingly. 'And her promotion means a vacancy in this department. Room for a good man.'

Arnold had kept his counsel. Councillor Raby had grimaced, a little put out that Arnold had not seized eagerly at the hint. 'Miss Stannard will be starting as Chief Executive immediately.'

Silence reigned between them. Councillor Raby humphed. He scowled, annoyed that the dangling carrot had not been snapped at. He rose grumpily from the seat he had taken only minutes earlier. 'I'll leave it to Miss Stannard to discuss the matter with you.'

She had not merely discussed it with Arnold. She had come close to raging at him on account of his diffident attitude.

'Don't you see what an opportunity this is? It's not just the promotion; it's the chance to do things the way you want to do them. Come on, Arnold, I'm well aware you've had views about my way of doing things, we've had our disagreements, but I've never had any doubts as to your ability!'

He could have pointed to various moments when she had vociferously displayed such doubts but he held the comment back, rather than enter into an unproductive argument. 'I'm simply not interested in the job,' he had replied calmly.

The storm had then broken about his head. He had always recognized her beauty. In a rage that beauty was amazingly enhanced: she was all fire, her green eyes seemed to flash scorn, the lines of her body seemed to become even more provocative, and the passion in her

17

voice brought back brief recollections of the past, the single evening when there had been passion of a different kind between them, in a darkened hotel room in Morpeth. He was shaken by it, disoriented.

'How can I get through to you on this?' she demanded challengingly. 'This isn't just about you, and what *you* want. We have a number of important projects running, and I've been asked to take over as Chief Executive with immediate effect. I can't keep two jobs going, not least now that Portia has handed in her notice and is taking up a research post at York! The department needs someone at the helm, and it can't be me. If we went for someone from the outside there could be months of upheaval. There's no one else with the experience, the acumen, the common sense, the ability, the drive to do the job, not inside the department!'

'I didn't realize you held me in such high regard,' Arnold had muttered sarcastically.

'There's no one else to do the job,' she hissed, 'until we can get around in due course to advertise nationally and find someone suitable! I repeat, Arnold: this is not about what *you* want out of life. This is a matter of duty!'

She had folded her arms across her splendid, heaving bosom. She glared at him. 'I've been informed by the Council that I can take whatever steps I deem necessary to organize the department. As far as I'm concerned, there is only one way forward. You have to take over, Arnold. And you *will.'*

She had been right: there was no other choice he could make, if he was to remain loyal to himself and the department. He had invested too much time and effort and commitment to the work over the years to act otherwise. So eventually, reluctantly, he had agreed to her demands.

But, as he should have guessed, there was a sting in the tail, nevertheless.

Sweetly, she had added after his capitulation, 'So I'll inform the Council that you've agreed to take over as Acting Head of Museums and Antiquities. We'll not rush to make a formal appointment, or advertise nationally just yet. And of course, there are a few things I'll still need to retain an involvement with: we'll sort of be in harness on some of the projects. Working together, as it were. Unfinished business, that sort of thing.'

The celebratory whisky she had offered him from the Chief Executive's drinks cabinet had not mollified him as the implications of her comment sank in. Acting head he would be; but she would still be looking over his shoulder, would still have a guiding hand on the rudder.

Not least in the appointment of a successor to Portia Tyrell, who would undertake her duties and those relinquished by Arnold himself.

'So, Mr Spedding,' Karen was purring, almost to herself, 'according to your curriculum vitae you were employed for five years as an assistant curator at the Pradak Museum in Rome. Your MA –'

'London University.'

'And your Ph.D.?'

'University of Prague. My thesis was on classical archaeology. I also have a doctorate awarded by Pennsylvania University.'

In the brief pause that followed, Arnold cleared his throat. 'According to your CV you were also a Fulbright Scholar in Rome.'

Spedding glanced almost casually in his direction. 'That is correct.'

Arnold thought he detected a slight query in the man's tone, as though he was questioning Arnold's role in the interview.

'I note you also have interesting fieldwork experience,' Karen continued. 'You've taken part in archaeological digs at Mesa Verde, Colorado, Gordion . . . You've also worked in Turkey and at five sites in Iran.'

'Widely travelled,' Arnold commented drily.

Karen shot him a warning glance. She turned back to Spedding. 'I've actually read two of the articles you've written, and you've produced two books also, I understand.'

'Two books, eighteen articles,' Spedding observed easily.

Karen glanced at Arnold triumphantly, as though she had played a personal role in Spedding's academic and professional history. 'Well, Mr Spedding, the position is that we've received a number of applications, have interviewed other candidates, but it is perfectly clear that you are well ahead of the field. I'm in a position to offer you the post on the terms and conditions already communicated to you, and all I need to ask is that if you were offered the post, would you be prepared to accept it?'

Spedding opened his mouth but irritably Arnold cut in before he could speak.

'Before we proceed further, might I just ask a few questions, Miss Stannard?'

She froze for a moment, then turned her head to look at him, a falsely obliging smile lighting up her beautiful features. 'But of course, Mr Landon. Forgive me. You are *acting* head of department, after all.'

Arnold ignored the subtle jibe. He leaned forward, one elbow on his knee. He fixed Spedding with a cool gaze. 'I'm puzzled, Mr Spedding.'

'Why would that be, Mr Landon?'

'To come and join us here, you would be leaving a lucrative and certainly more high profile post at the Pradak Museum.'

'That is so.' Spedding's tone was careless.

'Perhaps you could tell us the reason for your wishing to make such a move?'

'I needed a change.'

There was a short silence. Arnold grimaced. 'That doesn't tell us much about your motivation, Mr Spedding. Were there any . . . difficulties with your previous employers?'

Stiffly, Spedding replied, 'You have seen my references.'

'Glowing,' Karen intervened in a warning tone. Arnold gained the impression she did not wish to lose this particular fish and was annoyed by his questions. Nevertheless, he persisted.

'References are sometimes given in order to get rid of someone who is proving . . . difficult, shall we say?'

Spedding's eyes were icy. 'I think you'll find my record at the Pradak is well documented, and more than satisfactory. If you have any specific doubts you might wish to share –'

'How did you get on with the directors of the museum?'

There was a short pause. Spedding shifted his glance to Karen Stannard. His tone was carefully reflective. 'I have no hesitation in revealing that over the years I had certain disagreements with the directors. They were amicably resolved. But, more recently, I came to the view that it was perhaps best that I should consider a change of direction, a career move, if you like.'

'Why?' Arnold demanded to know. 'What was the basis for these . . . disagreements?'

Karl Spedding remained silent for a few moments but he held Arnold's glance: the frown on his forehead became more pronounced, and there was an element of steel in his tone when he finally replied. 'My advice was ignored, when I made certain recommendations.'

'Such as?'

Spedding grimaced his displeasure at Arnold's tenacity. He raised a supercilious eyebrow. 'I was against certain policies being pursued by the directors.'

'I'm not certain what you mean.'

'Let me simply say that I did not entirely approve of the acquisition policies of the board.'

Arnold had not finished, but Karen had had enough. 'I think that can be put behind us,' she announced in a firm tone. 'We would not wish to enter into any controversial areas, and we're more than happy with your credentials and experience, Mr Spedding. I will repeat the question. Would you be prepared to accept the post on the terms offered?'

'I would be more than happy to accept,' Spedding replied gravely.

Karen rose, and as Spedding rose with her she extended her hand, smiled. 'Then I will make the necessary recommendations to the authority, and we can confirm it all in writing within two days. As you'll appreciate, we would want the appointment to take effect as soon as possible –'

Spedding nodded in agreement, but held up a warning hand. 'I'm happy about that, but I must explain that I have one or two outstanding commitments that I need to honour before I could join the department.'

'Such as?'

'One in particular, at least. I am due to present a paper to the Antiquities Association Conference at the end of the month.'

'In La Rochelle? What an agreeable coincidence,' Karen said, flashing a radiant smile in Arnold's direction. 'We shall have the pleasure of hearing you. Mr Landon and I, we shall also be attending the same conference.'

It was the first Arnold had heard about it.

When Arnold saw the notes in Karen's appointment book his heart dropped. It was as he had feared: there was a long list of meetings scheduled, and his worst anxieties were confirmed: the old days when he had been able to spend time at exploratory excavations at sites in the hills, and on the sea-coast, would now seem to be over. Council meetings; sub-committee meetings; funding groups, press releases and conferences . . . the list seemed endless. And it was already starting with the meeting scheduled for today.

'I'll be coming along with you,' Karen had explained briskly, 'because this is something left over that I need to deal with. The approach was made to me personally so I should in all conscience come along for the first meeting at least.' She smiled at him, arching one elegant eyebrow. 'You might find it entertaining, sitting in on a discussion with three women.'

At least it would get him out of the office, he reasoned irritably. In the meantime, he spent the morning going through Karen's desk diary, scratching out as many of the appointments as he reasonably could, and rearranging the priority of some of the project submissions that she had been intending to make. The meeting he was to attend with her was to take place at Stanhope, in Weardale: somewhat outside their territory, to be sure, but there were probably good reasons for that. Karen had not deigned to explain: she was far too busy dealing with her new role as Chief Executive.

It made her a little late in calling at his office. 'You ready?' she asked. 'Perhaps you wouldn't mind driving.'

'On your expense account?' Arnold queried.

'My, my, Arnold, aren't you aware you're in charge of departmental expense accounts now? And this is the business of the Department of Museums and Antiquities – not the Chief Executive's. I'm coming along to introduce you to the people we're dealing with: I'm just along to ease you in. You should take it as a compliment.'

He knew his mood would improve once they were out of the Morpeth office. They took the A1 south to Newcastle, swung on to the western bypass, followed the sweeping road towards Hexham and Corbridge. It was a warm, cloudy day and the folded hills glowed gold above valleys that were cloaked in the low-lying fog that had gathered since lunchtime. As they left Corbridge, crossed the Tyne and ascended the steep hill past Slaley Hall the mist came down about them and Arnold was forced to slow, turn on his lights and drive with care. Karen shivered.

'Makes you wonder what all those Syrians and Italians and Arab mercenaries made of service in the legions on Hadrian's Wall.'

'Climate would have been better in those days. And at least they weren't stuck in an office.'

'Aw, come on Arnold,' Karen complained, flashing an irritated glance in his direction. 'You'll get used to it. And believe me, the challenges will still be there. Even if they are somewhat different.'

Stray sheep wandered across the road, dimly seen in the mist, forcing Arnold to brake sharply at intervals. On the summit of the fell, to their right the moorland fell away steeply in a deep declivity but the road was fairly straight and soon they were dropping into the steep slope of Crawley Bank. 'Where's this meeting to take place?' Arnold asked.

'In the castle, no less,' Karen replied. 'It's a ground-floor apartment. Mrs Fenchurch. She's an old lady, I understand, and semi-paralysed, but we'll be talking with her grand-daughter and someone you probably know . . . or at least will have heard of.' She glanced at him curiously. 'Isabella Portland.'

Arnold frowned. Then his mind cleared rapidly. He knew of Isabella Portland. Her husband had committed suicide, when faced with the consequences of his criminal activity. He had murdered someone he had assumed was his wife's lover. When the enormity of his error had come home to him, and he had been confronted by the police, he had turned a handgun on himself. 'Portland . . .' he murmured almost to himself.

'You remember the case. Bad business,' Karen said quietly. 'But the widow was left with a considerable amount of money and the collection her dead husband had amassed.'

They were turning into the main street: the castle gate lay across the road from them and Arnold drove carefully through the archway to the gravelled area beyond. The castle was really an eighteenth-century manor house that had been built on the site of a medieval motte and bailey construction. Some years ago, the building had been developed to create a series of individual apartments. Arnold parked, cut the engine, turned to look at Karen. 'So what's this meeting about?'

Karen adjusted the rear mirror and inspected herself, pursing her lips, running an exploratory finger over one eyebrow. 'Isabella Portland rang me, asked to meet me – as Head of the DMA – to undertake some valuations for her, and give her some advice. It seems that she's going into some kind of partnership, setting up a business selling antiques, though why the meeting is to be here rather than the Portland home at Belton Hall I'm not very clear.' She flashed Arnold a swift, mocking smile. 'But I'm sure that now we're here all will be revealed.'

Arnold caught a flash of her long legs as she opened the car door and stepped out on to the gravel. As she gave him a sardonic glance and slammed the door Arnold got out and locked the car. Karen was already making her way towards the entrance to the castle. Standing in the doorway, waiting for them, was a young woman.

She was about twenty-two years of age, Arnold guessed. Perhaps less. She was tall, striking in appearance, her long legs sheathed in casual jeans. Her hair was raven black, her features regular, her nose slightly crooked, her mouth wide, smiling a welcome. The light sweater she wore did not detract from her figure. She was a very attractive young woman, in his view. She was extending a hand to Karen.

'You must be Miss Stannard. I'm Angela Fenchurch.' She glanced past Karen towards Arnold. 'And you will be Mr Landon. I've heard of you.'

'Evil things, I'm sure,' Karen muttered.

'Oh, not at all!' Angela Fenchurch laughed. 'In my archaeological studies some of his activity was commented upon. You're quite famous, you know, Mr Landon.'

'Lucky, actually,' Karen growled, somewhat irritated by the attention being paid to her companion.

'Well, you know what they say in archaeology,' the young woman commented breezily. 'In the field it's luck you need, not qualifications.'

Arnold was not sure he should take that entirely as a compliment, but Angela Fenchurch had turned away, leading them into the castle hallway. 'My grandmother and the others are waiting. It's in here.'

The ground-floor apartment was large: Arnold guessed there would be at least two bedrooms as well as the sitting room which was considerable in size, with a view over the expanse of the front lawns. The room was well furnished, though somewhat spartan, and the furniture was certainly not new but Arnold guessed that little expense had been spared in its original purchase. There were three people in the room.

Angela Fenchurch's grandmother was perhaps eighty years of age. She was seated in a wheelchair: dressed rather severely in black, with a light blanket over her knees, she stared at Arnold with sharp, piercing, intelligent eyes. Her hair was silver, thick, tied back tightly in a bun. Her face was heavily lined now, but there was an air of determination about the way she held her chin high.

Isabella Portland was rising from an easy chair, holding out a hand to Karen. The man standing beside the woman in the wheelchair stepped forward to be introduced. 'This is my grandmother's lawyer,' Angela Fenchurch explained.

'And friend,' he said smoothly. 'James Detorius.'

He was perhaps in his late fifties, squarely built with a ruddy complexion and round features. His eyes were small and restless, shifting glances rapidly around the group even as he was shaking hands with Arnold. He was dressed formally in a dark business suit, white shirt, grey tie, and his handshake was limp, uncommunicative, as though he was unwilling to give anything of himself away. Like all lawyers, Arnold thought, then pulled himself together mentally. It had become a bad habit of his, making snap judgements. He turned towards the old lady and moved forward, extending his hand. Detorius interrupted him dextrously, moving almost to block off his access to her. He raised a hand. 'Mrs Fenchurch welcomes you here to her home.' He lowered his voice slightly. 'Unfortunately, Mrs Fenchurch is unable to communicate verbally, or to move freely, since her latest attacks. I tend to act on her behalf in business transactions . . .' He glanced briefly back towards the old lady, who nodded slightly. 'But my presence here is not really required now. I will take Mrs Fenchurch out to the sunroom – even though there's not much sun at the moment.' He stepped back behind the wheelchair, and began to move it towards the door. 'Miss Stannard, Mr Landon, Mrs Portland, I wish you success in your discussions.'

As the wheelchair was swept past him Arnold caught the glance that the old lady gave him: he was surprised by the intensity of her eyes. She would have been a beautiful woman in her youth, he guessed: high cheekbones, straight, classical nose. He could imagine the imperious manner in which she would have held herself, confident, beautiful, assured. Now she stared at him he gained the impression that she was summing him up. She might be frail, stricken with illness, but she still had her wits about her, he was convinced. She would be no fool. There was something else in that glance that puzzled him. A sparkle. A sense of mischief.

Isabella Portland was walking towards him. She was a beautiful woman; her movements were easy, elegant; her olive skin tones betrayed her Mediterranean origins, Italian he guessed; when she spoke there was a slightly husky, melodious tone to her voice. He caught a slight accent, but her English was perfect. 'Mr Landon. I understand you are now the head of the department at Morpeth. May I offer my congratulations?' She glanced at Karen. 'When I arranged this meeting I had not expected to have the advice of two eminent archaeologists. Angela, perhaps our visitors would care for a coffee?'

It was a subtle way to delineate relationships. Isabella Portland was in the home of Angela Fenchurch's grandmother but she was making it clear just who was to be in control of the meeting. When both Arnold and Karen refused the offer Isabella returned to her chair and smiled at Angela. The young woman sat down in the chair alongside while Arnold and Karen seated themselves side by side on the leather settee.

Angela Fenchurch. She bore the same surname as her grandmother. Arnold wondered about her background . . .

'I am grateful for your coming to Stanhope for this meeting,' Isabella Portland was saying huskily, smiling at Arnold and Karen in turn. 'I decided it would be better here than at Belton Hall in view of the arrangements that I'm making with the assistance of Mr Detorius. To put you briefly into the picture, the situation is this.' She paused, lowered her eyes thoughtfully. 'I have no doubt that you will have been made aware of my recent . . . difficulties. There was enough publicity about it.' She raised her head in defiance. 'My husband's death was traumatic, and for a while I was in considerable despair. But, well, life must go on. My husband was a man involved in numerous business activities, most of them a matter of mystery to me. I knew that he was a collector of antiques, some of which were valuable, and many of which he kept at our home, but I was never really very interested in his collections. Indeed, shortly after his death I sold most of them to a dealer. My husband had left me adequately provided for irrespective of these items, and I started work for charity . . . but I did not find this emotionally rewarding.'

Arnold glanced at Karen. He could not see where this discussion was going. He wondered what earlier discussions had taken place between Isabella Portland and the

28

new Chief Executive. Karen had said in the car the meeting was about valuations . . .

'Then, to my considerable surprise, when the estate of my husband was being wound up I received a visit from his lawyers. It seems that my husband had not only held a collection of antiques at Belton Hall; he had also been *dealing* in antiquities, and more seriously than I would have guessed. The lawyers told me that I now had title to the contents of an apartment in Edinburgh. When I visited it, I discovered to my considerable surprise that the collection housed in Belton Hall, our home, was dwarfed by the other holdings he had obtained over the years. There was a considerable number of artefacts . . .' She shrugged. 'I am no expert; I was never interested; but now I needed advice. So, that is when I met Angela, who was introduced to me as someone who could help me. Angela . . .?'

The young woman seated beside her smiled. 'I had come back to England, looking for a job, after my grandmother fell ill. It was my grandmother's lawyer, Mr Detorius, who introduced me to Isabella. I was raised here in Stanhope by my grandmother, after my mother died. Grandmother looked after me well: she wanted what was best for me, spared no expense, sent me to school in Switzerland and she supported me in my aspirations and interests. I was fascinated by history and particularly interested in archaeology. I spent a great deal of my time in museums, enjoying my reading of the past. When Isabella mentioned her problem to me, I jumped at the chance to work with her. I am unqualified, of course, but it's been my dream to work with things from ancient times . . .'

'Not just work with me, go into business with me,' Isabella Portland corrected her with a smile. 'The fact is, I needed an assistant to help me set up a new business – to give me an objective in life again – and to sell the antiques in my possession now that my husband was dead. But I didn't really know where to start.' She glanced at the door through which the lawyer had wheeled the elderly Mrs Fenchurch. 'Mr Detorius was able to offer basic advice, and undertake the necessary legal formalities in setting up

Portland Holdings Ltd; Angela came on board as a director with knowledge of the world of archaeology; and Angela's grandmother was also able to put in some finance, by way of some items of her own.'

'You seem to be well enough organized,' Arnold intervened. 'I'm not clear where our department comes in.' He was irritated at his words as soon as they emerged: he was still unable to say *my* department. He wondered when he would become properly reconciled to his new position.

Angela glanced at Isabella Portland, who nodded agreement. 'From my reading, I have some understanding and knowledge of Grecian and Italian artefacts, but in Mrs Portland's collection are items that may well be valuable, but which I obviously cannot identify. Also, I'm of the opinion that some of these items of local origin should really be in a local museum. So I had suggested to Isabella that we should seek to take advantage of your expertise, perhaps place some items by way of donations into your museums, and take advice on the value of those items beyond my expertise.'

'Where do you intend opening your sale rooms?' Karen asked.

'Morpeth and Alnwick.'

'And the items are still in Edinburgh?' Arnold asked.

Isabella Portland shook her head. 'No, I've sold the apartment there to help finance the business and transferred the collection to my home at Belton Hall. There are some items held here at the castle, belonging to Mrs Fenchurch, which I shall take today, but meanwhile we can make available to you a number of photographs, which are records of my husband's Edinburgh collection. They were kept with the artefacts themselves. If we can reach agreement with you today, we can let you have these photographs, and you can get back to us in due course.' She nodded to Angela, who rose, left the room and returned a few moments later with a leather-bound photograph album. She placed it on the table, opened it. As she removed some plastic sheets from the album Arnold caught a brief glimpse of what seemed to be family photographs, a woman who may well have been the young Mrs Fenchurch, another of a blonde woman holding a child, a dark-haired, unsmiling man standing behind with one possessive hand on the blonde woman's shoulder.

Angela handed the sheets of plastic holders to Karen, closed the album and hesitated, then left the room briefly to replace it where she had found it. Karen briefly inspected the photographs held within the pockets of the plastic wallets and then passed them over to Arnold before resuming her conversation with Isabella. As she continued to discuss the proposal with Isabella, Arnold inspected the photographs filed inside the plastic covers. He became engrossed; the pictures were fascinating, not least because of the curious variance in background to the artefacts shown. Some seemed to have been taken at moments of discovery, dirt-encrusted, with vague backgrounds of hills and destroyed stone walls; others had been taken in studios, or rooms where he could make out tables, repair and cleaning materials. A few had been duplicated, but with different backgrounds. Suddenly he was jerked back to the present as Karen coughed lightly; he looked up and realized that the three women were staring at him expectantly in silence.

'I'm sorry. I've been caught up . . . This will take time,' he muttered. 'The range of artefacts displayed here . . .'

He did not finish. He did not want to use the word *astonishing*.

When the discussions were concluded, Isabella and Karen went to the sunroom to say goodbye to Angela's grandmother. Clutching the folder that Angela had provided to hold the collection of plastic wallets containing the photographs, Arnold wandered out to the gravelled drive. James Detorius was standing in the doorway, arms folded across his chest. He straightened as Arnold approached, glanced at the folder. 'Business concluded?' he asked cheerily.

'More or less.'

31

'I thought it best not to intrude. Angela, she has a good head on her shoulders.' He leered confidentially at Arnold. 'Lovely girl, too. But your companion, Miss Stannard, she's quite something, isn't she? Stunning, I'd say.'

'She's a colleague,' Arnold muttered.

'I wouldn't mind working closely with her,' Detorius chuckled. He looked Arnold up and down as though considering whether he presented any competition. 'I hear you'll be sending a delegation to La Rochelle next week.'

'That's right.'

'Miss Stannard?'

'She'll be there.'

'That's good. I'll be going myself,' Detorius informed him, smiling his gratification. 'I have some clients to see . . . and there's the work for Mrs Fenchurch.' He stopped abruptly, frowned slightly, as though annoyed with himself for saying too much, then continued, 'Anyway, I look forward to seeing you there. And making the further acquaintance of Miss Stannard also, I hope.'

As though on cue, Karen Stannard emerged on to the steps. Detorius immediately turned to her, smiling obsequiously, clearly attempting to smarm his way into her attention. An ageing Lothario, Arnold concluded: he'd seen plenty of them on the Council, fluttering ineffectively moth-like around the flame of Karen Stannard.

The new Chief Executive could eat men like Detorius for breakfast. Disgusted, Arnold turned away and headed for the car.

During the next few days Arnold managed to further clear his diary of a number of commitments but he also took the first steps in familiarizing himself, and coming to terms, with his new duties. After a while, he was forced to admit to himself that some of the committee work was largely satisfying, not least because he found himself working on the Local Culture Group with councillors who appeared to have a real interest in their northern heritage and to be prepared to strongly support the scheduled activity of the department for which Arnold was now responsible. Additionally, Karen stayed out of his hair: clearly she had enough on her own new plate to have little time to bother him or interfere with his own work schedules.

He did manage to squeeze in one visit to the Roman site his colleagues were working on in the rolling hills near Rothbury: it was a location he knew well, and a drive he enjoyed greatly. He was able to spend an hour or so there, inspecting the shards that the team had unearthed, and poring over the planning papers that the group were preparing, before he took a roundabout route for his return to Morpeth. As a consequence Friday had come around before he found time to check again through the folder containing the photographs that he had received from Angela Fenchurch.

It was clear from his perusal that Gordon Portland, Isabella's deceased husband, had been a somewhat eclectic dealer and collector. The range of artefacts was wide, and Arnold spent some time listing into groups the various items shown in the photographs. He was able to ascertain fairly quickly the less valuable pieces shown: if Isabella Portland was hoping to establish a good business in antique dealing she would hardly be able to rely on much of the collection. Valuation would be fairly easy, he concluded, apart from certain items that made him frown, sit back and consider at some length. Finally, he rang Isabella Portland and suggested they might meet to discuss the matter. She suggested it would perhaps be a good idea if he were to call at her home, on the Sunday afternoon. It suited him: he would be able to breathe the sea-coast air afterwards, in a stroll on the cliff tops at Craster, perhaps visit the dramatic cliff-top location of Dunstanburgh Castle, where the sea pounded the great cleft in the headland, sending booming, crashing sounds upwards to scatter the mewing gulls that inhabited the bare rock.

Early on the Sunday afternoon he left Morpeth and made his way to the house lived in by Isabella Portland.

He was impressed by the location of Belton Hall with its background of the northern hills; he admired the giant portico with its Ionic columns and recognized it as a residence of character. He was equally impressed by the demeanour of the grave-featured, softly spoken butler who greeted him at the imposing entrance. Both man and building gave him the impression of another world, a time-locked period that had doggedly refused to face up to the twenty-first century. The butler led the way across the echoing hallway, lit by the cupola in the roof, past the magnificent curving staircase to the impressively proportioned room designated as the library. Isabella Portland was waiting for him there. She rose to greet him, placing on the long mahogany table the book she had been reading. She extended her hand.

'Mr Landon. I'm grateful you could find time for this call.'

Her voice was attractively husky. She wore an open-necked shirt that emphasized both the graceful line of her throat and the splendour of her bosom. Her hair was in slight disarray, wind-blown perhaps from a walk in the extensive gardens of the Hall; her eyes were luminous, her hand-pressure firm. As she walked away from him he was aware of a certain sensuousness in her movements, the sway of her hips: he recalled that the death of her husband had been occasioned in part by the man's jealousy. He had killed for it, before he ended his own life. Arnold could understand how Gordon Portland might have felt possessive: Isabella Portland exuded a sensuous sexuality to which few men would fail to respond.

'I asked for coffee to be brought in as soon as you arrived, Mr Landon. Unless you would like something stronger?'

'Coffee will be fine.'

She directed him towards the settee and then, surprisingly, sat down beside him as he placed the folder containing the photographs on the low coffee table in front of him. Her shoulder touched his lightly, and he was very conscious of her nearness as he leaned forward and opened the folder.

34

'I've gone through all these photos and I've made notes on most of the artefacts shown,' he said hurriedly, conscious of her nearness as she leaned closer to him. 'I've made various valuations, which I've noted on the sheet I've slipped into the back of the folder. However, there are certain items I'm not very certain about.' He paused. 'Do you know where your husband might have obtained his pieces?'

She shrugged carelessly, pursed her lips in thought. They were very full, he noted distractedly, and soft. 'I was never very interested in the collection he always kept here at the Hall. And I have to say, all these pieces turning up the way they did in Edinburgh, well, it was a surprise to me. My guess now is that this wasn't stuff he intended retaining in a collection ... I think he was dealing in these items. Buying and selling. But it was an activity I wasn't even aware of at the time.' She half turned, looked directly at him. Her eyes were very beautiful; her eyebrows dark, arching perfectly. 'Which items are bothering you, particularly?'

He dragged his attention back to the folder. He separated the plastic sheets, identifying each object in turn. 'First of all, this gold *phiale* decorated with acorns ... and this gold platter. This vase here seems to me to be Attic in origin, as is this black-figure amphora. Then again, this bronze mirror ... Did Mr Portland keep any documentation in connection with these items? Apart from these photos, I mean. The reason is, I suspect some of these artefacts may be of considerable value but they should have been accompanied by details relating to their purchase.'

She considered the matter thoughtfully for a moment, then rose, walked across the room to a mahogany desk. She paused beside it briefly, and a shadow crossed her face. Arnold suspected the desk held unhappy memories for her. A vague recollection of the manner of her husband's death touched him. The man had died in this very room. He brushed the thought aside as Isabella Portland unlocked the desk drawer, rummaged through its contents and then drew out a leather-covered file. 'Maybe this will be what you're thinking about.'

The coffee arrived, brought on silent, stately feet by the butler. He placed the tray in front of Arnold and withdrew without saying a word. Isabella poured the cups of coffee as Arnold studied the papers within the leather-backed folder. They both remained silent for several minutes, as Arnold attempted to link up the documentation with the items he had mentioned. Isabella Portland sipped her coffee, admonishing Arnold when he appeared to be allowing his own coffee to become cold. At last, he placed the file on the table in front of them. He shrugged, not certain what to say.

'Is it helpful?' she asked.

Arnold nodded. 'The links are there. Short descriptions. And the accompanying documents, the export licences, they all seem to be in order.'

'Export licences?' she asked, frowning.

'Approvals such as these are necessary in some instances, to allow artefacts to be sold outside the country of origin, such as Italy and Greece.' He hesitated, thinking. 'I'm afraid I can't really place a valuation on these items I've mentioned, but I think I know someone who can. It would be helpful, however, if I could also have copies of the documentation to show.'

'That raises no problem. Which documents are you referring to?'

Arnold selected the sheets and Isabella Portland left the room to copy them, presumably in some office elsewhere on the ground floor. Arnold finished his coffee during her absence. He rose, walked across to the window to admire the lawned area outside, the prolific shrubberies, and the distant view of the Northumberland hills. Perhaps he'd take a run up there later, rather than drive out to the coast . . .

Near the shrubberies he noticed the bonnet of a car. It was a strange place to park, when there was so much room at the gravelled front of the house, or beside the former coach house to one side of the Hall, where he had placed his own car. It was almost as though the vehicle had been deliberately placed to avoid prying eyes.

He heard the library door open behind him. Isabella Portland came towards him, her stride elegant, sensuous. She held out the document copies. Arnold extracted the relevant photographs and promised to return them as soon as possible. When he left, the grave-featured butler remained standing on the front steps, watching him drive away.

Isabella Portland remained in the library after her visitor had gone. She waited, and after a little while she was joined by the man who had arrived earlier that morning. Detective Chief Inspector Jack O'Connor placed a hand on her shoulder and she smiled up at him. 'I hope you didn't mind waiting upstairs.'

He had, but he shrugged. 'Hole and corner stuff. Inevitable, in view of the situation.'

'It's in your hands,' she rejoined. 'You could change the *situation*, as you call it.'

He knew it. They had already discussed it. Somehow, he could not bring himself to make the decision, in spite of the passion that reigned between them, the desire that flamed when they were together, the longing he experienced when they were apart for any length of time. But there was a history, experiences they had shared, and on his side suspicions that still stained his mind. After a short silence, he changed the subject. 'So is Landon able to help?'

'I think so.'

'I don't know why you're bothering to set up this business with Angela Fenchurch. It's not as though you need it, financially.'

She held his glance directly. 'I need something to take up my time, and my attention. After all, there is no man in my life, on whom I could concentrate my attention.'

And that, she was making clear once again, was in his hands to correct.

3

The conference of the International Antiquities Association was to be held in the *salle des spectacles* of the former Carmelite chapel La Coursive, with its imposing seventeenth-century portal surmounted by a magnificent carved scallop shell, facing the sweep of the harbour at Cours de Dames. Karen and Arnold had booked in at the Hôtel de la Monnaie, close to the beach at the Plage de Concurrence and within short walking distance of the conference hall. The afternoon session was to commence at 2 p.m.; Karen announced that she would be doing some shopping in the late morning so after a quick lunch Arnold took the opportunity to walk alone through the Parc Charruyer beside the ancient fortifications that had repulsed Cardinal Richelieu during the sixteenth-century siege of the city. He followed the winding paths along the river; caught sight of swans and a solitary, tensely poised heron, then turned back to stroll in the hot afternoon sunshine towards the Mail where he paused beside the monument to the dead, the master work of Joachim Costa, before crossing through the narrow hedges towards the flower-bedecked memorial to the Resistance. He was surprised to realize for the first time how many concentration camps had been set up by the Nazis in France: they were listed on the memorial. Also listed were names of Rochelais resistance fighters who had died during the years of the Occupation.

Now, the more recent invasion of La Rochelle was more welcome, he guessed: the tourist industry was booming.

Arnold lingered at the memorial, then walked to the promenade above the beach and sat down, gazing out over the dark waters of the river mouth, towards the huge marina at Les Minimes, the largest on the Atlantic coast. He had the vague recollection that the area had been the setting for the attempts on the life of d'Artagnan by Cardinal Richelieu in *The Three Musketeers*. At that time, it would have been a bare peninsula, covered in scrawny, wind-blasted scrub and ramshackle wooden fishing huts.

38

Now the peninsula housed blocks of flats, and the University of La Rochelle.

He glanced at his watch. He had been daydreaming too long. He rose, made his way quickly along the promenade, past the beach and along the Rue des Murs, hurrying down the steps near the tower and turning towards the conference hall.

The marbled entrance lobby was cool and quiet. The conference hall of La Coursive itself was crowded. Arnold was clearly a little late in arriving. Proceedings had already begun and a small group of speakers was assembled on the platform at the far end of the high-ceilinged room. Arnold stood at the back and looked around: after a little while he caught sight of Karen, seated beside and in animated discussion with James Detorius. He was disinclined to join them: there was something he disliked about the middle-aged lawyer. It was nothing he could put his finger on: perhaps it was the man's servile manner, his eagerness to please. Whatever it was, it was like an irritation at the back of the neck, difficult to scratch, impossible to relieve. He looked about him and found a seat near the back of the hall. As one of the speakers in the first session, Karl Spedding was already at the dais, notes stacked neatly in front of him. There was a brief introduction from the conference chairman, outlining Karl Spedding's background and achievements, a scattering of applause.

Arnold wrinkled his nose: there was still something that niggled at him about Spedding. Suspicion still stained his mind – the former curator was too good to be true. Karen Stannard saw the appointment of such a well-qualified man as a great acquisition for the department, a feather in its cap, raising the status of the group she had now left in Arnold's hands, but Arnold still smelt a rat somewhere.

He didn't like Spedding. And he didn't like James Detorius either.

He smiled suddenly, critical of his own feelings. Both men paid open court to Karen Stannard, both made no secret of their admiration. Maybe it was the regard they showed that soured his feelings towards them. He was jealous. He smiled again, at the thought. He had known Karen too long; he was aware of her manipulative personality; he knew it was all a game to her. Jealousy? The thought was a ludicrous one. Or maybe it wasn't. Maybe it was true.

Spedding had launched into his speech to the delegates.

'Attitudes towards unprovenanced, and probably illegally excavated and smuggled, antiquities have been changing slowly over the years,' he was saying. 'The source countries – such as Central and South America, the Mediterranean countries, West Africa, India – have all been taking a clearer line since the Second World War, not least because archaeological sites can provide considerable tourist revenue.'

He raised his head, looked about him at the silent audience. 'Greece began the legislative controls in 1834; Italy followed in 1872 and France in 1887. The League of Nations introduced the Treaty of Sèvres to control and stamp out looting, but it was never ratified. So what have we seen since? Generally speaking, a concerted attempt by what we can describe as the market countries – Britain, the USA, the Netherlands – to prevent, slow down, even impede the impact of controlling legislation. Even when UNESCO introduced its Convention against Illicit Export, Import and Transfer of Ownership of Cultural Property in 1970 many countries were slow to ratify it. The UK only came on board thirty years after the event; Denmark, Holland and Germany have still not ratified it. This is in spite of the fact that there is a considerable body of evidence to demonstrate that our archaeological heritage, the material remains of past human activities, is being destroyed at an undiminished pace.'

Arnold leaned back in his seat as Spedding reeled off the statistics: over fifty per cent of Mayan sites looted, 830 sites in Mali destroyed, half the Buddhist shrines, stupas and monasteries in northern Pakistan damaged. Karl Spedding made reference to Andalucia and Peru, China and Inner Mongolia, 'And we are all aware of the looting that went on in Iraq between the first Gulf War in 1991 and 1994

40

when eleven regional museums were broken into. And after the fall of Saddam Hussein, the Baghdad Museum in April 2003 was broken into and over thirteen thousand objects were stolen. To date, only four thousand have been recovered . . .'

Arnold looked towards where Karen Stannard was seated. James Detorius, beside her, had lowered his head and seemed to be nodding off, but Karen was leaning forward, her attention riveted on the man whom she had just appointed as second-in-command to Arnold. No doubt she would be quick to boast to the Council back home that her new acquisition had produced a splendid effect at the international conference in La Rochelle. It would help justify the expenses, anyway, he considered cynically.

Now thoroughly warmed to his theme, Karl Spedding pushed his notes aside. He leaned forward, one elbow on the lectern in front of him, and his voice rose accusingly. 'My own view is that it's all very well passing legislation – even if it is largely unenforced – and making it more difficult for looters such as the *tombaroli* in Italy to place their ill-gotten pieces in the market place. But it's equally important that we should direct our attention, and our ire, towards the shadowy people who make millions of dollars, feeding off the looters. To their credit, the army-linked Art Squad in Italy have recently carried out persistent enquiries – in the teeth of disobliging governments, including that of Great Britain it must be said – that have led to some high-profile cases, both against prominent dealers in looted antiquities, and against the curators of internationally respected museums who have turned a blind eye to the provenance of the objects they purchase. Even as I speak, certain high-profile cases are being heard in Italy, with dealers and curators on trial. But what about the unseen collectors, the private, extremely wealthy individuals who purchase directly from these criminal go-betweens, retain priceless objects in their private collections, then years later do deals with the museums, forge documents to suggest legitimate acquisitions with appropriate export licences, lending support right along the line in both directions – downwards to the *tombaroli* who loot the tombs and up the chain to the museums who lend their names and international respectability to the destruction of our archaeological heritage . . .'

Arnold was feeling uncomfortably warm. He glanced up to the ceiling: the light was bright, the afternoon sunny. He was hearing nothing new, nothing that was startling, and he felt vaguely irritated at the thrust of Spedding's speech. The man had been a curator himself – and Arnold was still unconvinced that he had left his recent post entirely voluntarily. Moreover, for Arnold there was a false ring to his proselytizing. His irritability, underlined perhaps by the fact that Spedding was now to be working to Arnold at the department, made him decide to skip the rest of the lecture.

The decision made him feel a little guilty – perhaps he was not giving Spedding a fair crack of the whip. But he rose, nevertheless. Spedding was well launched, getting even more enthusiastic in his denunciation of the vast industry they all knew about, the delegates were attentive, but Arnold felt that he had heard enough. A little fresh air was required.

Placed near the back of the hall, he disturbed few as he made his way out, down the marble steps to the cool reception hall that housed the ticket office. He stood there for a few minutes, reading the posters proclaiming coming theatrical attractions, and feeling somewhat less irritated he decided to step out into the street, and take a walk.

The harbour was crowded. As he walked past the cafés that lined the walk he became aware of the sweet, sharp scent from the lime trees that arched above his head. The tide was in, and the numerous boats at their moorings lifted rhythmically, their lines tinkling merrily in the light breeze. The passenger cruise ship was casting off from the quayside on her afternoon trip to the Isle d'Aix, the island where Napoleon had spent his final days on French soil before being arrested by the British captain of the *Bellerephon*. Elderly couples sat sunning themselves on the wooden benches under the trees, and a scattering of bearded young men lay with their dogs near one of the benches, drinking dark-coloured liquid from bottles. The drinks could have been Coke, but Arnold doubted it. He took a deep breath: he was feeling relaxed, the trip was a good break from the office and he felt at ease under the influence of the limes, and the sunshine, and the clean salty air.

He sat for a while on a wall between the twin guardians of the harbour, the St Nicolas Tower and the Tour de la Lanterne, then strolled through the archway of the Porte de Grosse Horloge, and entered the Cours de Templiers. The shops in the narrow medieval streets beyond were busy, tourists in shorts meandering along, smart-suited men brushing past them, hurrying to business appointments. Reluctant to leave the harbour side Arnold turned, made his way down Rue Passeport and found himself facing the harbour again.

And a face, and a figure he knew well.

She was seated at the café immediately opposite the entrance to the harbour, a wineglass in front of her, in conversation with her male companion. Her full voluptuous figure drew admiring glances from strolling passers-by. She was a well-built woman with finely sculpted features, a generous mouth and sparkling brown eyes. Her fair hair was carefully cut, slightly tousled with one lock falling over her tanned forehead. She had broad, peasant arms that had received a long exposure to the sun, working on archaeological sites throughout Italy: he remembered her handshake, her rough, calloused fingers. He also remembered her earthy warmth, the enthusiastic way she had hugged him on the last occasion he had seen her, when they had said goodbye at Newcastle Airport. As Arnold stopped and stared at her, she turned her head, breaking off her conversation as she caught sight of him. Surprise and pleasure immediately shone in her eyes.

'Arnold!'

'Carmela Cacciatore!'

'DeeDee!' she corrected him and laughed boisterously. It had been a nickname bestowed upon her by her macho

Italian colleagues in the Carabinieri Art Squad, a sexist joke based on the size of her bra cups, but Arnold had preferred to use her given name. It was something she appreciated, he was sure; now she rose, came towards him, threw her arms around his neck and crushed her large bosom against him. She planted two vigorous kisses on his cheeks, then stepped back. 'I wondered whether you might be here in La Rochelle. You are at the conference?'

'That's right. But I haven't seen your name among the list of delegates.'

'No, no . . .' She hesitated, then glanced sideways at the slim, middle-aged man who had risen from his chair and was standing silently, regarding them. 'No, I am here on business. Ah . . . this is . . . Arnold, may I present my friend Jean-Pierre Leconte?' She gestured towards the lean, moustached man silently standing there. 'This is my friend Mr Arnold Landon. He was of much assistance during the recent business in England that I told you about, the matter of the calyx krater . . .'

'I am pleased to make your acquaintance,' her companion said in accented English, bowing slightly but making no attempt to shake Arnold's hand. He was perhaps fifty years of age, narrow-featured, with experienced eyes and the gravelly voice of a man who smoked fifty Gauloises a day. He glanced briefly at Carmela. 'However, please take my seat, monsieur. Mademoiselle Carmela and I have completed our business, I have matters to attend to, and now that my charming companion has company I can leave her in good conscience.'

He smiled at Carmela, leaned forward and kissed her twice on the cheek, then nodded to Arnold and moved away, strolling casually along the Quai Duperre, glancing across the harbour to the twin towers that guarded the entrance.

'He is a hardworking man,' Carmela murmured, eyeing his easy walk appraisingly. 'For a Frenchman. Committed . . .'

'What's he do?' Arnold asked as he settled into the chair beside Carmela.

She hesitated. 'He is a policeman.'

A young waiter was hovering. 'Monsieur?'

Arnold glanced at Carmela, who shook her head, gesturing towards the half-empty glass of white wine in front of her, so Arnold ordered for himself. *'Grande crème, s'il vous plaît.'*

'So French is among your considerable accomplishments,' Carmela teased him.

'Restaurant French only,' he replied. He turned his attention to her. She was a buxom woman, but as with many large women her face was small, beautifully proportioned, and her skin was soft, unlined. 'So you're not at the conference. Here on business, you say. The Carabinieri Art Squad?'

He was well aware of the group she worked for. Faced with considerable looting of artefacts from Italian sites, Etruscan tombs and Roman palaces, some forty years earlier the Italian government had established an elite squad, linked to the army rather than the police, operating from their headquarters in the ornate, four-storey, ochre-and-white baroque Piazzale Clodio on the Piazza Sant' Ignazio in Rome. The Comando Carabinieri Ministro Pubblica Istruzione. Creating the squad had been a public demonstration of the importance the government placed upon protection of their heritage. And Arnold had been able to lend some assistance to their work, in England, eighteen months previously.

Carmela hesitated, clearly a little careful about what she was about to say. 'Certainly, I am not here on holiday.' She shrugged, and smiled broadly, flashing perfect white teeth in his direction. 'You know it is my life, Arnold. And things have moved on since we last met and you helped us recover the calyx krater. The old days, when there were just sixty officers in the squad, they are gone. We have now developed into twelve regional units, and I have been so fortunate as to receive promotion.'

'Congratulations,' Arnold murmured. 'I'm sure it was well deserved.'

'You had a part to play in it. And at least I don't get called DeeDee any more . . . except by my special friends.' She regarded him with a raised eyebrow. 'You always used my proper name. I wouldn't have minded, from you, but . . .'

Arnold shrugged. 'Carmela is more professional.'

'And to you, personal also,' she replied in acknowledgement. 'But the success of the recovery of the calyx krater, it has had wider implications merely than my promotion. Our operations have now been considerably extended further into the international field.'

'How do you mean?'

The waiter had returned; the coffee was placed in front of Arnold. Carmela sipped her wine, and squinted about her in the glaring sunshine. 'We have taken the attack into the field in a more systematic way. Yes, the *tombaroli* still operate – and in spite of their protests that they love antiquities, that they excavate carefully, that they preserve sites that would otherwise languish undiscovered, we know that this is all one great lie. They are active for the money they receive . . . and we root them out still, but also our efforts are now more clearly directed towards the other end of the market.'

'The dealers, you mean?' Arnold asked. When she raised an inquisitive eyebrow, he explained, 'I've just come out of a lecture at the conference. My new colleague is giving a paper on the sins of the private collectors, and the insidious part they play in the market for looted antiques.'

Carmela brushed the errant lock of fair hair from her eyes. She nodded. 'He is right, this colleague of yours. The recent Monticelli trial – he got four years for conspiracy to rob – it has exposed some of the secrets of the looting organizations. But it has also made public the methods we in the Carabinieri have been using.' She grinned at Arnold. 'Your own government and courts, they are slow to accept the necessity for phone-tapping, but in Italy now, in view of the seriousness of the loss of our heritage, we have had permission to use this method of investigation.'

'You eavesdrop on the looters?'

'They use phones, like everyone. It is true the *tombaroli* are very ... how do you say ... cagey, when they use the phone, but we are very patient and just occasionally, when they let their guard slip, we are able to obtain nuggets of information that allow us to proceed to the next level.'

'The dealers,' Arnold guessed.

'Not just the dealers. The collectors also. And even the museums.'

Arnold grimaced. 'I'm aware that there are items of doubtful provenance in many of the most famous museums, but I've always assumed that this is the result of fraud. Are you now suggesting that some of the curators have been consciously dealing directly with *tombaroli*?'

Carmela Cacciatore shook her head. 'No. Not directly. The *tombaroli* work at a different level – and get paid at a lower level also. No, as a result of our wire-tapping, and information obtained in the Monticelli case, we have been able to discover a great deal about the *cordata*, the inter-linked men and women involved in the purchase and sale arrangements of looted artefacts. What has happened is that we have in our possession lists of people who are employed in the trade worldwide ...'

Arnold's coffee grew cold as he listened, fascinated, to Carmela's account of how the Art Squad's offices in Piazzale Clodio in Rome had now expanded, how vast amounts of documentation were being studied and ana-lysed, and how new laws and agreements internationally had recently begun to be implemented.

'It's not just the market countries, and the source coun-tries like my own,' she said earnestly. 'Others such as Egypt, Jordan and China have become more assertive in their attempts to clamp down on the illicit trade. They are adopting a common stance. So what Italy began thirty years ago, it is now coming to fruition.' She leaned back, drained her wineglass in evident satisfaction. 'French wine is famous, but I prefer Italian. That is chauvinism, no? Chauvinism ... a French word, no?'

'Your English has improved,' Arnold noted.

'It is the time I have recently spent in America,' Carmela asserted. 'We have a big investigation pending there, with the Metropolitan Museum, and the Getty . . . but you have allowed me to talk more than I should. You have encouraged me to climb my hobby-horse. Hobby-horse . . . that is correct?'

'Certainly. But I am interested.'

'Still, I talk too much. Give away too many secrets, perhaps.' She smiled broadly. 'But you are a friend. *Molto simpatico*. As to which, how is your other little friend, Miss Karen Stannard?'

Arnold grinned at the thought of how Karen would have winced at the description given to her. 'She's now Chief Executive. She's placed me in charge of the department.'

Carmela beamed. 'Promotion for you also! I am pleased. You deserve.'

'She's here at the moment,' Arnold remarked.

'Unwilling to release strings?' Carmela teased.

'Something like that,' Arnold admitted, draining the cool coffee. He leaned back in his chair, and they were silent for a while, enjoying the sunshine, observing the crowds sauntering along the Quai Duperre.

'This colleague you mention,' Carmela said after a little while. 'It is not Miss Tyrell?'

Arnold shook his head. 'No. She's left the department. She had a rough time . . . I won't go into the details.'

'Affair of the heart?' Carmela enquired, raising an eyebrow.

'Something like that. No, don't give me that knowing look. It wasn't me. And it was a messy business . . .' He hesitated. 'No, the colleague who is presenting a paper today is a new appointment, working under me.'

'So why is it you do not present the paper?'

'He was already scheduled to do it. And he's far better qualified than I am.' Arnold glanced at his friend from the Carabinieri Art Squad. 'He's a former assistant curator at the Pradak Museum.'

'The Pradak?' She frowned in thought. 'His name?'

'Karl Spedding. Long list of qualifications. Considerable experience.'

There was something in Arnold's tone that caused Carmela to glance at him suspiciously. 'You don't like him.'

'It's not that. I'm just curious . . . Why would a man of such ability wish to take a second-rate job in a department in the north of England?'

'Spedding . . .'she murmured thoughtfully, almost to herself.

Arnold glanced at his watch. 'Anyway, I'd better get back to the conference. The first lecture will be finished by now. I hope we'll be able to meet again this week, Carmela. Maybe for dinner? I'm staying at the Hôtel de la Monnaie.'

'More than the Art Police can afford,' she said flashing him a smile. 'Dinner will be difficult. But I will be in touch. And this man Spedding . . . his name is known to me, but the context . . . I am not sure. The Pradak, you say . . .' She rose, kissed him on the cheek. '*Arrivederci*, Arnold. Till the next time. And in the meantime, I will make some enquiries about this man who is so well qualified – but wants to work for you!'

Arnold began to walk away, then stopped, looked back at her. 'Hell, I almost forgot! You're still operating out of the palazzo?'

'That is so,' she concurred.

'I recently sent you a package, some photographs and supporting documentation. Seeking your advice. You've not received it yet?'

'It will be waiting for me at Piazza Sant' Ignazio, I expect.' She raised an eyebrow. 'It is important, this package?'

He shrugged. 'I don't think so. But I'd appreciate your advice in due course.'

'I will pick up the package when I return to Rome. Then, you will owe me, Mr Arnold Landon. And I will exact a heavy price.' She grinned. 'But I assure you it will be a pleasurable one!'

Chapter Two

1

Arnold managed to slip back into the conference room just in time; the afternoon session was ending and there was a general exodus towards the lobby. As the crowd of delegates drifted past him Arnold waited there, just inside the doors, until he caught sight of Karen and James Detorius. Karen was walking with lowered head, listening: the pompous lawyer was chattering to her, one hand resting on her bare arm possessively. She caught sight of Arnold and raised a hand: he made his way towards them.

'Well, I thought that went very well,' she exclaimed, divesting herself of the clinging hand above her elbow with a practised ease. 'Karl Spedding's contribution was extremely well received, wasn't it . . . not least because of the hard things he had to say about the private collectors who hoard these unprovenanced artefacts. He certainly laid into them with gusto, hey? What did you think of it, Arnold?'

'I'm sure you've made a very good appointment for the department,' he muttered evasively, glowering at Detorius, hovering eagerly at Karen's shoulder. In case Karen continued to ask for his reaction to Spedding's paper, Arnold changed the subject smoothly. 'Anyway, the conference is over for the day now. Karen, I was wondering what you wanted to do about dinner tonight. It would be a pity to confine ourselves to the hotel restaurant: maybe we ought to seek out some place along the quayside.'

'That would be nice,' Karen said, smiling. She turned to Detorius. 'What do you think, James?'

Arnold was taken aback at her turning to Detorius, but then relieved by the lawyer's hesitation. 'I . . . er . . . I'm not sure. What time are you thinking of meeting up?'

Karen was clearly surprised by his diffidence. She turned to Arnold, eyed him uncertainly, then shrugged. 'Well, I don't know, but maybe I also ought to have a word with Karl Spedding first, to see if he'd like to join us. Make a party of it, hey? How about we leave a note at reception for you later, James, if you're going to be busy? Or perhaps we could give you a ring at your hotel. Hôtel Résidence de France, isn't it? Four stars, you know, Arnold. Not like us poor public servants.'

Detorius was still hesitant, he chewed his lip thoughtfully. 'Well, er, I need to get back to my hotel to deal with some papers and early this evening there's a business client I need to see . . . After that I guess I could join you, if you let me know where you're likely to be.'

'Don't let us press you,' Karen replied a little tartly, irritated by his indecision. She was not accustomed to men hesitating over a dinner invitation from her.

'No, no,' Detorius said hurriedly, 'don't get me wrong. I'd love to join you. It's just that I was expecting . . . Look, why not leave a note at reception, as you suggested? Maybe my business meeting will be concluded before you leave the hotel.'

Arnold was also a little irritated. If the truth be known he would have preferred to have wandered the town alone and found a restaurant to suit himself. He had asked Karen what her plans were, out of politeness – and he knew that, away from work, she would have made a pleasant dinner companion – but now it seemed he had saddled himself not only with Karen, but with Spedding and possibly even Detorius. He should have stayed away from the conference hall longer. But even so, if Karen had seen him in the hotel no doubt she would have called upon him to join her dinner party.

As they walked back to the Hôtel de la Monnaie Detorius made his excuses and left them. The Hôtel Résidence de France was in the centre of town, between the Place Verdun and the market. After he had gone Karen strolled with Arnold along the Plage de la Concurrence and they sat for a while in the early evening sunshine, watching a group of university students playing touch rugby on the beach. 'What do you make of James Detorius?' Karen suddenly asked Arnold.

Arnold was hesitant. He shrugged. 'Not a lot, really. He's a lawyer, the usual dry-as-dust character. But I'm surprised he has such an academic interest in antiquities, turning up at La Coursive. I mean, what in particular has drawn him here to the conference?'

'He did say he had meetings with clients here in La Rochelle. And law and archaeology ... the two aren't mutually exclusive as interests,' Karen replied, glancing at him sharply.

'I suppose not,' he replied in a grudging tone. 'But it still seems to me to be an odd combination: legal business and conference attendance.'

'One's a hobby, one's a profession.'

'Either way, I think he's a creep.' When he saw the irritation in her green eyes he muttered defensively, 'You did ask me.'

Back in his room at the Hôtel de la Monnaie Arnold took a shower and relaxed for a while, sprawling on the bed in the towelling bathrobe provided by the hotel. He extracted a tiny measure of brandy from the room minibar, poured it into the cut-glass tumbler and topped it with soda water. He turned on the television. The news programme was difficult to follow: his fluency in French was too constrained to follow the commentary. Eventually he gave up and as he sipped at his drink he turned his attention to the conference brochure: apart from the schedule of events and lectures for the three following days there were pen-portraits of the main participants. Karl Spedding's professional details and photograph were there. Arnold frowned. He still felt uneasy about the man's appointment to the department: something about the whole situation did not ring true.

The phone rang. It was Karen.

'I've talked to Spedding and arranged to meet him in the bar at seven thirty. And Detorius rang, somewhat apologetically: he'll try to join us in time for dinner. As for a choice of restaurants, I've had a look at a city guide: there's a restaurant called Les 4 Sergents which is close by and is highly recommended.'

'Sounds fine. I'll see you in the hotel bar,' Arnold agreed.

Arnold arrived at the bar shortly after the appointed time. He saw that Karl Spedding was already there, seated on a high stool at the curved, polished-wood counter with what appeared to be a gin and tonic in front of him. Arnold hesitated: he had no great desire to spend time in the man's sole company, but his problem was resolved almost immediately as he felt a hand pressing against the small of his back. It was Karen. She grinned at him mischievously and gave him a little push. 'Go on, you're quite safe. He won't bite.'

There was a scattering of other conference delegates in the bar, seated at tables around the room. As Karen and Arnold walked forward to join Karl Spedding a man seated in the corner of the room got up to leave his table, and seemed to be headed in the same direction. Karl Spedding glanced around and caught sight of Karen and Arnold; he rose from his stool to greet them but as he did so the man who had risen from his table stopped just behind Spedding. He tapped him on the shoulder.

Surprised, Karl Spedding turned. Arnold glanced at the stranger as he and Karen approached. The man was middle-aged, burly in his build, with short-cropped, greying hair. His heavy jaw betrayed an aggressive thrust: Arnold gained the impression he would be a man who was accustomed to getting his own way. Behind his light spectacles the stranger's heavily pouched eyes were sharp, narrowed purposively; he hooked one large hand into the waist of his trousers and leant his elbow against the bar as he held Spedding's glance.

'Mr Spedding. I don't think we've met.'

Spedding was clearly aware of the studied insolence in the man's tone. He stared at him, took in the heavy, baggy sweater, the craggy features, raising one eyebrow. There was a short silence, and then Spedding nodded. Coolly, he responded, 'That's right. We haven't.' Then, as Karen reached him, he turned back to greet her, ignoring the man who had spoken to him. 'Miss Stannard . . . Mr Landon. What would you like to drink?'

There was more than coldness in his ignoring of the stranger; it was a deliberate slight. But as Arnold and Karen ranged themselves beside Spedding, the burly man in the casual sweater tapped his shoulder again, undeterred. 'Spedding. I don't think you know who I am.'

There was a short pause. Karl Spedding stared at Karen, then Arnold, as though he hadn't heard the stranger. With a studied casualness he resumed his position on the stool. He swung slowly around until he was facing the man who had accosted him. 'On the contrary,' he stated in an icy tone. 'I know exactly who you are. Miss Stannard, Mr Landon, may I introduce you to Adam Shearbright, MA Harvard, erstwhile heir to the Kontakt department store chain, owner of the Shearbright Trucking Corporation and consequently very well-heeled, chairman of the Attic Galleries organization, and a noted dealer in antiquities.' He turned his back on the man he had acknowledged. 'Now then, the drinks . . .'

Karen asked for a gin and tonic; slightly embarrassed, facing an empurpling Adam Shearbright, Arnold settled for a brandy and soda to follow the one he had already imbibed in his room. The foxy-featured barman was standing close by, hands on the bar, openly observing the group, aware of the tension between them. As the man accepted the orders and turned away Adam Shearbright spoke again, ignoring the presence of Spedding's colleagues, concentrating a fierce, belligerent gaze on the museum ex-curator.

'I listened to your presentation today,' he growled.

'I trust you were duly enlightened,' Spedding replied, without deigning to turn to face the man. The barman glanced over his shoulder, clearly interested in hearing what was likely to transpire, even as he poured the drinks. Hotel barmen, Arnold guessed, were swift to recognize trouble when it was looming.

Shearbright's tone was aggressive. 'That speech of yours. You made some pretty wide-ranging attacks against the people who work in the business, Spedding. As someone who's been involved for a number of years, I take personal exception to some of the generalizations you made.'

'Well, how's this for a generalization?' Spedding asked coolly, swivelling slowly on his stool to stare straight into his interlocutor's face. 'Although we've never met, I know who you are and am aware that you are deeply involved in the collection of ancient artefacts. A noted dealer with an international reputation, an organizer of important exhibitions in your spare time. Well, in my view, the whole antiquities business is a mess – it's nothing more than a commercial cesspool of greed and vanity, founded on looted tombs and consumed with greed at every level.'

The man facing him gripped the edge of the bar and his brow became thunderous. 'That's a gross misrepresentation of the work we do, the preservation, the vast amounts of money philanthropists like me spend to seek out the heritage –'

'Philanthropists?' Spedding cut in remorselessly. ' Come off it! It's well known that many of you are driven by the tax breaks you can obtain: buy at one price, then gift the item to a museum at an inflated price, five times the value you paid, and save a huge amount in taxes. But it's not just the *profit* motive, is it, to fifty per cent tax bracket people like you! Collectors of your ilk, Mr Shearbright, are dogged with wish fulfilment: in mounting your acquisitions in exhibitions the wishes of you, the collector, which may have no basis in fact or reality, take precedence over the work of better-informed scholars. The reality is that collectors' conceit takes over from disinterested scholarship.'

'That's just not true,' the big man said fiercely. 'The purchases I make, they are always with the provenance clearly stated –'

Spedding shook his head in contempt, twisted his glass of gin and tonic in his left hand as the barman hovered just in earshot. There was a sneering smile on Spedding's lips. 'Come, come, Mr Shearbright. You know as well as I that the vast majority of provenances are inventions, convenient fictions concocted to add to the value of individual pieces and to hide the fact they've been looted and smuggled.'

A little alarmed by the contempt in Spedding's tone, Karen attempted to intervene. 'Karl, I think that's being somewhat too harsh –'

Spedding was adamant. He turned on her, his face slowly flushing. 'Miss Stannard, the wide spread of unprovenanced artefacts, in collections such as those amassed by Mr Shearbright, allied to the massive jumble of fakes acquired by museums, means that whole categories of acquisitions may be spurious.'

Shearbright grunted in growing annoyance; he lowered his head like a charging bull. He ignored Karen's attempt to cool the situation and glared at Spedding. 'Fakes! Are you suggesting –'

But Spedding was well launched. '*Suggesting*? Not at all. Look at your own reaction to my statement. I'm putting it forward now, perhaps more bluntly than I did in my presentation at La Coursive today: it is a *fact* that few collectors seem willing to acknowledge even the *possibility* that some of the objects they hold are fake.'

Shearbright stiffened, squared his broad shoulders. 'Even if that were the case – which I deny – your comments are a slander against private collectors. We support the acquisition of knowledge about the ancient world. You know damn well the items that appear in auctions, the kind of artefacts that I purchase, they are usually of small value and importance and –'

Spedding's interruption was cutting. 'What I do know *damn well*, as you colourfully put it, is that objects of lesser importance at auction are often placed there merely to launder antiquities so that dealers can claim they've bought objects in open sale – though they are actually, more often than not, in reality buying from themselves – thus providing these objects with a spurious auction room provenance. And as for the documented provenance itself, well, in my view it's often nothing more than a euphemism, a document using phrases that are so vague as in reality to be archaeologically meaningless. It's all a charade, an invention generated by commercial considerations.' He eyed Shearbright ironically, sipped at his gin and tonic. 'And tax breaks.'

Shearbright was speechless with rage. The barman was close by, listening, probably waiting for the explosion. Spedding put down his glass. His lip curled in contempt.

'Take the case of the *tombaroli*: they use the same arguments as you do, Shearbright. They protest that they love antiquities and excavate unimportant objects with great care, objects that would otherwise be lost to all. Excavate with care? With mechanical diggers? Their argument is false and everyone knows it. And so do you. The fiction that the traffic in illicit antiquities is only about unimportant objects has long been exploded. No, it's obvious that the traffic is continued because of the demand from some rogue museums and rogue collectors.'

'Are you classifying me in that category?' Shearbright snarled, balling his fists.

'Wear the cap that fits,' Spedding remarked with indifference.

Adam Shearbright laid a hand on Spedding's shoulder, gripping it tightly. 'I came across to you to dispute the comments you made in your address to the conference. But I now see that your bias against the people who bring history to life, the museums, the private collectors, it's almost paranoid – it allows you to spit out the most outrageous views.'

The barman was still hovering close by, nervously, as Spedding slowly peeled Shearbright's fingers from his shoulder. His jaw was set; his lips tight. 'Here's another paranoid view. I consider that the actions of some museums and *most* private collectors are no less to blame than the looters themselves in causing such damage to our understanding of the past. They – and you – believe that as long as objects are beautiful the original archaeological context is irrelevant – so that context is then lost and irrecoverable. This is an attitude that encourages the market and private collectors to continue the destruction.'

In the brief silence that followed, Arnold glanced around the bar. Others nearby were listening, even though the conversation had been conducted without raised voices. He realized that James Detorius had arrived: the lawyer was standing uncertainly in the doorway, watching them. Perhaps he was aware of the argument that was brewing among the tight group at the bar, and was reluctant to become involved. He caught Arnold's glance, nodded, and moved away back to the reception lobby. Arnold looked back at Shearbright.

The wealthy American dealer's features were suffused with rage. 'What you've said . . . that's another way of saying that collectors like me are the real looters!'

'Perhaps they are, Mr Shearbright,' Spedding countered calmly. 'Let's consider the antiquities you hold in your own collection, the Italian marbles, for instance –'

'Italy, Italy!' Adam Shearbright gave a snort of contempt. 'You're obsessed with that damned country! Your emphasis in your talk was all about what's been going on in Italy – just because of the recent publicity given to the *tombaroli*, the recent court cases, the Monticelli affair –'

Spedding shook his head and placed his glass down carefully on the bar. There was a slight tremor in his hand. Despite his cool exterior, Arnold could see the ex-curator was only just managing to hold his temper at the American's persistence.

'It's not just Italy, Mr Shearbright. I made the point in my presentation. Look at the baleful influence the demand from collectors like you has had on the African heritage; check out the passion among collectors for Asian artefacts. Then there's Nepal : it's lost half its Buddhist and

Hindu sculptures. To whom? To private collectors! Look at the recent reliefs that were looted from the Sennacherib Palace in Nineveh. And the relief from the palace of Tiglath-pileser at Nimrud. All ten reliefs appeared on the open market. Auctions held for private dealers. And we all know what happened after the looting of the Baghdad Museum, after the fall of Saddam Hussein: the antiquities started appearing in Western collections. If you want my view, it's not even *possible* any longer to form a collection of classical antiquities by legitimate means!' He paused, took a deep, measured breath. 'Christopher Chippindale was right when he said that as far as the trade in antiquities is concerned, however bad you feared this state of affairs might be, the truth is worse.'

'Chippindale! Academic poseurs,' Shearbright muttered scornfully.

'Who are probably right.' Spedding looked the American straight in the eye. 'It is my considered view that private collectors are dogged with wish fulfilment: that's what I meant when I said earlier that the wishes of the individual collector take precedence over the work of better-informed scholars. Collectors' conceit takes over from disinterested scholarship.'

'Disinterested scholarship!' the American dealer snarled. 'The kind, I suppose, that got you sacked from the Pradak!'

Karl Spedding went white. His lips tightened and he half moved from his seat. It was time to bring an end to the argument. But before Arnold could step forward, Karen Stannard intervened. The smile she turned on the American antiquities dealer was dazzlingly insincere. 'You'll forgive us, Mr Shearbright. A most interesting discussion, but we must leave it there. We have a dinner appointment.' She replaced her glass on the bar, the drink barely touched. Imperiously, she walked away towards the door. 'Arnold, Mr Spedding, it's time we left.'

Arnold followed sheepishly. After a moment's hesitation, Karl Spedding followed just behind him. At the doorway, Arnold glanced back. The burly American dealer was still staring at them; his features were contorted with suppressed rage. Arnold gained the impression that in a less public place Shearbright might well have resorted to violence.

'I think you've made a serious enemy there, Spedding,' Arnold remarked, as they moved out of the bar.

The ex-curator shook his head, dogged, unrepentant. 'It didn't take that discussion to make us enemies. I despise that man and all he stands for. It's time someone told these people the facts of life. Private collectors like Shearbright, they throw their money at anything of beauty that appears on the market. They have no interest it its provenance; no interest in the archaeological context. They simply want to *acquire*, come hell or high water. It's an attitude that's destroyed thousands of tombs, damaged hundreds of archaeological environments. And the collectors, they simply don't care!'

Karen turned her head, glanced at him; Arnold could see she was irritated, but she held her tongue.

James Detorius was waiting for them in the lobby. He had taken an easy chair, half hidden by an immense potted plant. He rose as they approached. He seemed edgy, oddly nervous, glanced past them as though worried that the man they had left would come in pursuit. 'I saw you in the bar. Things seemed to be getting somewhat . . . heated.' He glanced at Karen Stannard. 'What was it all about?'

'Don't ask,' Karen replied gloomily. 'Let's hope our visit to Les 4 Sergents is less tempestuous.'

Arnold merely hoped Adam Shearbright wouldn't follow them to continue the argument.

'Apparently, the restaurant is named after four sergeants who were incarcerated in the Chain Tower, a few hundred years ago, and scratched some graffiti on the walls. I'm not certain whether their incarceration was anything to do with the king's attempt to restore Catholicism to the city.' Arnold hesitated, glanced around at the morose little group, aware they were barely listening to him. 'Cardinal Richelieu laid siege to the city: La Rochelle was a stronghold of Protestants ... or Huguenots, as they were then known.'

The dinner was not working out successfully. The surroundings were exquisite, dining under the splendid domed ceiling; the meal was excellent and the service perfect, but the atmosphere had clearly been soured by the argument in the hotel bar. Karl Spedding seemed distracted, frowning, obviously still upset by Shearbright and perhaps his own lack of control in the company of his colleagues. James Detorius was still curiously ill at ease, perhaps affected by the long silences of his companions: he kept glancing at his watch surreptitiously, as though wishing he could find an excuse to leave the group and go elsewhere. When Arnold spoke in an attempt to get a conversation going Karen merely glanced at him in irritated fashion and then remained silent, uninterested in his comments, merely picking at her food: Arnold guessed she was annoyed with Spedding's performance, railing against Adam Shearbright. As for Arnold himself, his thoughts kept returning to the American dealer's sarcastic comment about Spedding's being sacked from the Pradak Museum.

Spedding had told them he had left the museum of his own volition, to seek a change of career. Now, Arnold wondered whether Shearbright knew of other reasons for Spedding's leaving. The curiosity tended to confirm his own feelings about Spedding: something in the man's behaviour was out of kilter with his statements.

Everyone seemed relieved when the dinner came to an end. By mutual consent they refused coffee. Karen insisted on paying the bill from her own subsistence account: she was fierce in her insistence. All three men backed off. When they emerged into the street the lights of the cafés and restaurants along the Cours de Dames beckoned to them but Karen muttered, 'I'm tired. I'm going back to the hotel. Arnold?'

Dispirited, he shook his head. 'I think I'll go along for a nightcap in one of the cafés.'

James Detorius hesitated, then said quickly, 'I'll take my leave. I'll see you all in the morning.'

As Detorius hurried away down a side street Karl Spedding, to Arnold's relief, frowned and muttered, 'It's not a drink I need. I think I'll just take a walk, blow away some cobwebs.'

He turned on his heel and marched along towards the Quai Duperre. Arnold turned to Karen. 'Shall I see you back to the hotel?'

She was snappish in her refusal. 'I'm a big girl now, Arnold.'

He bade her goodnight and then stood for a little while between the twin towers at the entrance to the harbour. Eventually he strolled quietly along the front, choosing one of the less frequented pavement cafés to order a brandy and soda. It was really only his second that evening, he consoled himself: he had not managed to drink the one bought by Spedding at the hotel. Karen's order to leave had been peremptory, though he could not blame her.

But as he sat in the café under a starlit sky, and watched the lights glittering and dancing on the dark water of the harbour while the yachts rocked gently on the incoming tide, he gradually began to unwind, and in a little while realized he was completely relaxed.

For the first time that evening.

2

The pale light of a rosy dawn stained the sky beyond the window. Inspector Jean-Pierre Leconte leaned forward and switched off the table lamp that had been the only illumination in the narrow room through the long night hours. He glanced at Carmela, sprawled in her chair, but said nothing.

Jean-Pierre Leconte was not a man given to small talk. He was an introspective, self-contained person who kept his thoughts to himself and rarely spoke of anything other than the business at hand. He sat across the room from Carmela, behind his desk in the small office in the police headquarters at Place Verdun, overlooking the square, the opulent, fin-de-siècle Café de la Paix and the bus terminal. While she sat uncomfortably in the hard-seated chair against the wall he seemed at ease: Jean-Pierre leaned back in his chair, his small dark moustache twitching occasionally as he fastidiously cleaned his fingernails with a nail file, then clipped the nails by biting at them, carefully, so that they did not tear. His teeth were small, and very white. His movements were precise and lacking in extravagance.

Carmela was eager for action and the long sojourn during the hours of darkness had seemed interminable. But they had to wait for the decision of the magistrate. She leaned her head back against the wall and closed her eyes, urging herself to remain calm, patient, in control. Emulate Jean-Pierre Leconte.

It had been a long trail she had followed, culminating in this small office in La Rochelle. She had no great expectation that the raid they were about to make would be the end of the whole business, but hopefully it would provide another link in the chain of international conspiracy and corruption that had exercised the Art Squad for the past three years. The *cordata* . . . the men linked as though by a rope, stretching through Italy and France, Germany and Switzerland.

It had begun with a car crash high in the mountains on the Swiss border: the dead man had been killed instantly,

2

but when the police arrived and clambered down to the car in the ravine he had been quickly identified as an Italian citizen. And when the contents of his glove compartment had been inspected, the Carabinieri Art Squad had been contacted immediately. The set of photographs they had discovered in the car had been startling: a ceremonial table with griffins, a chalice-krater, several marble heads, a lunette with a mask of Hercules, a marble statute of Tyche, the list had seemed endless. Some of the artefacts shown on the photographs were still encrusted with dirt; it was clear they had been looted from Etruscan and Roman tombs. But perhaps most important of all was the notebook. For the Carabinieri Art Squad it was a gold mine: the notebook contained details of purchases, prices paid, and the name of the seller.

A well-known name: Antonio Sapienza. A noted *tombarolo*.

Carmela folded her arms against her generous bosom, shifted in her chair, straightened, glanced at Jean-Pierre. He was still engrossed with his nails. He seemed indifferent to the passage of time, but the French police had not been as closely involved in this affair as Carmela and the rest of the Italian squad had been. Long years of investigation had taken place, until suddenly the breakthrough on the Swiss border had occurred. She could still see in her mind's eye the building yard in the tiny village near Lake Bolsano: it was no different from any other small enterprise with its litter of timber and bags of cement, piles of sand, blocks of concrete and girders, tiles, wooden pallets. And the builder, di Stefano, seemed unconcerned by their visit. He was a big, slow-moving man, bald, large-bellied, muscular in the arms and shoulders, but reserved and quiet in manner. He expressed considerable surprise at receiving a visit from the Carabinieri Art Squad officers, but appeared unconcerned and invited them freely to look around his yard and the office premises.

His wife was different: a small, excitable woman, she had appeared edgy, nervous, and while the officers looked around the yard they overheard her shrill, frightened tones as she execrated her stolid husband. The officers gathered, from what they could make out, that she had been warning her husband for years, but he had paid her no heed. And after that, when they confronted di Stefano with the photographs, he thought the matter over silently for a while and then, still badgered by his wife, he had led them, without a protest, into the woods behind the yard. The track was narrow and winding, overgrown with brambles, but there was a clearly marked passageway. Finally, deep among the overhanging trees, he pointed to a tin-roofed garage. He gave them the key. He stood by silently, a little hangdog in his attitude as they entered.

Electric light had been installed by way of a cable: when they switched on the bright light it was like entering an Aladdin's cave. Carmela recalled gasping as she saw the piles of looted antiquities scattered carelessly about on the garage floor, many still broken as they had been dragged out of the earth, some still encrusted with soil, clearly local in origin; there were fragments shoved into sacks and fruit boxes, ceramic pieces, bronzes. But the greatest surprise was the table at the far end of the garage: it had been used for restoration work, with palettes, brushes and technical equipment, reference books on archaeology. And on a shelf above the table was a small pile of notebooks.

Carmela opened her eyes, blinked, glanced at the quiescent Jean-Pierre. It still amazed her how the *tombaroli* and the dealers had almost compulsively committed themselves to recording their transactions in detail, in records that were bound to expose their criminal lootings to anyone who might find them. In the notebook found in the car of Sapienza were details of business dealings, prices, names – including the links that pointed the way up the chain, and down to the man who owned the isolated village construction business. Di Stefano might be a simple builder in a small way, but it was clear from his own records that his night-time activity among the Etruscan tombs was his real passion – and the source of his personal finances. He too had kept meticulous lists in his notebooks, and unusually he had even recorded not just what he had found, but the location of the finds.

The Art Squad had struck gold in more senses than one. It meant they could identify the fields that had been excavated and their owners – with whom di Stefano had shared some of the sale proceeds – as well as match the individual items with the specific looted tombs. And most important of all, the notebook identified the dealer to whom di Stefano had sold the stolen items.

It was this information that had led to the arrest and prosecution of the dealer Monticelli in Italy, but the Sapienza notebook revealed he was only one of a wide, international network, groups of *tombaroli* and interlinked dealers. For the moment the Art Squad was following up the leads in raiding those dealers who had worked directly with the *tombaroli*: Monticelli in Rome was only the first. There was an Englishman in London who was in their sights, and there was Ernest Carpentier, here in La Rochelle. They were all part of the *cordata*, the rope-linked conspirators dealing directly with the *tombaroli*, selling to each other and buying back at auctions, trading with each other to manufacture a provenance for the items for sale and then selling upwards thereafter to private collectors and museum curators. It was a well-organized operation. But the collectors and the curators, they would be the next to expose to the world, to bring to book. . .

The telephone shrilled suddenly, startling Carmela out of her vengeful reverie. She caught the glance of Jean-Pierre, who reached for the phone. He picked it up, listened briefly, then straightened. He nodded, replaced the phone on its cradle and stood up.

'*Allons-y*. All is in place.'

There were three unmarked police cars waiting in the Place Verdun. Inspector Leconte gestured to Carmela to get into the back seat of the first vehicle; he took a seat behind the driver. As they drove away from the square she glanced out of the back window: the two other cars were following them closely. The roads were quiet and the lights of the city centre faded behind them as they crossed the *périphérique*, proceeded into the suburbs of Jericho and soon reached their destination at Rue de Général Leclerc. The street was empty. The nineteenth-century houses, four storeys high, lined up ahead of them, regimented, slightly shabby, shutters closed. The driver pulled in at the kerb and Leconte got out. As Carmela alighted she heard the doors slam behind her: there were five other men walking towards her.

Leconte mounted the short flight of steps up to the front door of the house they were targeting. He rang the bell. There was no response. He rang again, three times, as the group waited expectantly. Finally he stepped back, and nodded to one of the group. The door would have to be forced.

At that moment a smartly dressed woman appeared from around the corner. She hesitated when she saw the group of plain-clothes policemen at the door and then she hurried forward. '*Qu'est-ce que vous faites?*' she called anxiously. '*Que voulez-vous?*'

Carmela's French was sufficiently sound to follow the brief conversation. Leconte observed the woman carefully for a few moments then asked, 'Do you live here?'

'Of course! What is it you want? Why are all these people –'

'We have here an order from the magistrate,' Leconte interrupted her soberly. 'It permits us to search these premises.'

'Search?' The woman was bristling with indignation. She pushed past them, glared at Carmela as though she was furious that a woman would stoop to be involved in such outrage as this assault upon her house, and stood in front of the door, arms flung wide in a futile gesture of defiance. 'This is my house. I live here. You have no right to enter.'

'You are Madame Carpentier?'

'Of course!' Her voice cracked slightly: her defiance was uncertain.

'Here is the documentation. It permits us to enter. By force if necessary.' Leconte touched his moustache lightly with one finger. 'If you open the house to us, I can promise you we will be careful, discreet in our search. If not ... I fear there might be considerable damage.'

Madame Carpentier was silent, various emotions chasing across her narrow features. Her eyes darted desperately around the group facing her. Carmela guessed she was thinking swiftly, anxious to find a way of deterring them. It was a lost cause. Finally, reluctantly, she turned and unlocked the door and led the way into the house.

They walked along a narrow passageway. Beyond was a large, high-ceilinged dining room. On the other side of the corridor was the kitchen: one of the officers walked into the area and glanced around. 'The next floor?' Leconte enquired.

The woman's mouth was set stubbornly. She scowled. 'There is another sitting room, and two bedrooms.'

'And the floor above?'

'Two bedrooms again. What is it you are looking for?' Her eyes were quick, darting sharp glances around the officers.

Leconte ignored her. He spoke quickly to the other officers, assigning them to the floors above. Then he turned back to the owner. 'Monsieur Carpentier is in town?'

She hesitated, reluctant to say anything, and then shrugged. 'He is away on business. In Switzerland. I do not expect him to return for several days.'

Carmela left the dining room and climbed the stairs to the first floor. It was soon apparent that the information in the notebooks had been correct: their search was not to be fruitless. The glass top of the table in front of the window was supported by a stone pedestal. Carmela could see at a glance that it was part of an ancient stone pillar. On the table top itself were two terracotta heads. On the heavy wooden sideboard against the wall was a red-figure Attic kylix. As Carmela watched, one of the searching officers opened the sideboard: the shelves within were strewn with glazed ceramics, shards of pottery, coins, glass and jewellery. She heard a man shout down from the floor above. 'This room up here – it's furnished like a restorer's laboratory.'

Carmela heard a step behind her. It was Madame Carpentier. Her finely drawn features were ashen, her eyes panicked. She was silent. Carmela walked towards her. 'Do you have somewhere to stay? It's clear we shall be here for some time.'

The woman glared at her, rejecting her sympathy, then turned and went back downstairs. She had a brief conversation with Inspector Leconte and then Carmela heard the front door slam. She looked out of the window. One of the police drivers was taking Madame Carpentier away, presumably to the police headquarters where she would be asked to make a statement. As Leconte joined Carmela on the first floor he raised his eyebrows at the sight of the artefacts that were being taken out of the sideboard. 'There are some in the bedroom as well. It is a cornucopia.'

It was loot, Carmela thought bitterly. She looked about her at the increasing pile of antiquities. Carpentier had clearly established a close and direct link with the *tombaroli*: she could see at a glance that many of the items were of Italian origin. The trail had been well worth following. She climbed the stairs to the rooms above and wandered through them. They were sparsely furnished.

Apart from the collection of looted antiquities. She shook her head in despair at the range of works there: a red-figured Attic phiale; a Corinthian olpe drew her attention; on the restorer's table was an Etruscan antefix in the shape of a dancing Menades and Silenus, partially burned at some time in the recent past. Pushed carelessly into one corner was a ceremonial marble table, a scattering of ceramics on its grubby surface; near the window was a Roman lunette with a mask of Hercules; scattered about the room haphazardly were Pontic and Attic amphorae and Apulian terracotta vases. It was clear to her that Carpentier was a shadowy, but obviously well-established link in the *cordata*. Whatever his business might be in Switzerland, Carmela had no doubt it would be lucrative . . . and illegal. With a sigh she moved on to inspect the other rooms. Soon, she would have to start the recording, along with the other officers.

It was going to take days.

The group worked doggedly for the rest of the morning. There was a break at lunchtime while sandwiches and coffee were brought in, and throughout the afternoon men sneezed constantly as the dust rose in their nostrils during their search. Painstakingly, they catalogued the items as they emerged: the house was clearly rarely used as living accommodation, if at all. Rather, it was a warehouse and a workshop for the French antiquities dealer. He was due for a surprise when he returned: steps had already been taken to prevent his wife warning him by telephone.

The officers finally finished work for the day at nine thirty in the evening. That night, after a late dinner, back in her hotel room Carmela was unable to sleep. She tossed and turned, uneasy, concerned about something. A piece of the jigsaw in her mind was missing: as she had worked at the house in Rue de Général Leclerc she had felt there was something wrong. It was like a shadow, a butterfly, half-seen, fluttering at the back of her mind. During the search of the premises she had broken off several times, wandered around the rooms, watched the others working, before returning to her own cataloguing activity, still worried.

It was the same the next day. Teams of men now began carrying away the antiquities for safe storage after the initial listing: they would continue to be worked on with some expert advice from local museum curators and other members of the Carabinieri Art Squad and the French authorities. Carmela had been to see Madame Carpentier but she was saying nothing, remaining tight-lipped in the absence of her husband. That she was as deeply involved as her husband Carmela had no doubt.

The group finally finished their work in the late afternoon. Once the items were safely stored Inspector Leconte, in a grateful gesture, invited the group as a whole to join him for dinner in his favourite restaurant: they dined off langoustines and crab, asparagus and palm hearts. The wine was not Italian, but Carmela admitted it was good. The party broke up at midnight, and Leconte escorted Carmela back to her hotel.

'It has been a successful raid.'

'But only one of many to come, I fear,' Carmela admitted.

Leconte nodded. 'You are right. Italy, France, Switzerland . . . and then there is the American connection. The web, it is widely cast.'

He bade her goodnight courteously, and she went up to her room. She had enjoyed dinner and the companionship of the tired yet exultant searchers but there still remained at the back of her mind something that worried her, something obvious and yet amorphous, dancing away from her each time she tried to grasp it, concentrate, identify what it was that concerned her.

Pacing the narrow confines of her room, she knew she would not get to sleep. At last, she went downstairs, got in her car and drove back to Place Verdun. She explained to the officer at the desk, who was unable to keep his eyes off her bosom, that she wanted to return to the now empty house, and she signed for a set of keys. She made her way once more to the house in Rue de Général Leclerc.

The street was deserted. At the doorway she paused, inserted the keys, and as she did so her fingers strayed lightly over the lock. There were scratches there, sharp edges. At some point the lock had been interfered with. She unlocked the door and stepped into the darkness of the hall and corridor. She made no attempt immediately to switch on the light: she wanted to get the feel of the house, sharpen her own senses to discover what it might be that was worrying her.

A faint light filtered through the fanlight at the top of the stairs, producing a ghostly luminescence on the stairwell. She ascended quietly, one hand on the solid, heavy oak balustrade. On the first landing she paused, thinking, then moved again towards the stairs leading to the floor above. When she reached the bedroom, which was now stripped of all the antiquities that had been stored there, she stopped, stood still, listened to the silence.

And finally, slowly, the question that had been bothering her unconscious mind filtered through in the close darkness of the room. They had searched three floors of the

71

house, but there were four storeys to the building. Yet there had been no sign of an attic entrance, no trapdoor in the ceiling, no visible entry point. She walked to the door, pressed the light switch. Nothing: the ceiling was bare, and she knew from her earlier wanderings that the other rooms were the same. She stood there uncertainly, and the light flickered uncertainly, as though the bulb, or the connection, was faulty.

She cast around, staring at the bare boards of the flooring. Dust had been scuffed up, the looted treasures all removed. The heavy mahogany wardrobe against the side wall gaped open, empty-mouthed, stripped of its illicit contents, unhelpful. Her glance dropped; there was something odd about the flooring at its base. She stepped forward, frowning, noted the smoothness of the wood, the scrapes that had scoured some of the varnished surface, and just as the light flickered briefly, flared again and then suddenly went out to leave her in darkness she guessed at the truth.

She waited several seconds until her eyes became used to the faint light from the window and then she moved to the wardrobe. It was solid, heavy, but she was a strong woman of sound peasant stock and as she pulled and heaved at the wardrobe it began to move. It had been moved before, and often.

Carmela swore at herself for failing to bring a pocket torch with her but she hesitated only a moment. She pulled again at the wardrobe and as it slid back sideways she extended her hand, felt nothing but space. Dropping to one knee she felt along the floorboards. Her groping fingers touched an uncarpeted step. And then, above it, another.

A staircase, leading to the attic room above. A concealed staircase . . . so who knew what treasures might lie above?

Her heart began to race with suppressed excitement; she squeezed herself through the gap and placed one foot on the step, was about to climb the stairs when a slight sound reached her. It came from below. Someone was entering the house.

Carmela froze. As she stood there, unmoving for several moments, listening, she realized at least two people had entered the house, through the front door. She could not remember whether she had locked it behind her: the keys remained in her pocket. She remained where she was, listening intently, and then finally she heard the sound of someone, perhaps two people, slowly, deliberately ascending the staircase in the darkness.

She had never regarded herself as a weak, faint-hearted woman: she had seen enough violence in the back streets of Naples as a child, and dealt with enough hard-handed, vicious *tombaroli* since, not to fear violence. She was a strong woman, determined, and confident in her own abilities. Nevertheless, there in the darkness, as the cautious footsteps came stealthily up towards her, it was as though a cold fist squeezed at her heart.

She waited breathlessly in the darkness. She clearly heard the echoing footsteps on the floor below, moving from room to room. Then, after an interval the sounds of movement changed, the steps had turned towards the stairs and she became aware of the thin pencil of light that flashed in the stairwell. She remained motionless, trying to quell the quickness of her breathing, aware of the thunder of the blood in her panicked veins, unreasoning.

There were definitely two of them; two men. Their heavy tread sounded on the landing outside the room that concealed her. They were silent. She wanted to cry out, but her tongue was thick, her mouth dry. She pressed herself back into the narrow stairs, hard against the wall, and the footsteps advanced into the room. There was a short pause, and the light was brighter now, as the beam of the torch flickered about the room. It settled on the wardrobe she had moved, steadied, and then the steps came forward, the light flashed violently into her eyes.

Half-blinded, she raised a hand to shield her eyes; there was a sharply hissed intake of breath and then the light held her, shaken in its beam, before it dropped, the narrow pencil of light focusing away from her, on to the dark stairway that led to the attic. Now, Carmela could make out the forms of the men who stood there, the lean one holding the torch, the other a big, broad-shouldered heavy shadow behind him.

When the man standing in front of her finally spoke, his tone was harsh, edged with menace, but it was a voice she recognized.

'What the hell are you doing here in the darkness?'

It was Inspector Jean-Pierre Leconte.

The narrow room at the Hôtel de Police was harshly lit by a strip lamp set in the ceiling: the white-painted walls added to the glare. The windows overlooking Place Verdun were shuttered, as though emphasizing the secrecy of the briefing they were about to receive. It seemed to Carmela Cacciatore to be an unnecessary precaution.

Carmela, the only woman present, sat at the back of the room when the group was assembled. The audience no longer consisted of the men who had been with her when they searched the house in Rue de Général Leclerc. There were new officers here now, hard-faced men who would have spent their lives dealing with the scum of the underworld, searching for the violent criminals who would stop at nothing to carry out their nefarious activity in the city *banlieues*. Nothing, not even murder.

She lowered her head, closed her eyes.

Carmela's thoughts jarred back to the earlier hours of the previous evening, her own entrance to the house and the darkness of the stairway to the attic, Inspector Leconte standing in front of her, astonished. 'They told me at headquarters that you had come back here to the house. What for? And what have you found here?'

The flashlight flickered around the narrow staircase again. Hastily, angry with herself for her earlier childish fears, and yet still aware of the cold perspiration along her back, Carmela stammered out, 'I've been ill at ease. When we came to the house earlier, I had this feeling all along there was something wrong, something we were missing. And it should have been so obvious. A four-storeyed house. The attic floor: we'd found no entrance to it.'

'Until now, it seems,' Jean-Pierre Leconte murmured softly. The flashlight wavered; the beam danced up the narrow stairs stretching upwards behind Carmela. 'When we came in and found the lights did not work we wondered what was happening. I feared the worst.'

'It was a faulty bulb,' Carmela explained hurriedly. 'It must have fused the whole system. But I found this hidden staircase, concealed by the wardrobe – and that means, if it's concealed like this, there'll be more to be discovered in the attic.'

She had been right. She led the two men up the stairs, the light from the torch preceding them.

The beam of Leconte's flashlight only dimly illuminated the room as a whole, but it quickly picked out the clutter of antiquities that lay scattered around the bare-boarded floor of the long, low-ceilinged room. Carmela noted that many of the objects were still dirt-encrusted and as the beam flashed cursorily over them she became aware that in this storeroom were retained more valuable items, recent lootings that would have been hidden away here until the appropriate time came for them to be taken to the room below, cleaned, restored and then released, slowly, piece by piece, on to the market.

Leconte stepped past her, flickering the beam around the room. 'It looks as though . . .' His voice suddenly died away and he stood still, stiff, the flashlight beam fixed on a dark crumpled heap behind the door. For a moment Carmela thought it was a large bag that might have contained a heavy piece of looted statuary but then she realized that the pallid head held in the steady brightness of the beam was not statuary, it was not an ancient bust. Her mouth was suddenly dry.

'What . . . who is it?' she murmured shakily.

The steady beam did not move from the face. Stepping forward, reluctantly, Carmela could see that there was a small wound, a dark hole in the centre of the forehead. The bullet would have entered there; its exit would have created a larger hole, at the back of the head.

Leconte was silent for a few seconds, then quietly he said, 'I think it is Carpentier.'

The dead man's wife had told them he was in Switzerland on business. But he had returned, clearly without her knowledge. To his death.

Carmela put out one hand against the wall. She felt dizzy. She was suddenly conscious now of a faint, sickly odour in the heavy, fetid atmosphere of the attic. The scent of blood and decay and death. She was aware of the large frame of the stranger who had accompanied Leconte, standing behind her. A heavy hand touched her arm. 'Are you all right?' He spoke in English; she detected an American accent.

She made no reply, but nodded, straightened, pulled herself together. Leconte was still staring at the corpse behind the door. Then, slowly, he directed the beam of the flashlight away from the crumpled form of the owner of the house, wavering across the litter of scattered antiquities. She heard the startled sucking in of breath as the flashlight was stilled again.

'There is another here.'

Reluctantly, in spite of her anxiety, Carmela willed herself to step forward, until she was standing just behind Leconte. She looked past him to the thing that had once been a man, slumped in a half-seated position against the wall. The head was back, the eyes wide, staring, almost bulging out of their sockets. The mouth was open and the dark stain of blood coagulated around the jaw.

'I think this one was strangled,' Leconte said in a quiet, dispassionate tone. He kept the beam fixed on the dead man's face. 'I wonder what's gone on here. Can this be another dealer, like Carpentier?'

Carmela continued to stare at the swollen mouth, the bloated features, the glaring eyes that seemed to demand attention with an aggressive insistence. In spite of the effects of the strangulation Carmela felt a shudder of recognition pass through her: she believed she knew who this man was. It was a face she had seen in catalogues, in articles, in newspapers. She touched Leconte lightly on the sleeve.

'No. Not a dealer in antiquities.'

The flashlight beam danced around the room as Leconte glanced back over his shoulder to stare at her in the dimness. 'You know this man? You recognize him?'

Carmela nodded. Her mind was in a whirl, but her conviction was growing.

77

'I think so. But he is not a dealer,' she murmured. 'He is a collector. He is . . . was . . . well known in the world of antiquities. He is a wealthy American.'

'His wealth is meaningless now,' Leclerc muttered. 'But you know his name?'

Carmela nodded. 'He is from New York. His name is Adam Shearbright.'

There was a hiss, a sharp intake of breath from the big man, half hidden behind her. Carmela glanced back at him curiously, then turned again to Leconte. She was an expert in looted antiques; she was a hunter of criminal dealers and tomb robbers. Murder was not her specialization. 'What can have happened here?' she queried in a shaky voice. 'Who can have done this?'

There was a short silence. It was finally broken by the broad-shouldered stranger standing just behind her in the attic darkness. 'I think there can be little doubt about that. I've been trailing the man who did this, for the last two years.'

The stranger's breathing seemed harsh, and frustrated. 'His name is Anwar Zahiri.'

Carmela clenched her fists, hearing again in her memory the later hysterical screaming of Madame Carpentier back at headquarters, when she had been told of the death of her husband. She had been inconsolable, but continued to cling to the panicked fiction that she knew nothing about her husband's criminal dealings in looted antiquities. And still insisting she had no idea why he had been killed. No doubt that would change in due course, when reality thrust in upon her and she came to understand that denials would have no effect upon her future . . .

Carmela opened her eyes, looked about her, thrust away the recollections of the smell of blood in the attic and the sobbing screams of the widowed woman in the interview cell, and concentrated on what Inspector Leconte was saying in the briefing room to the assembled policemen.

'I have here copies of the photograph of the man we are seeking in regard to the murders of the two men, Carpentier and the American Shearbright. Please take one each.'

Leconte remained silent as the photographs were doled out around the murmuring room. Carmela received hers. She stared at it. The face was unfamiliar to her. She guessed the man would be perhaps late-forties; it was a narrow face, hard determined eyes, high Slavic cheekbones, moustache, neatly trimmed beard. His dark, greying hair was curly, greased back from his bony forehead. She looked again at the eyes: she felt she detected there a hint of fanaticism, a fierce commitment. She looked up.

Inspector Leconte was standing on a small dais. Behind him was the burly American who had been with Leconte and Carmela when they discovered the two bodies in the attic in Rue de Général Leclerc. He was perhaps six feet in height with the shoulders of an American football player. Carmela guessed he was at least fifty years of age but he had looked after himself well: his stomach under the sharp suit was trim, his stance was upright, his bearing confident. His greying hair was carelessly tousled, growing thickly at the back of his head, and his grey eyes were sharp, intelligent; his wide mouth had laughter lines at the corners and she gained the impression he would be a man easy to get on with, a man who would be attractive to women. He would know it too. But he was also a man who would know his own mind, and would follow through a quest with determination and aggressive commitment. Like his quest for Anwar Zahiri.

'We now have two major investigations on our hands here in La Rochelle,' Inspector Leconte was saying. 'The team investigating the criminal trade in antiquities, which has included our Italian friends from the Carabinieri Art Squad, will now necessarily become somewhat attenuated: we are unable to devote as considerable a part of our resources to this investigation as was previously the case, and we have been forced to draft in additional officers now that we have a double murder to deal with. On the other hand, we have the additional resource granted to us by the American government.'

Carmela thought she detected a slight irony in Leconte's remarks.

'This is Monsieur Richard Gonzalez. He describes himself as a field officer of the American Central Intelligence Agency. I will leave it to him to explain the reason for his presence here ... and for his belief that he is able to identify the man who murdered the dealer Carpentier and the antiquities collector Shearbright.'

Leconte stepped back to the rear of the dais and selected a chair. He sat down, folded his arms: his features were expressionless, but Carmela felt she detected a certain disapproval in his demeanour. She became aware of murmuring among the assembled officers as Richard Gonzalez stepped forward.

'As Inspector Leconte explained,' he began in reasonably fluent, though accented and somewhat stilted, French, 'I work for the CIA.'

The police officer beside Carmela cleared his throat surreptitiously and muttered to his fellow officer on his left, 'That stands for Criminal Incompetence Agency.'

Carmela grimaced. It was clear there was resentment in the room at the presence of Gonzalez in this investigation. It was not new to her: French and American relationships could be subtly hostile: there was a love–hate attitude between the two nations, exacerbated by recent political events. If the attitude came to be reflected in individual behaviour the result could be the kind of turf war that could hinder the successful prosecution of an investigation.

'I need to fill you in on a few things ... sketch a background for you. I have for the last two years,' Gonzalez was saying, 'been in pursuit of a man called Anwar Zahiri. It is in my view highly likely that he is the assassin responsible for the killing of the two men last night. You have in your possession a photograph of this individual: he is extremely dangerous, a killer who was trained in his techniques and attitudes by the organization known in the West as SAVAK.'

The room was silent, and Gonzalez clearly became aware of a number of blank looks.

'SAVAK,' he repeated, scanning the room. 'Or to use its original name: *Sazeman-e Ettala't va Amnyat-e Keshvar.*'

'Quite a linguist,' the officer beside Carmela muttered sarcastically, 'for a man from the CIA.'

'Perhaps I'd better put in a little of the context, the background of Anwar Zahiri,' Gonzalez was continuing. 'He was trained as a killer by SAVAK, the organization which was established by the Shah of Persia to act in support of his reign. And perhaps it goes without saying that like all such secret forces operating in an autocratic state it routinely used murder and torture to pursue its ends.'

An officer in the front row near the dais spoke up. 'SAVAK was a secret police force?'

'That describes it in a nutshell,' Gonzalez nodded firmly. 'The organization can be seen as on a par with the KGB in Russia or the STASI in East Germany. Nominally, it was run by a certain General Nassiri, who was slavishly obedient to the Shah. Nominally, I say, because Nassiri acted only on the authority of the Peacock Throne. But it needs to be said that although the organization was basically a secret police force supporting the Shah it had a wider brief too: it was never quite so completely inward-looking as other such organizations. It also maintained close liaison with Israel and its counterpart Mossad.'

'And the CIA?' the chauvinistic officer beside Carmela asked pointedly.

Gonzalez permitted himself a wry smile. 'There were contacts certainly. It's always as well to find out what the opposition might be doing.'

'I don't suppose the Arab world would have been happy about SAVAK contacts with Israel,' another officer suggested.

'It was never fully disclosed, or admitted to the Arabs. As for the Shah, well, he was always in secret contact with the Israelis, throughout his reign. But that is of little significance here at the moment. Though you are right to note that SAVAK had extensive contacts with the CIA, not least through the American Embassy in Tehran.'

Carmela guessed she knew the answer to such behaviour: during his reign the Shah would have played all ends against the middle.

'The Shah of Iran was a realist,' Gonzalez continued. 'A pragmatist. And he had considerable admiration for the West, which gave him much support during his reign, even if the Western governments let him down badly in the end when he was seeking asylum after the revolution of the mullahs . . .' He paused. 'The Peacock Throne obtained significant amounts of arms from the West. Supplies came from Britain and the USA. Even,' he added after an ironic hesitation. 'from France. The fact is, all these countries scrambled over each other to obtain lucrative contracts. And Mossad used SAVAK extensively to obtain information.'

Carmela wondered where the mysterious Anwar Zahiri fitted into this business.

'SAVAK was personally controlled by the Shah, so he must be held responsible for its savagery, but the West turned a blind eye to its activities. The West saw him as dragging Iran into the modern world with humanitarian projects, and land reform, but the peasantry in the country were well aware that he was turning a blind eye to the more savage of SAVAK activities – torture, murder, pursuit of dissidents at home and abroad.'

The officer beside Carmela spoke up again. 'Yet the CIA supported him?'

'Of course,' Gonzalez admitted blandly. 'The Shah was seen as a bulwark. And he was oil-rich. That always counts, I am forced to admit. Yes, the CIA supported the Shah, were also involved in the background, and until quite a late stage were in fact still financing the Shah's son, Reza Pahlavi, when he fled to the States.'

'So you tell us SAVAK was a feared organization,' someone at the front of the room called out, impatiently. 'But what about this Anwar character?'

'I'm coming to that,' Gonzalez asserted seriously. 'As I said at the beginning, Anwar was trained by SAVAK but it was late in the days of the regime. It was at the time when the Shah was tottering on his throne. SAVAK began to develop a modern face, secretive though it might be. It went about the recruitment of young mullahs who changed sides and brought in religious infrastructure; it developed modern techniques and thought; it set up an impressive PR structure and modern press relations. Under the leadership of General Nassiri, who in reality was personally responsible for organizing real estate, SAVAK had an acceptable public face, as far as the West was concerned. But the rest of it . . . the gathering of intelligence was left to the shadowy figure of a man called Parviz Sabeti. It was he who established and organized the co-operative links with the CIA, obtained intelligence and sowed fear. He set up agency arrangements throughout the country, and had spies located in every embassy abroad. He acted through thousands of informers. And in particular he recruited a young sixteen-year-old who showed a remarkable aptitude for carrying out the organization's principal objects: to gather intelligence and sow fear. Anwar Zahiri.'

Gonzalez paused, glanced around the room before he continued. 'Once a victim fell into the hands of SAVAK there was nowhere to turn: they disappeared, after whipping and beatings; the agents used electric shocks, nail and teeth-pulling, pumping boiling water into the rectum. Zahiri also learned the other favoured techniques, which included hanging heavy weights on testicles, tying prisoners to slowly heating bed frames, inserting broken bottles into the anus, and, as a matter of course, rape. All new recruits were introduced to the delights of such activities. But it was the next phase that completed the education of the young Anwar Zahiri. When the mullahs came to power, after the Shah abdicated the throne and Ayatollah Khomeini took control, SAVAK set up an assassination squad as a blackmailing and money-making terrorist organization. It was tailor-made for Anwar's talents. He became a murderous assassin motivated by a heady mixture of religious zeal and fanaticism.'

Carmela frowned. All this must have taken place decades ago. She could not see how it fitted in with the murder of the French antiquities dealer and the American collector. She realized suddenly that Gonzalez had fixed his glance on her at the back of the room. Perhaps he was prescient; perhaps he had guessed at her puzzlement.

'Iran today,' he went on, 'is a very different place since the death of the Shah. The lengthy war with Iraq, the Gulf War, the fall of Saddam Hussein, recent political changes in Iran, all these had an impact upon the Shah's secret police. Age and death took account of many of the active officers; many slunk back into the community, some were executed, some went into hiding, others went abroad. But a hard core remained, men who had access to secrets that were known to only a very few. One of those secrets concerned the hidden wealth of the Shah himself.'

The officer beside Carmela snorted. 'A treasure hunt! An old fantasy,' he muttered, more loudly than before.

Gonzalez heard the comment and permitted himself a wry smile. 'I should make it clear from the outset that when one speaks of the hidden wealth of the Shah, it is now widely recognized that much of it is mythical. The sojourn of the Shah in the West was costly; also many of his bank accounts were really those of the State and claimed by them. On the other hand there were certain *personal* items that were of incredible value. Some of these were not merely valuable in financial terms: they also had considerable religious significance.' He paused, and his eyes seemed to seek out Carmela again.

'Our attention was directed to some of these items when the Baghdad Museum was ransacked in April 2003. Some fifteen thousand items vanished in the aftermath of the US invasion.'

American troops had stood by, Carmela recalled bitterly, while the looters went in, grabbing priceless items such as the 5200-year-old sacred vase of Warka, the world's oldest known carved stone ritual vessel. It had been returned, finally, in the back of a car, no thanks to the US troops.

'The lootings from the museum helped terrorist activity, helped fund the insurgency in Iraq: for instance, US troops found more than thirty items in a raid in Anbar province in 2005. But CIA informants drew our attention to a specific cache that had been hidden in the Assyrian Room. It had gone missing, but it was believed the particular item we are interested in was taken *before* the looting of the museum. SAVAK agents, and Anwar Zahiri in particular, have been searching for it ever since.'

Carmela was aware that more than ten thousand pieces looted from the Baghdad Museum were still being sought, including an eighth-century plaque of a lioness attacking a Nubian, inlaid with lapis and carnelian and overlaid with gold. But Gonzalez was talking about something more specific; of religious significance and once held by the Shah.

Gonzalez cleared his throat. 'These killings last night, I am convinced, were the work of Anwar Zahiri. For some years he has been obsessed, as others were in his group, with the recovery of items from the personal wealth, which also had religious significance, of the now defunct Shah. The CIA has been aware of the search, and we have managed to ... ah ... shall we say, head off some of the searchers. Occasionally we were forced to take extreme measures.'

The meaning was not lost upon his audience. The euphemism *extreme measures* was well known to them. And no doubt, Carmela considered, the CIA hunting of the terrorists would be partly due to their desire to hide its own secrets.

'But of the small group that remains, the hard core of SAVAK thugs, turned religious zealots, one man has been given the specific task of recovery of a certain item . . . I do not intend telling you what this artefact is, it is of no relevance to this part of the investigation, but I am convinced that Anwar Zahiri is behind these killings because, as I've been following his activities, so he has been following the travels of the American collector Adam Shearbright. It's my opinion that Shearbright came to La Rochelle to buy what Anwar Zahiri himself was looking for. It was possibly in the hands of the French dealer Carpentier. And when Shearbright went to an assignation with Carpentier last night, he was followed by the SAVAK-trained killer Zahiri.'

There was a short silence, followed by some subdued murmuring among the assembled officers. Finally, one of them called out, 'So has this man achieved what he was after? This . . . item you do not disclose to us, it is in the hands of this Zahiri?'

Gonzalez looked grim, thoughtful. Behind him Inspector Jean-Pierre Leconte rose from his seat and came forward to stand beside the man from the CIA. He held up a hand. 'This is something we cannot know. In one sense, it is of no relevance to our enquiries. Mr Gonzalez has suggested to us a suspect – and a motive – for the murders last night. What we have to do is seek out the *truth*. And it may be that Mr Gonzalez is correct in his assumptions. He has given us a name, and a photograph. We would be foolish to ignore this lead that the CIA has given us. We search for this man, this Anwar Zahiri. The *alleged* killer.' He paused, smiled briefly and somewhat apologetically at Gonzalez. 'But we do not close our mind to other possibilities. We shall in addition, as they say, interview the usual suspects.'

His final remarks could have been addressed directly to Carmela at the back of the room. 'The remaining and ongoing investigation, concerning the dealers in looted antiquities, will continue, of course, and we shall still render assistance to our friends from Italy, the Carabinieri Art Squad, but this can no longer be a matter of the greatest priority in the Département of Charente-Maritime.' He smiled, nodded to Carmela. 'That does not mean that we shall raise any obstacles to the ongoing activities of our Italian friends. That, I repeat, goes without saying. But we must now devote our greatest activities and our resources to the murders of Carpentier and Shearbright . . .'

Chapter Three

1

The group that flew back to Newcastle was in a subdued mood. Their return from La Rochelle had been delayed for twenty-four hours after the end of the conference by the requirement for each of them to be interviewed by the police. The news of the death of Adam Shearbright had naturally shaken Arnold and Karen: they had no knowledge of the other murdered man, but had guessed from what was said that he had been involved in the sale of looted antiquities. As for Karl Spedding, he had seemed withdrawn, reserved; he had kept his thoughts to himself when he had learned of Shearbright's death. He had already made clear his opinion of Shearbright, in the hotel bar, but he seemed disinclined to make any further comment to Arnold or Karen since the man's death.

'What about this other man?' Arnold had asked him, as they waited at Stansted Airport for their connection to Newcastle. 'This dealer, Carpentier.'

Spedding had shrugged, shaken his head. 'We've simply been told he was a dealer, but I've no knowledge of him. I don't think he would have been acting directly with museums.'

Presumably he had said the same to the police, when each of them was interviewed separately at the head-quarters in Place Verdun.

The man who had introduced himself to Arnold as Inspector Jean-Pierre Leconte asked all the questions; behind him sat a big man in a well-cut suit who said nothing. It was as though he was not directly involved in the investigation, but was holding a watching brief. Something about him made Arnold feel he was not French.

'So you insist that you did not know this dealer Carpentier, that you are here merely for this conference, and that the other dead man, the American Adam Shearbright, was also not known to you.'

'That is correct.'

Leconte's forefinger reached up to caress his small moustache. His eyes were riveted upon Arnold. His English was as precise as his manner. 'You did not know him, yet we are told you had a conversation with the American, only a matter of hours before he died.'

Arnold frowned, and shook his head. 'No, I did not converse with him. I was merely present when he was talking to a colleague of mine.'

'Ah, yes ... Monsieur Karl Spedding,' Leconte mused. 'They were talking, you say. And you did not know Shearbright previously.'

Arnold nodded. 'Karl Spedding merely announced his name. Sort of introduced him. But Shearbright actually ignored us ... me and Miss Stannard. It was as though we weren't there. His discussion was exclusively with Spedding.'

'Discussion, you say.' Leconte's eyes narrowed. 'Other observers say it was more in the nature of a quarrel.'

The inquisitive barman, Arnold guessed. He shook his head. 'I wouldn't exactly describe it as a quarrel. There were ... high words from Shearbright, certainly. He was angry. He was annoyed at things that Karl Spedding had said during the presentation of his paper at the conference. But Spedding himself, well, he remained cool.'

'But Monsieur Spedding repeated during the discussion the comments he had earlier made?'

'I suppose so,' Arnold agreed defensively. 'But he did not lose his temper; he maintained control; he did not quarrel with Shearbright. He merely kept to his position, reiterated his beliefs.'

'Which nevertheless angered the American,' Leconte murmured. 'And after this confrontation in the bar, you and your colleagues went to dinner?'

'That's right. At Les 4 Sergents.'

Leconte smiled approvingly. 'A good choice. And after dinner . . .?'

Arnold hesitated. 'We . . . well, we went our separate ways. Miss Stannard said she was tired, and went back to our hotel. I strolled towards the Place de la Chaîne and the two towers, then took a I coffee in a café on Quai Duperre.'

'Mr Spedding was with you?'

'No. He was staying at the same hotel as us, but I believe he took a walk.'

'Alone?'

'I believe so.'

The eyes of the police inspector were hooded. 'There was a fourth member of your party.'

Arnold nodded. 'Well, yes, though not exactly of our party. He was known to us. He attended the same conference, though wasn't staying at the Hôtel de la Monnaie. A lawyer, James Detorius.' Arnold hesitated. 'He had arranged to join us for dinner, provided he could get away. But he wasn't in the bar with us. He joined us after the . . . discussion: he was waiting for us in the reception area. He wasn't with us when Shearbright got angry with Karl Spedding.'

'And none of you saw the American after that incident in the bar?'

Arnold shrugged. 'I certainly did not. Obviously, I can't speak for the others.'

Thoughtfully, Leconte permitted himself a slight smile. 'So in fact, none of you can corroborate an alibi for the other . . .'

When they reached Newcastle Karen and Arnold took a taxi back to Morpeth. Spedding intimated he would be going into Newcastle to attend to some personal business that evening so declined an offer of a lift. 'But you'll be able to start work at the office tomorrow?' Karen asked.

Spedding nodded. 'I'll be there.'

In fact, he arrived before Arnold. By the time Arnold reached the office Spedding had already begun his move into the room that had formerly been used by Arnold: there were two cardboard boxes placed in the middle of the room, and various personal items had been neatly arranged in the centre of the desk: a leather-bound diary, a miniature clock encased in Waterford glass, a laptop computer. Spedding himself was not present. Arnold guessed he would be with Karen Stannard, being given an outline of his duties. It would save Arnold the trouble. It was clear Karen would be slow to release the strings she had held as Head of the Department of Museums and Antiquities.

Arnold still felt uneasy at the thought that he was now working in that capacity.

At ten o'clock he walked along to the committee room for a meeting with the Museums Sub-Committee. He did not enjoy committee work but there was a presentation to be made on a report he had earlier prepared on a Roman dig at Rothbury, so at least he was able to make a good impression on this first task: the work had been done by him personally, not by Karen.

For most of the afternoon thereafter he was involved with Karl Spedding, introducing him to the rest of the staff in the department, and then discussing with him the range of current field activities, in particular those which Spedding himself would have to take under his wing. Arnold found it a difficult task: he was having to give up responsibility for sites in which he had taken a personal interest for so long. It was almost like losing a part of himself. It did not help that he found the uncommunicative Spedding difficult to deal with.

The remainder of the week passed swiftly. Spedding called in to see him several times, for clarification of certain issues; he had a session with Karen when she handed over to him the outstanding files still in her possession, but it was not until the Friday afternoon that she mentioned their experience in La Rochelle. Arnold was in her office; her secretary had brought in coffee, and she was relaxing.

When the secretary had gone, Karen frowned. 'So, Arnold, how's your new assistant settled in?'

Arnold thought for a moment, then admitted, 'He seems to have taken to the work easily enough. I suppose that's to be expected, from a man of his experience.'

Karen's green eyes were fixed on him, contemplatively. 'You don't like him, do you?'

'I didn't say so,' he retorted defensively.

'No, I just said so. Just what is it about him that gets under your skin?'

Arnold hesitated. 'It's nothing . . . definite. He's settled in; he is well informed; but there's a certain reserve about him. He seems to sort of hug things to himself; doesn't seem to relax. And I don't know, but I still think it's fishy, this move from such a prestigious post as assistant curator at the Pradak. Then there's what Shearbright said, about him being sacked . . . That doesn't appear in Spedding's application. In his CV he stated he had resigned. For a career change.'

Karen's glance slipped away. 'Well,' she muttered at last, 'I don't suppose you need to like him. Just work with him without friction.' She glanced at Arnold again, as though thinking about the friction that had existed between the two of them over the years, but then shrugged. 'Has he said anything to you about Shearbright?'

Arnold shook his head. 'Nothing. It's as though it never happened.'

'You heard anything else from the French police? I certainly haven't.'

'I'm in the same boat. But then, we had seen Shearbright only for a matter of minutes, and didn't even speak to him.'

Her gaze became reflective. 'Spedding certainly pulled no punches that evening at the bar. He clearly holds strong views about the antiquities trade . . . It was almost as though he took things personally.' She shook her head dismissively. 'Anyway, have you been able to get on with that business of identification for Isabella Portland? I promised her we'd give her some answers as quickly as possible.'

'I've arranged to call to see her at Belton Hall tomorrow morning.'

'That's good.' Karen eyed him mockingly. 'She's a widow, Arnold, and very attractive. You'd better be careful. Maybe I shouldn't let you go by yourself.'

He left his bungalow at ten the following morning and drove into the Northumberland hills. The sky was a pale, washed-out blue, a slight haze lying over the Cheviots, and the air was fresh and clean. A group of strutting partridges scuttered away into the hedgerow; on one of the dry stone walls that stretched along the winding road a haughty male pheasant observed his progress with regal detachment. The almost inevitable buzzard soared on the thermals above the hill, mounting higher and higher, and as Arnold dropped into the valley that held Belton Hall sheep scampered away to the higher fells.

He had done some research. The Hall itself had been redesigned in the nineteenth century to accommodate the grandiose desires of a nouveau riche coal magnate. Its origins were early eighteenth century, Arnold now knew; it was circular in plan with the giant portico flanked by Ionic columns a later addition. The long gravelled drive curved between magnificent oaks and well-established rhododendrons. As Arnold made his way along the drive he saw another car coming towards him, leaving the house. It slowed, drew level and stopped as he did. The electric window of the Mercedes whirred down. In the driving seat was Isabella Portland, glossy hair framing her elegant features. She leaned across the passenger seat to speak to him.

'Mr Landon. I'm sorry, I know we'd made an appointment, but I have to go and see my lawyer unexpectedly. Something's come up; it's to do with the sale of the Edinburgh flat. Scottish law and all that.'

'Shall we make another appointment? I could call back another time.'

She shook her head. 'No, that won't be necessary. Angela Fenchurch is up at the house. She's expecting you. She can deal with the business in hand. Hope to see you soon.'

The window closed, she drove off and vanished around the bend into the main road. Arnold realized he was far from disappointed: he had been looking forward to meeting Isabella Portland's young assistant and partner. The opportunity to spend time with her alone was a pleasant surprise.

He left his car in the gravelled drive. He walked up to the great doors flanked by the marble statues of Autumn and Spring. The whole place was redolent of wealth, and the stern-visaged, elderly butler who opened the door to him asked no questions: it was as though he recognized Arnold in spite of his vague gaze. Arnold asked to see Miss Fenchurch.

She met him in the hallway, at the foot of the stairs. She had tied back her hair, her face was a perfect oval. She was more tanned than he recalled and her welcoming smile was clear and unaffected. There was a smile in her eyes and when she extended her hand her grip was firm. She was dressed in jeans, flat shoes and a loose, light blue sweater. 'It's good to see you again.'

'Good to see you, also. And the drive was pleasant.' He felt oddly ill at ease, unable to make small talk, and stood there diffidently, the folder of photographs and documents under his arm.

'I'm working upstairs,' she said, 'in the exhibition room. Perhaps we could talk up there.'

He nodded agreement and followed her up the broad stairway, acutely conscious of the movement of her hips in the tight jeans she wore. The room they entered was, he guessed, immediately above the library on the ground floor and was proportionately large. The walls were lined with books and tapestries: the volumes would probably have been brought up from the library downstairs, for reference purposes. Some of them were lying on the long table in the centre of the room. Also placed on the table were several bronzes. Ranged along the walls were numerous other pieces, neatly placed and ticketed. They would comprise the collection Isabella Portland had acquired from the Edinburgh premises. Angela Fenchurch followed the line of his glance. 'The Edinburgh flat was a surprise to her – she had no idea her husband kept items up there. She's selling the apartment, of course, but these items . . . it was quite a windfall. I've been cataloguing them during this last week and there are some interesting pieces, and some idiosyncratic ones too – like this thing here.' She smiled at him. 'You recognize it?'

'I can't say I do,' Arnold admitted.

'I've seen one before in the museum at Carlisle. It's a Roman implement, for the removal of cataracts. Quite how it was used, with only wine as an anaesthetic, and with this blade and cup . . .'

Arnold shuddered. Hastily, he said, 'I'd rather not know! There's quite a wide range of stuff here. You'll be able to deal with most of it yourself, I imagine. As for the items that had been photographed . . .'

'You've been able to identify them?'

'Shall we sit down?' Arnold suggested. She nodded, waved him to a chair at the mahogany table and sat down herself, facing him expectantly. Arnold placed the folder on the table between them, and opened it. 'I've been able to identify most of the items we had queries about, and I've appended some notes regarding their likely uses. Karen has also made a few notes: I agree with them in the main; they're concerned with the likely sites that they might have come from.' He paused, glanced at the young woman, uncertainly. 'This collection of Mrs Portland's . . . it's a bit light on provenance. And some of the attributions are vague. This one, from a dealer, for instance . . . acquired during World War II by the vendor's mother. It doesn't exactly inspire confidence.'

Angela nodded vigorously. 'It's something I've already discussed with Isabella. This statement here, for instance, on this bronze . . . believed to be of Pontic origin. That tells us something and nothing.' She leaned back, folded her arms across her breasts and shook her head. 'I've told Isabella that if we hope to sell some of these items we might have a problem. There are dealers, of course, who are all for secrecy –'

'Commercial secrecy is often nothing more than a smokescreen for unacceptable practices,' Arnold advised.

'I know it. The fact is,' Angela acknowledged with a sigh, 'Isabella's husband built up this collection without her knowledge.' She hesitated, glancing at Arnold doubtfully. 'I believe you've heard that he was involved in some shady business practices.'

'I know the story,' Arnold admitted.

'And the secrecy of this collection,' Angela continued, 'would lead me to believe that there might be some dicey stuff here. Which is one of the reasons why I suggested Isabella take advice from your department.' She nodded towards the folder in front of Arnold. 'And check on the photographs.'

Arnold riffled through the pages of the folder, pausing over various items in the plastic covers. 'Well, I can tell you that a number of these have doubtful origins, and the attributions are perhaps a little suspect, so you might have difficulty in selling them to a reputable buyer. On the other hand, there are museums who might take them for exhibition purposes, and maybe root around for stronger provenances. However, the pieces on this list would seem to be pretty genuine, with appropriate provenance ... and Isabella and yourself, well, you could build up a reasonably sound business, selling them. On the other hand ...'

Arnold selected a sheet from the folder and passed it to Angela. 'This is a list of photographs I've extracted from the file. I've been unable to identify some of them, and the provenance of all of them is to say the least hazy. I would guess that a number of them are Italian in origin, and I know someone who'll be very interested to see the photographs, and help in identifying the pieces.' He paused, choosing his words with care. 'In at least two cases, I suspect they've actually been stolen.'

'Stolen?'

Arnold nodded. 'I don't mean looted at illegal excavations. I mean stolen from private collections. This statuette, for instance. I'm pretty sure I've seen it in a catalogue. And there are some others . . . Anyway, I've taken the liberty of sending a selection of photographs of the items concerned to a friend of mine in Rome. I actually met her this last week, unexpectedly, in France. She will be able to pick up the photographs on her return to her headquarters –'

'A museum?'

'No. She works for the Carabineri Art Squad.'

Angela was quiet for a little while, staring at the list Arnold had given her. At last she sighed, looked up at him and smiled. 'I'm sure Isabella will be grateful for the trouble you've taken. You'll let us know what happens in due course?'

'Of course,' Arnold assured her.

'Right,' she said breezily, setting aside her anxieties, 'we can take a look at the artefacts that pass muster now, and perhaps you'd like to give me some advice on valuations, and possible placements. Karen Stannard said you'd be able to help.'

Arnold was only too pleased to oblige.

The collection was an eclectic one. It was clear that Isabella Portland's dead husband had had no clear aim in his collection, as far as grouping was concerned. He had been no specialist. He had had an eye, without doubt, and Arnold was certain that some of the artefacts displayed in the room would command considerable prices at auction, while there were at least three objects, which seemed to have appropriate provenance, which would raise considerable interest among international museums.

'Provided they haven't been stolen,' Angela observed ironically.

It was a pleasant morning's work. Apart from the fact that Arnold was interested in the display, he enjoyed the presence of Angela Fenchurch; her enthusiasm was infectious, her sense of humour bubbling, and he appreciated the combination of intellectual ability, physical beauty and cheerful personality. As their work came to an end, he felt a certain disappointment that it was finished.

'So, Arnold,' she said with a smile, 'Isabella thought we'd see the morning out, so she's arranged for lunch here, if you wish.'

Arnold was more than pleased with the suggestion. Angela led the way back down the stairs to the dining room where cold meats and a splendid salad had been laid for them. Angela giggled as she handed a bottle of chilled Chardonnay to Arnold, for him to open. 'I should make it clear we don't always take a break of this kind when we're working.'

The wine was excellent. As they snacked on the cold collation Angela told him a little more about herself. She had not really known her mother: she had died when Angela was still an infant. Consequently she had been raised by her grandmother in Stanhope.

'Was that your mother I caught a glimpse of, in the album where you were keeping the photographs? I just happened to catch sight of a picture . . .'

Angela nodded, sipped at her wine. 'Yes, there's an old shot of her with me as a babe in arms. And my father behind us.' She frowned. 'It's the only one I have – or rather, that Grandmother has kept.'

She was very close to the old lady, grateful for her support, her kindness, her wisdom and her insistence that no expense should be spared in providing Angela with a sound education. 'The final icing on the cake was the time I spent in Paris, after school in Lausanne,' Angela added, toying with wineglass. 'It was a remarkable experience. I enjoyed the access to the Louvre, the architecture of the city blew my mind, the night life on the Left Bank was exhilarating . . .' She smiled confidingly. 'And Frenchmen, well, I have to admit they have a certain *je ne sais quoi* . . .'

'But you came back to England, and the north,' Arnold said.

She nodded. 'I had made no commitments in Paris, and I felt I owed so much to my grandmother. She's getting old, and I thought I should come back to be with her during her declining years. And then, fortunately, I was introduced to Isabella, we got on well together, she talked to me about this amazing collection her husband had developed in the Edinburgh flat, and it seemed to fit so perfectly, we could go into business together and –'

The telephone extension in the dining room shrilled, cutting her off. She hesitated, glanced at Arnold, apologized then rose from the dining table, walked to the telephone and picked it up. 'Hello? This is Angela Fenchurch.'

There was a short silence. When Angela said no more Arnold glanced up at her. He saw the colour had gone from her face, her eyes were wide with shock, and he rose quickly from the table. He was moving towards her as she deliberately replaced the receiver. Her eyes were blank. Arnold touched her arm. 'Are you all right?'

She stared at him, almost unseeing. Then he felt her arm begin to shake. He led her back to the table, seated her. She said nothing as he poured some cold water from a decanter into a glass, and offered it to her. She took the glass almost mechanically, sipped it, still saying nothing.

'Angela,' he urged, 'what's happened? Are you all right?'

Slowly she turned her head; tears glistened on her eyelashes. Quietly, she said, 'We were talking about my grandmother.'

Arnold took her hand; it lay in his, then slowly her fingers tensed, gripping his fiercely. 'That phone call,' she murmured. 'It was about her.'

She closed her eyes in despair. 'That was James Detorius. My grandmother has just died.'

2

The nurse was middle-aged, homely in appearance, comfortable in build. She had an air of competence mingled with compassion. She sat down in front of Arnold, hands folded in her lap, large-lidded brown eyes fixed on him. 'When I went in to give her the lunch I'd prepared, she had already gone, you know. Peaceful, like. She was a nice woman, you know: caring, compassionate, and she loved her granddaughter so much. You could tell, by the way she looked at her. She brought her up from a very young age, you know. They were very close, like mother and daughter, really. I've been looking after the old lady now, for seven years, give or take. So I ought to know. And Angela, she's badly broken up at the moment, but she'll come through. She's a strong young woman . . .'

Arnold didn't doubt it, and the closeness of the relationship was clear from the way Angela had taken the news of her grandmother's death. The nurse had phoned Detorius; he had traced Angela to Belton Hall. Angela's eyes had been red-rimmed when she explained to Arnold, 'It isn't as though it's unexpected, she was an old lady, she's had several strokes and her recent life can't have been pleasant, restricted to her wheelchair. She's been frustrated by her condition, her inability to do anything for herself, the need for constant nursing. And there was the difficulty of communicating. But the fact that she's gone, I don't know, it isn't sinking in yet, I can't handle it . . .'

She was still shaking. Aware that she was suffering from delayed shock Arnold had made the decision for them. 'I'll drive you back to Stanhope. You need to be there. You're in no condition to drive yourself; you can leave your car here and I'm sure Mrs Portland will be able to make arrangements for it to be collected later, brought to you.'

She had protested weakly that she did not wish to put him out, but he had quickly overridden her objections. The drive to Stanhope had been a quiet one. Once they arrived at the castle apartment Arnold had gone in with her; when she went into the bedroom to see her grandmother, the nurse had emerged, closed the door quietly behind her and sat down to talk to Arnold.

'Come through to the kitchen, love, and I'll make you a cup of tea.'

'I'm not sure I should stay,' Arnold murmured. 'I mean, if there are family members . . .'

The nurse rose, shaking her head, and in a firm tone that denied further argument said, 'There is no family. The old lady, she had only Angela. It's best you wait for a while. You were kind enough to drive Angela; she'll want to thank you, I'm sure, once she's paid her respects to the old lady.'

Arnold followed her into the kitchen. He sat down at the table while the nurse filled the electric kettle with water and switched it on. 'I hadn't realized she was the only relative,' he murmured.

'No other family,' the nurse replied. 'The poor girl has always been alone in the world, apart from her grandmother.' She leaned against the marble worktop, folded her arms and stared thoughtfully out of the window. 'The old lady lived all her life here in Stanhope. And for the last twenty-odd years that life revolved around her granddaughter. They used to live in a big house top of the bank, but that was sold years ago, and then they moved into this apartment. More suitable for Mrs Fenchurch really, especially when Angela was away at school. She was a boarder at Durham, you know, and then there was the school in Switzerland, and later, Paris. The old lady was very proud of Angela. Would do anything for her.' The nurse sighed, shook her head. 'I think Angela's more distressed, really, because she wasn't here when the old lady passed away. After all, Angela came back here to Stanhope just to be close to her grandmother.'

'Her mother died young, I believe.'

The nurse nodded. 'Ovarian cancer, I believe. There's never been much talk about her at all, really. I mean, all the time I've been with the old lady, she never once mentioned her daughter. Maybe because she never married: Angela's surname is the same as her grandmother's, isn't it, so, well, you know, these things matter to the older generation, don't they? Different nowadays, of course.' She sniffed critically, then sighed. 'Angela couldn't have been more than two, if that, when her mother died and she came to live back here in Stanhope. She was lucky, I guess, that her grandmother was in a position to be able to look after her. She wasn't short of a few quid, the old lady . . .'

Arnold nodded. He watched as the nurse turned back to the kettle, poured the water into a teapot. It was not a drink Arnold normally indulged in but the nurse was very firm in her instructions. He accepted the cup, agreed to a little milk, refused sugar, and watched while the nurse stirred two teaspoons of sugar into her own tea. 'So what about Angela's father?'

'What about him?' There was a certain defensive note in her voice.

Arnold hesitated. 'I just wondered. I mean, no one seems to have mentioned him.'

There was a short silence. The nurse sipped her tea reflectively. 'Well, there's no harm in talking about him, I suppose. Not that anyone seems to know much anyway, though there was a certain amount of gossip at one time. He's dead, that's for sure. And Angela never knew him . . . I mean, he died when she was young, but quite when and where no one seems to know. He sent money, it seems, for a while, but then it dried up. At least, that's what I've assumed from things the old lady mentioned from time to time.' She stared at her half-empty cup, swirled the liquid around. 'I always got the feeling the old lady had no time for him. He was a gambler or something shady like that. And foreign. Anyway, whatever he was, he didn't play any real part in Angela's life. He was just never there, you know what I mean?'

She started suddenly, as the chimes rang in the hallway. 'Someone at the door,' she exclaimed, and rose hastily.

Arnold was not sure what to do. He finished his tea quickly and walked back into the sitting room. He felt redundant here at the Stanhope apartment, but thought he should not leave until he had seen Angela again, in case there was anything else he could do to help her.

He heard voices in the hallway. After a short delay, the door from the hallway opened, the nurse bustled in, nodded, and headed for the kitchen, clearly wishing to be out of the way. Behind her was the portly, pinstripe-suited figure of James Detorius.

The lawyer seemed taken aback when he saw Arnold. 'Landon! I didn't realize . . .'

'I was with Angela when she heard the news from you. I brought her home,' Arnold explained.

Detorius frowned in abstracted fashion, as though he had hardly heard what Arnold had said. He turned away and headed for a cabinet in the corner of the room. He opened it, took out a bottle of whisky, poured himself a stiff shot of the amber liquid. He glanced back at Arnold and raised his eyebrows. Arnold shook his head. James Detorius was clearly very much at home.

The lawyer walked stiff-legged across to the window, looked out over the lawns, shadowed in the early afternoon sunshine. He sipped at the whisky. Quietly, he said, 'She hated being so restricted. Stuck in that wheelchair. Now, the old lady's gone . . .'

Arnold remained silent. After a few moments Detorius looked back over his shoulder. 'How is Angela taking it?'

'Badly,' Arnold replied.

Detorius nodded. He too seemed affected by the death of the old lady. Some of the cockiness of his manner seemed to have drained from him; there was a new anxiety in his furrowed brow, and his eyes were restless, darting glances around the room as though he was seeking solutions to some problem that was on his mind. He wandered about, his left hand stroking the furniture in an almost proprietorial fashion, almost weighing up its valuation. His glance slipped back to Arnold, and it was as though he suddenly became conscious of the glass in his hand, the apparent freedom with which he had helped himself to the old lady's alcohol. 'We used to have a regular glass together, whenever I called,' he explained hurriedly, reddening.

It was no concern of Arnold's.

'I've actually known her for seventeen years,' Detorius continued. 'My senior partner dealt with her affairs until he died. I've been her lawyer for the last twelve years. But it developed into more than a lawyer–client relationship. We became friends, and she trusted me. I arranged all her affairs.' His frown became more pronounced. 'I . . . I came as soon as the nurse rang me, then I rang Angela. I had to go back to the office, but as soon as I was free –'

He turned as the door to the sitting room opened. It was Angela. She was pale, her eyes were red, she had clearly been crying, but she was now more in control of her feelings. She came forward to Arnold, slipped her hand into his and squeezed. 'Thanks for bringing me home, Arnold; and thank you for staying.' She glanced at the lawyer, standing quietly near the window. 'And thanks to you also, James, for coming back.'

He saw her eyes note the glass in her hand. He put it down and came forward solicitously. 'I think you could do with a stiff drink too,' he suggested.

She hesitated, frowned, then nodded. 'Yes, I'll have one. And for Arnold also, please.'

Her hand slid up, gripping Arnold's forearm. She was still not relaxed, however calm her tone appeared. Arnold was aware of the controlled tension in her body, and they stood there silently as Detorius poured two more glasses of whisky.

'I'll drink this,' Arnold said quietly, 'and then I'll be on my way. There'll be others who'll want to pay their respects.'

Angela stared at him, and slowly shook her head. 'I don't think so. My grandmother . . . I think it's right to say her life almost revolved around me. She had no real friends in the village. I think people had a view about her when she lived in the big house, and then when she came down to this apartment they tended to keep their distance. There were no close friends.'

103

There was a brief, strained silence. Detorius grimaced. 'Well, you must remember she was seen as somewhat . . . isolated when she lived on the hill. And when she moved to the castle, she kept herself to herself. She was a woman of independent mind; she had no need of friends.'

'*You* were her friend,' Angela asserted.

Detorius appeared to be uncomfortable at her words. He ducked his head in deprecation. 'Well, I was in a partnership, and the principal acted for her for years and when he died I sort of took over and yes, I guess you could say we became sort of friends.'

'You would be the keeper of all her secrets,' Angela remarked with a wan smile.

Detorius stiffened, stared at her for a moment as though surprised, almost alarmed, and then his glance slipped away. 'Secrets . . . well, I suppose lawyers are always seen as the keeper of a client's secrets. If there are any.'

Angela sipped her drink and grimaced as the fiery liquid burned her throat. She released Arnold's arm and sat down in the easy chair, crossed her legs, gestured to Arnold to take the other easy chair. 'And were there?' she asked dully.

'What?' There was an edgy, underlying note of concern in Detorius's voice.

'Secrets,' Angela repeated. 'My grandmother was in her eighties. She must have had *some* secrets.'

Detorius glanced nervously at Arnold. 'I don't think –'

'For instance, she never talked much about my mother and father.' Angela stared at her glass, frowning. 'When I was young she sort of skirted around it and when I came home from school and asked her about them she was always evasive. And then, later, as I got used to the situation I suppose it mattered less and less to me.'

Arnold could guess it would be the natural thing to do; the old lady would seem to have lived for her granddaughter. She would have taken the place of father and mother to Angela. The rest would have been in the perhaps murky past, to some extent irrelevant to their lives.

Particularly if, as the nurse had earlier hinted, the father had led a chequered existence.

Angela shook her head as though discarding old memories. She looked around the room, almost as if seeing it for the first time. 'They weren't married, were they? My parents.'

Detorius looked at his whisky glass. 'I don't believe so.'

Angela shook her head. 'At least, Grandmother gave me a home. Looked after me. Denied me nothing.'

James Detorius cleared his throat nervously. He glanced again at Arnold, as though questioning whether he should raise the matter in front of a stranger, but the issue was clearly burning at him.

'Did your grandmother leave a will?' Detorius asked suddenly.

Angela raised her head, stared at him with something bordering on astonishment. 'Why on earth do you ask that? Don't you know? You're her lawyer! You've been her lawyer for years!'

Detorius drained his glass, walked to the cabinet, poured himself another whisky. There was a nervousness about him that puzzled Arnold; he did not like the man for his bumptiousness, his self-confidence, but Detorius gave the impression now that he was walking on eggs. It was almost as though he was guilt-ridden.

The lawyer swung around. He waved his glass uncertainly. 'Her lawyer. That's true. Twelve years. I've been acting as her lawyer, as her confidant, and I've been advising her ...' Detorius hesitated, grimaced, glanced uncertainly at Arnold but then ploughed on. 'But she's not always taken my advice. The fact is, I've been advising her to make a will for some time. Her situation ... her age ...'

'But if Grandmother had made a will, surely she would have asked you to draw it up,' Angela protested.

'That's so,' Detorius asserted. 'But the fact is, she never used me in that capacity.'

'Why ever not?'

Detorius shrugged unhappily. 'Old people can be funny in that respect. They can feel that to make a will is a sign of their own mortality, like making themselves a hostage to fortune, I don't know. Or maybe it was because she didn't want to face reality, because she still felt you needed support, and . . .' Detorius made a helpless gesture. 'As I said, she never instructed me so I have no copy of her will. But now I would strongly suggest, Angela, that you go through her things, check her personal belongings, find out whether she had made a holograph will –'

'A what?'

'Written out her last wishes in her own hand. Such a document would not require the usual witness formalities.'

'But you know Grandmother was paralysed by a series of strokes!' Angela snapped, in disbelief.

Detorius wriggled uncomfortably. He clearly realized he was not explaining himself very well. He sipped his drink, then went on in the face of Angela's growing exasperation. 'What I mean to say is that she might have made a will years ago, before the strokes disabled her. Maybe even before I became her legal representative. I was only suggesting . . .'

His voice died away miserably. He sat down, stared at the half-empty glass in his hand. 'I'm just suggesting you should look for a will, Angela,' he muttered weakly. 'It will make things easier. Or, if you wish, I could do it for you.'

Arnold felt it was time he should leave: this was nothing to do with him. He finished his drink in the heavy silence, and began to rise. Angela placed a hand on his arm, restraining him. Her tone was cool, her voice controlled. She looked back to the perspiring lawyer. 'Why is it so important, James? Why do you think I should search immediately?'

The lawyer remained silent for a little while, avoiding her glance. There was a slight tremor in his hands; Arnold wondered briefly whether it was anxiety or excitement. At last Detorius gathered himself together. 'I'd better explain things clearly to you, Angela.'

Her tone was cool. 'That would be helpful.'

After a short silence, Detorius said, 'I won't go into your family background . . . indeed, I don't know the full story myself. But as far as I've been able to make out from old office files held by my predecessor in the firm your grandmother was raised in middle-class circumstances, but she was never a wealthy woman. I believe her father was a shopkeeper in Durham.'

'So?' Angela asked in a puzzled voice.

Detorius shifted uncomfortably in his chair. 'Her financial situation was all set up before my senior partner died and I took over the firm, but it seems your grandmother was able to move into the house on the hill because her daughter – your mother – made certain dispositions in her favour.'

'You mean sent her money?'

'That's right,' Detorius nodded. 'Then, when you were sent to be looked after by your grandmother, financial support was provided for a few more years –'

'After my mother died?'

Detorius grimaced. 'That's right. By your father, it would seem. But . . . well, the payments ended abruptly.'

Angela glanced at Arnold, clearly puzzled. 'You're losing me, James,' she muttered.

'I'm not certain I can explain it more clearly,' the lawyer assured her. 'Your mother set up your grandmother in the big house; she sent her regular sums of money; a short while later you were sent to stay with her; then after your mother died your father continued that financial support but it suddenly dried up. Perhaps . . . perhaps when he himself died.' Detorius paused, then added hurriedly, 'I've no information on that matter, of course.'

'Haven't you discovered details in the files of your predecessor?' Arnold asked curiously.

Detorius shook his head. 'After his death they were handed to the old lady. A few months later she contacted me, asked me to act for her in some minor matters. Then, some time later, when she gained confidence in me, well, she and I became friends . . .'

'I'm still not certain where this discussion is leading,' Angela admitted.

Arnold was not getting the drift either.

Detorius was sweating. His discomfort was clear, but Arnold could not understand why the lawyer was so nervous and upset. It was as though he was concerned about his own part in the story . . . perhaps, Arnold wondered, because there was evidence of incompetence in his advice to the old lady. 'The fact is, Angela, the old lady was in financial trouble. She has been for some time. And though I was her lawyer and we were friends she was always somewhat secretive about some things. It would be useful if we could find she made a will, in case there are assets she mentioned there which I know nothing about.' The lawyer shuffled, turned around, looked about the room as though it held the secrets he sought. 'If there is no will it means we'll have to scout around to try to discover any outstanding assets, and letters of administration can be taken out . . .'

He paused, glanced uncertainly at Angela. 'There's no need for you to worry your head about such things. There are no other heirs that I'm aware of; if you wish to instruct me I can make the necessary searches and then proceed with the grant of intestacy. In the circumstances, I'll make no charge for my legal services: I've known you and your grandmother a long time.'

'James, that's very kind of you,' Angela murmured.

'When I've taken out letters of administration I'll wind up the estate,' Detorius confided. 'Then, whatever's left can be made over to you.' He hesitated, awkwardly. 'But I need to warn you, if my understanding is right, there will be little or nothing left.'

Angela shook her head silently. Arnold guessed the situation was something she did not care to discuss at this time: the death of the woman who had raised her was too recent. The realization came to Detorius at the same time. He nodded sympathetically. 'We can talk about all this some other time, once I've made out a list of assets and . . . er . . . debts. There's just one thing.'

Angela raised her head. 'Yes?'

'The business you're setting up with Isabella Portland.' Detorius was uneasy again, licking his lips anxiously. 'I think you'd better hold fire on that for the time being.'

'Why?' Angela's tone was still puzzled.

Detorius glanced at Arnold and squared his shoulders. He hesitated, searching for the right words. 'I had my doubts at the time . . . I tried to warn your grandmother, because the debts had piled up. But she gave you certain items of jewellery –'

'That's right. She told me they were heirlooms. They are to be my stake, my contribution to the business with Isabella.'

Detorius shook his head sadly. 'I'm afraid she misled you . . . or misled herself. Wishful thinking, perhaps. The fact is, your grandmother has been living beyond her means for years, ever since the income from your parents dried up. The big house on the hill was heavily mortgaged: that's why she moved down here to this apartment. She had a negative equity in this place too, I believe. And the jewellery, you'll have to recover it from Isabella Portland's collection because I fear it may well have to be sold in order to pay off the debts –'

'But how could Grandmother have got into this situation?' Angela protested. 'She never said a word . . . she never mentioned anything to me about financial problems . . .'

James Detorius was silent for a little while, staring at the carpet. 'The money she had, it's been dribbling away for years. But she loved you; she wanted the best for you; she had lost her daughter, and you were her only relative. She wanted you to have everything. The private school at Durham . . . the finishing school in Switzerland . . . the time in Paris . . .'

'She never told me!' Angela burst out, with a catch in her throat. 'I never realized –'

'She didn't want you to know,' Detorius interrupted. 'But we'd better leave this for now. You're upset. Leave everything to me.'

'But the big house . . . and this apartment . . .'

'Mortgaged to the hilt. And there are other debts . . .'

'Does that mean the cottage has gone as well?'

There was a short silence. Detorius stared at the young woman, his eyes widening, a crease of anxiety on his forehead. He seemed shaken. It was clear he had no idea what she was talking about. 'Cottage? I wasn't aware your grandmother owned another piece of property.'

'It was a small place up near Elsdon. When I was a child, we used to go up there from the big house. Grandmother used to take me for walks on the moors, show me the pele tower and the site of the last gibbet in England, have cakes in a small teashop . . . I used to love those summer outings. But we haven't been there for years. It was just a small place, an isolated stone cottage.' She lowered her head, crying softly. 'I loved those summers, but it was all so long ago . . .'

Detorius rose, walked forward and laid a sympathetic hand on her shoulder. Arnold noted the slight shake in the hand; the lawyer was clearly moved, concerned. 'Don't worry about it, Angela. Leave it all to me.' He hesitated. 'I never knew about the cottage. She never mentioned it. Maybe it'll help save things. Hang fire on the jewellery until I've made enquiries. Just tell me precisely where the cottage is and I'll see what I can do.' He hesitated. 'Do you know where the keys are? I don't recall your grandmother . . .'

Angela shrugged. 'I have a set somewhere, but I'll have to look for them.'

It was time for Arnold to leave. He had already stayed longer than he should have done. He rose, stood awkwardly in front of the young woman. 'I'd better go. If there's anything I can do, Angela, you just have to let me know. And don't worry about the business with Isabella Portland. It'll get sorted out, I'm sure.'

When he left the apartment and drove back north over the winding road that crossed the moors dark clouds had gathered from the west, and the wind had risen.

Soon, the rain would come.

The group of officers gathered in the briefing room was silent.

Assistant Chief Constable Sid Cathery was in one of his ranting moods. He placed his thick, meaty hands on the table in front of him. His voice was raised into an angry roar. 'You know, I spent my two weeks' leave on the Costa Blanca last summer and all the waiters in the Spanish restaurants were Colombian! Then you take Italian restaurants in London: they're all bloody Spanish staff! Go into Newcastle, and what do you find? It's no better: I know a Greek restaurant run in the Bigg Market that's operated by Romanians; there's an Italian restaurant in Dean Street staffed by Poles; and don't talk to me about Indian Tandoori places – whether they're in South Shields or Tynemouth, Morpeth or Hexham, they're all staffed with Pakistanis or Bangladeshis! Even the Chinese takeaways – they're run by bloody ex-building workers from Korea! I tell you, nothing's right and proper any more. You just don't know where the hell you are.' His choleric mood calmed somewhat as he became aware of the extent of his rant. He blew out his cheeks, took a deep breath. The small group of seven senior detectives in front of him remained silent.

Detective Chief Inspector O'Connor glanced at Inspector Farnsby, seated at his side. He wondered what Farnsby would be making of this; Farnsby's saturnine features displayed no reaction as he stared straight ahead of him, his lips thinly set. He was a cold man. Nothing seemed to faze him. O'Connor wondered whether Farnsby knew the identity of the burly, pleasant-featured man seated beside the Assistant Chief Constable at the front of the briefing room. He was tousle-haired but greying, exuding an air of competence and confidence. He was sufficiently self-controlled not to display open amazement at the diatribe launched by the bulldog figure of the ex-rugby forward Sid Cathery. Perhaps like the rest of the officers in the audience he was not clear as to the direction in which Cathery was headed.

Cathery leaned back in his seat, his face ruddy, his brow thunderous, but he clearly imagined he'd made his point and was satisfied. 'But with all that,' he concluded, 'it's more than capped by the fact we've now, apparently, according to Mr Gonzalez here, got a bloody *foreign* assassin come in on our patch to do his thing.' He glared around the room in triumph. 'On our patch! A bloody Iraqi hitman, no less!'

'*Iranian*,' the big man corrected him. He hesitated, then pulled out a cigar from the top pocket of his jacket. He glanced around at the group, made a slight grimace. 'I guess you'll have a smoking ban here, like they do in most places these days. Trouble is, I got this addiction . . . cigars, and whisky.' He grinned. 'Women too, in fact, but we don't need to go into that.' He waved the cigar. 'If any of you object . . .' He glanced at Cathery, saw the disapproving jut of the Assistant Chief Constable's chin, and murmured, 'Well, I guess I'll just chomp on this. Kind of like a comforter, you know.'

The room remained silent as he inserted the thick cigar in his mouth, rolled it to one side of his mouth. He smiled in satisfaction. 'Fine Havana. We in the CIA kept up good contacts with Cuba right through the cold war, you know, in spite of our well-known efforts to unseat Castro.'

Unseat, O'Connor thought to himself, would be another CIA euphemism for murder.

'Anyway,' the burly CIA man said with a shrug, 'like Mr Cathery here just said, my name is Richard Gonzalez. I've just flown in from Paris. The police there, and in La Rochelle, are investigating a double murder: the killings of a French antiquities dealer and an American collector. I pointed the finger at the man I believe responsible for the killings, a guy called Anwar Zahiri. But the French authorities . . . well, let's just say they weren't convinced. I guess it's a matter of culture and history: they didn't like the idea of a CIA man muscling in on their patch, and they kind of ignored what I had to say.'

Recent political tensions between the French and the USA would have played their part in attitudes also, O'Connor thought. ACC Sid Cathery voiced the thought bluntly. 'Fact is, the Frogs don't like the Yanks.'

O'Connor grimaced. Clearly, the CIA man also considered the ACC could have put the view more delicately: he thought that he saw Gonzalez wince slightly. Otherwise the big man ignored the comment. 'The French are tying the killings into an investigation they're carrying out with the Italian government: it's concerned with the trade in smuggled and looted antiques. They're concentrating on the connections the murdered dealer made in the trade. But from my perspective – and that of the CIA – that's kinda missing the real point behind these killings. We don't believe it's about the general issue of the international trade. This is about something much more specific.' He paused, took out his cigar, stared at it for a moment as though wishing he could light up, then stuck it back into his mouth, rolled it from one side to the other. There was something false about the gesture: O'Connor felt the man was trying to show he was a simple, uncomplicated individual at heart. It was all part of a show. What the Americans would regard as pork-barrel stuff.

'I'm pretty certain that the man who killed those two guys in La Rochelle isn't involved in any international smuggling conspiracy,' Gonzalez went on confidently. 'The gendarmerie think different. That's up to them. It's their country. And in a sense it don't matter too much that they're running down a false trail. Thing is, I've been on the trail of Anwar Zahiri for two years, and I know what's going on here. He's an assassin, a religious zealot with an objective in mind. He's not dealing in ancient artefacts – but he is after something from the past. Something of an individual, irreplaceable character, and importance. To him, and to the shadowy men who back him.'

Sid Cathery was not to be left out of the limelight. 'And now it seems this Zahiri character has left France, and is here in England. In our jurisdiction. On our bloody stamping ground!'

113

Beside O'Connor, Inspector Farnsby shifted in his seat. He raised his head, cold eyes fixed on Gonzalez. 'Why has he come to England, if the French police don't see him as a suspect? If they're concentrating on the antiquities trade, what reason was there for him to come here?'

Gonzalez waved his cigar prop at his small audience. 'It's like I said, he's looking for something. And his quest would seem to have moved to this country. But before I tell you about this guy I'm hunting, and I've been on his heels a long time now, I need to fill you in on the background, talk to you about the organization called SAVAK . . .'

O'Connor was only half-listening as Gonzalez outlined the history of the secret police organization established by the Shah of Iran. It seemed to be a well-rehearsed account. He watched Gonzalez, trying to sum him up. He tried to think of him in a different milieu: he would be good company among friends. About his work, he would be enthusiastic. With women, maybe he would be ebullient, charming, charismatic. But as Gonzalez continued with his earnest account, there was something about his eyes that made O'Connor suspect that the CIA officer would be good at dissimulation: he would be well capable of holding something back. There was a caution, a hidden reserve in spite of his façade of charm. Probably, it went with CIA territory.

'My own personal passion,' Gonzalez admitted, 'lies in the prize-fighting world – I've been undercover with the mob there once or twice back in the States, and when you've seen what goes on behind the fight scene, you wouldn't ever bet on a prize fight again. But I have to say that when I was assigned to this case, and was given my briefing on SAVAK, well, there was nothing in the fight game to touch it.'

'Corruption,' Cathery offered sagely, nodding his head like a manic toy bulldog.

'Corruption on a different scale entirely,' Gonzalez affirmed. He chewed on his cigar, and eyed his audience thoughtfully. 'So what was going on in Iran thirty years ago?' He paused. 'My initial briefing from my handlers showed me how things were, and everything I learned later confirmed that in the 1970s the country was a wonderland for businessmen: kickbacks, agent fees, secret deals between princes, princesses, PR men and, I have to admit, my own bosses ... instructing CIA agents to act as middlemen, to set up stings, to infiltrate groups in order to obtain intelligence.' He shook his head. 'The country was awash in corruption. Guys were climbing aboard executive jets with Samsonite briefcases stuffed with cash; there were untraceable bank accounts in the Caribbean and Lichtenstein; the island of Kish was developed as a private resort financed by Panama President General Omar Torrijos. In exchange for providing a haven for the Shah, the US State Department even quashed a Miami gun-running indictment against a crony of General Noriega in Panama. When Noriega came to power, the island was sold to a Japanese development company.' He paused. 'But I'm getting ahead of my story.'

He caressed his stubbly chin and grimaced. 'The good times for businessmen in Iran couldn't last, of course. There were too many tensions; too many crooks; and there was no central control. Moreover, the Shah's family members were greedy. Satellite courts swirled jealously around the Shah's relations who controlled vast patronage, and members brought in drugs, cocaine: they could not obtain political power, they were merely agents of the Shah, but if they lacked the opportunity to gain power there was the alternative: wealth. Thousands of fixers prospered and displayed their wealth in cars, jewels, clothes, mansions – one built a home modelled on the Petit Trianon in Paris. I should have mentioned that to the French Sûreté,' he mused, ruefully. 'Maybe they'd have taken me more seriously.'

Sid Cathery was getting restless. Gonzalez recognized the impatient shifting of the man beside him and went on firmly: 'While the rich grew richer, half a million peasants were dispossessed of their land, had to sleep in shacks, holes in the ground, or sewers. Rebellion was in the air, and in Paris the exiled Ayatollah Khomeini railed against the ruler on the Peacock Throne. Finally, the Shah was toppled.'

The cigar rolled again, from one side of his mouth to the other. 'The Shah was in exile. He flew to Kish. His luggage – including six big packing cases – was carted to a little airstrip by the hotel to be loaded on light planes to the mainland. The operation was overseen by a trusted aide: a courtier, a guy called Mohamed Mehti.' Gonzalez paused. 'He got to play an important part in what then transpired. Anyway, Colonel Noriega saw the entourage off at the airport. The Shah went to Panama after a three-month stay, refuelled in Azores, headed for Cairo. Then, well, after surgery and chemotherapy the Shah died, in the middle of a hell of a lot of haggling, charges and counter charges from Parisian, American and Egyptian doctors – none of whom accepted responsibility for the botched treatment that led to his death. The Shah died in July 1980. But by that time, his trusted aide, our friend Mehti, he'd made himself scarce.'

The cigar had served its purpose. Gonzalez removed it, picked at a piece of tobacco on his lower lip, then laid the cigar aside on the table. Sid Cathery, with a gesture of distaste, retrieved the damply chewed item and placed it on a glass ashtray in front of him. His nostrils flared as he stared at it in gloomy disapproval.

'When the Shah fell from power it was a group of his super agents who were dictating the economic direction of the country and the government itself, though the Ministry of the Court and the High Economic Council followed their wishes and commands. One of those agents was Mehti.' He glanced around the silent room. 'He was one of those guys who seem to be all things to all men: aide to the Shah but a fixer, a wheeler-dealer in his own right. Mehti was not only a member of the inner court of the Shah, he was also a senior officer in SAVAK, and being so close to the Shah he knew many secrets. He was involved, most importantly for our purposes, in the operation where one of the Pahlavi family, nephew to the Shah, openly stole and exported for his own personal gain national art treasures, gold artefacts unearthed at the prehistoric archaeological site at Marlik.'

'Is it something from that site that this man Zahiri is after?' O'Connor asked impatiently.

Gonzalez frowned, stared at him for a moment as though irritated by the interruption, then ignored the question and went on with his history lesson. 'Let's just still concentrate on this guy, Mehti. The ex-courtier left his SAVAK links behind, tied in with the Shah's nephew, after the looting of the Marlik site, fled with him from Bandar Abbas port chased by Revolutionary Guards, and ended up in Kuwait. Mehti stayed at his side there but when the nephew went to Paris to meet Behbehanian, the Shah's money man, he wasn't with him. Which was lucky. The nephew ended up murdered in the street: a guy in a wrap-around crash helmet walked behind him, shot him in the back of the head, and again as he lay on the ground, then vanished among the crowd in Rue Pergolese.' Gonzalez leaned back in his chair. 'The lines were being drawn. The hitman had been employed by the group of men who had stayed on after the mullahs took over SAVAK. Mehti took the hint, and disappeared. He handed over to the money man what the assassins were after.'

'Which was?' an officer seated near O'Connor asked.

Gonzalez grimaced. 'At this point, I don't think I need to disclose that to you. It's classified information. Anyway, we in the CIA kept a close watch on events. The money man, Behbehanian, went to live in a *haut-bourgeois* villa in Basel, the banking capital of Switzerland, now fearing the forces the uprising had unleashed.' He shook his head. 'This guy, he looked like a pleasant, wealthy grandfather, resembled a retired dentist, small, round, grey moustache and friendly smile. But he was formerly the ruthless head of finance at court, held the purse strings to the Shah's private fortune, and now Mehti joined up with him. The Shah's former aide worked with the money man during the next decade, through the Iran–Iraq war, the Gulf War, the power of Saddam. But all the time the ex-SAVAK assassins employed by the mullahs were snapping at their heels.

Then, in 1991, things changed. You'll have heard of the collapse of the Bank of Credit and Commerce International . . . BCCI.'

'Known in the business as Bank of Crooks and Criminals International,' Sid Cathery muttered loudly.

Gonzalez grunted in acknowledgement. 'It was an apt description. They were money-launderers primarily, serving the global criminal community. When they finally got rumbled, BCCI branches were closed in London, Karachi, the US and Peru and senior bankers were indicted for fraud, money-laundering and dealing in dirty money – not least the proceeds of Colombian drug trading.'

'I seem to recall the CIA used that bank too,' O'Connor announced.

'That's true,' Gonzalez agreed a little ruefully. 'But using them ourselves, well, it did help us to keep tabs on what the criminals were up to. Including the Shah's ex-money man.'

'And Mehti?' Cathery asked, frowning.

'Exactly. It was through our BCCI contacts that we learned about Mehti, and what happened to him. You see, the problem for the money man Behbehanian was that he used the bank to hold all his looted assets. The mullahs' assassins were still after him and what he had, but the bank crash ruined him, and he decided to make peace with the mullahs, and their hired SAVAK killers. He went into retirement, handed over what was left of the Shah's fortune in his hands, and died a few years later.'

'Leaving Mehti high and dry?' Cathery queried.

'Exactly. And more or less penniless, it seems: his accounts in BCCI had been frozen. After that, things got a bit frenetic. Mehti was dashing around, Kuwait, Egypt, the US, and we kept an eye on him. But we couldn't prevent his murder in 1993.'

O'Connor wondered whether the CIA had even attempted to prevent it. He cleared his throat. 'What has all this got to do with Anwar Zahiri coming to the UK?' he asked.

Gonzalez was silent for a little while. Finally, he shrugged, glanced at Cathery and said, 'All I've said, it's to give you the background, to explain what's been going on, how committed these SAVAK killers are, how a group of them has been working in the US and Europe for some years . . . and one of them is now in England, a guy who must be seen as a dangerous and committed man. A guy to stay away from. And that's what I want to emphasize. I'm giving you all a dossier on this character. Your ACC has agreed that your group can make enquiries, keep an eye open for him. But lemme make it clear: in the long run . . . he's *mine*.'

There was a studied viciousness in the CIA man's tone that surprised O'Connor. Yet it seemed forced in a strange way. Insincere. Beside him, Farnsby murmured, 'Interesting . . .'

Sid Cathery put his meaty hands on the table in front of him and stood up. 'Okay, that's it for now. Pick up a dossier from the table here, get on top of the information it contains, use your contacts in the city, ask around, and look out for this Iranian character. But you don't play the hero. You find him, you contact us at the centre, call for back-up. Remember, this Zahiri character's left two corpses already in France.'

Murmuring, the group rose from their chairs and headed for the table, collected briefing documents and made for the exit. As O'Connor stood up Cathery called across the room. 'DCI O'Connor, you and Inspector Farnsby – I want to see you in my room right away.'

O'Connor raised his eyebrows in surprise, turned and glanced at Farnsby. His colleague failed to meet his eyes, and led the way from the room.

They were kept waiting outside Cathery's office for ten minutes. O'Connor was puzzled. Farnsby kept his own counsel, leaning against the wall with arms folded, head averted, gazing out of the window. They could catch the murmur of voices from inside the room, where Cathery was ensconced with the CIA man.

When they were finally admitted, O'Connor saw that Gonzalez had relaxed after his discourse: the room was wreathed in cigar smoke. Sid Cathery had failed to enforce his own dislike of smoking upon his guest, clearly overwhelmed by the thought of working with the CIA. But something about the whole affair bothered O'Connor: he had the feeling something was out of kilter in the situation presented to them.

'Sit down, gentlemen,' Cathery said generously. 'Take the weight off your feet.'

Gonzalez was having a greater effect than O'Connor would have anticipated. Cathery seemed almost mellow, puffed up with self-importance.

They took their seats, facing the Assistant Chief Constable behind his desk, Gonzalez seated on an easy chair just across the room from him. Cathery leaned back in his chair, linked his hands across his belly and exuded bonhomie. 'Right, now we four are here together in private we can fill in the rest of the story. Richard?'

First-name terms, O'Connor noted sourly. The CIA man was staring at him.

'You were the guy that spoke up, asking what Zahiri was after, in France, and now here.'

'That's right.'

'Ahuh . . . well, I was reluctant to tell the whole group. But in the present circumstances I guess I need to explain a bit further, amongst us here.' He paused, frowning slightly. 'The fact is, when the Shah's nephew looted the site at Marlik one of the things he came away with, and later lodged with the money man, was an important artefact. Very old, of incredible value . . . and of great significance to the jihadists.'

'The *what*?' O'Connor exclaimed.

Gonzalez ignored the exclamation. 'This item, it's of great religious significance. And it's been somewhere in the West for years. The ex-SAVAK zealots hate the idea of it lying somewhere in Europe. They want it back. They've always wanted it. It was something Behbehanian held back when he did a deal with the mullahs. He wanted insurance against the hit squads. While only he knew the location of the artefact, they wouldn't kill him. And he promised it would be handed over at his death.'

'So where had he kept it?' Farnsby asked curiously.

'First,' Gonzalez remarked calmly, 'it seems he placed it in safekeeping in Kuwait. Saddam's invasion put it at risk, so he got Mehti to go in and remove it. We in the CIA have pieced together what happened after that. The money man died of natural causes, the promise of return of the artefact wasn't kept because Mehti saw his chance and appropriated it, arranged for it to be hidden – for his own purposes – in the Baghdad Museum where it lay for some years. When trouble broke out after the fall of Saddam, Mehti went into Iraq again. But the insurance was no longer valid: the mullahs' assassins got tired of chasing him, unable to get their hands on what they wanted. Not long after, he was murdered.'

'And this mysterious artefact?' Farnsby asked.

'Disappeared again. But we'd been keeping tabs on the whole affair. And the electronic chatter we picked up told us that Anwar Zahiri was in Europe looking for it.'

'But how –'

'Mehti had arranged for it to be hidden in Europe. Probably Paris. But now, recently, it had surfaced suddenly. It had been put on the market. According to our information it was recently put up for sale.'

There was silence in the room. Gonzalez took out another cigar, lit it, puffed on it. The cigar smoke wreathed quietly to the ceiling. At last O'Connor asked, 'What exactly is this . . . artefact?'

Gonzalez gazed at him coolly. 'I didn't want to talk to the French police about it. And the group I've just briefed . . . they don't need to know. But you guys . . .' He contemplated the glowing tip of his fat cigar. 'The artefact? It's the only thing of its kind. Unique. It's an eleventh-century manuscript of the Koran, translated into Latin, and medieval French, as well as the original Arabic. Uniquely, it also contains a French Hebrew version of the biblical books of the Pentateuch, Lamentations, Ecclesiastes and the Lessons of the Prophets. It's priceless, but the religious zealots in Iran see it as something that belongs to their heritage. They want it back. They've commissioned Zahiri to carry out the mission of recovery: religious zealot as he is, he will kill to get it. Has killed already, I should say.'

'Priceless, you say,' O'Connor muttered.

'It's been compared to the Alexander sarcophagus in Istanbul, the Duke de Berry's illuminated Book of Hours, Albrecht Dürer's watercolour of a bird's wing in the Albertina in Vienna. These are all unique, master works, but they do not have the sense of soul that's to be found in the manuscript I'm talking about. As I say, it's priceless.'

'But you suggest it's up for sale.'

Gonzalez shrugged. 'The seller can't know its true value. Nor how dangerous a piece of history it is.'

'So what do you reckon happened in France?'

Gonzalez sighed. 'When it went out on the grapevine, the fact of the sale of the manuscript, an American dealer became interested. This man, Adam Shearbright, arranged to meet the seller in La Rochelle. Zahiri was on his trail. That's why I was sent to France, albeit always a little behind the game. Quite what happened then, I'm not sure. Like I said earlier, Shearbright ended up dead, and so did a dealer called Carpentier. Now maybe Carpentier was holding the manuscript, had arranged to sell it to Shearbright. In which case, maybe Zahiri got his hands on it after killing them both.'

There was a pause. Slowly, O'Connor said, 'But you don't think that's what happened.'

Gonzalez shook his heavy head, waved his cigar aimlessly, leaving a faint trail of smoke in the air. 'No, I don't think that's the way it went. I wouldn't be here otherwise. It's my belief that Shearbright was out to kill two birds with one stone when he went to France. He's been involved in the international antiquities scam for years, buying up stuff from looted tombs, in Italy in the main. He would have been doing some business with Carpentier, apart from the manuscript. I think it was Shearbright who identified the place of assignation with the seller of the manuscript. But something went wrong. Zahiri possibly acted too soon. He followed Shearbright, assumed the dealer Carpentier was the seller of the manuscript, and when he found out he'd got it wrong, he killed them both in a rage.'

'The French didn't buy into this scenario,' O'Connor challenged.

Gonzalez hesitated, then shook his head. 'They did not. But they're fixated, along with the Italian Carabinieri Art Squad, in smashing the illicit antiquities trade. They can't raise their head above that particular parapet. They don't even want to know about Zahiri. They don't even accept he *exists*. But he does.' Gonzalez's mouth was grim. 'Believe me, he does. I've been chasing him two years. And in La Rochelle I almost got my hands on him.'

It had become a personal quest.

'And his presence in England?' O'Connor asked.

'I'm sure he's here. In the north-east.'

'Why?'

'Because it looks like the seller is somewhere up here.'

Silence grew around them. Each man was lost in his own thoughts. O'Connor felt uneasy. There was something here that was wrong, but he was unable to put his finger on it. At last, he raised his head, stared challengingly at the CIA man. 'Why us? Why involve officers from this force? You're a CIA field officer. Your natural link in the UK would be with MI5. Particularly if, as you claim, this man Zahiri has terrorist associations. He's a jihadist, you say. Surely, you should be talking to the spooks in London, not us.'

A cynical smile touched Gonzalez's lips. 'And what would happen then? A general alert, new men coming into the area, guys rushing around blindly, armed SWAT teams charging into stuff they don't know about . . . You got to understand, DCI, as a CIA field officer I know what I'm doing. I know how Zahiri works. We've got to keep a low profile, if we're going to get our hands on him. And we're close, I'm damned sure. Very close!'

'But –'

'I need *local* men,' Gonzalez insisted. 'Guys with local information, local contacts. I know this character. He'll know of groups up here with Middle East sympathies: I'm told there are suspect cells here in the north-east, Yemenis, Senegalese, Arabs, because of long links with the East. He'll want to make use of these local guys. But he'll stand out up here. And he's so committed, so crazed, he'll make a mistake, and then I'll get him.'

O'Connor was silent for a while and then he asked, 'Right, so you've got our senior men now organized to look for Zahiri. So what's the point of talking to Farnsby and me, in private?'

Gonzalez switched his glance to DI Farnsby, seated beside O'Connor. Suddenly, O'Connor sensed Farnsby was uncomfortable. He glanced at him, and the Detective Inspector stared rigidly ahead. Gonzalez leaned back in his chair, drew on his glowing cigar, his story over.

Assistant Chief Constable Cathery cleared his throat. 'You and Farnsby, you'll be expected to do a trawl of the antiquities trade up here. The likelihood is that the seller of the manuscript will be involved in that kind of business, so you will find out what you can on the grapevine.'

O'Connor shook his head, puzzled, and uneasy. 'I don't see –'

Gonzalez intervened again quietly. 'The night Shearbright died, he got involved in a quarrel in a hotel bar. With a group of English people, attending a conference in La Rochelle. I had an informant working there. I've already given the names of the people involved to Mr Cathery.'

The eyes of the Assistant Chief Constable were hooded and cold. 'There was a delegation from Northumberland at the hotel: Karen Stannard and Arnold Landon.'

'They work for the local authority,' O'Connor argued. 'They're not involved in the antiquities trade.'

'There was another man with them. Karl Spedding.'

'An ex-curator at the Pradak Museum. We need to check on his background,' Gonzalez added.

'So, it's like this,' Sid Cathery announced. 'Farnsby, you'll make a check on Stannard and Landon –'

'I can't believe they're involved,' O'Connor snapped. 'I've had dealings with both of them and –'

Cathery glowered. 'Stannard, Landon, and this man Spedding. As for you, O'Connor, you'll be getting more *intimately* involved in things.'

There was a sneer in Cathery's voice. O'Connor bridled as he felt a cold fist grip his stomach. 'What's that supposed to mean?'

There was a short, pregnant silence when Cathery's eyes bored into O'Connor's. When he spoke, Cathery's tone was frigid. 'You'll make use of the close acquaintanceship you've apparently developed with a certain Mrs Isabella Portland.'

The silence that grew around them was electric. O'Connor felt a hot flush rising to his face. Farnsby sat stiffly beside him, his chin raised, staring straight ahead, hands clenched on his knees. A slow surge of anger moved through O'Connor's veins. Farnsby had betrayed him.

'It shouldn't be a problem,' Cathery commented icily. 'I'm informed from a reliable source that you've been sleeping with this Portland woman ever since her husband shot himself . . . and probably before that, as I understand it.' His mouth twisted, and he stood up, abruptly. 'Not one of the usual perquisites of the job. But in this case, perhaps a useful one.'

As O'Connor opened his mouth to protest, Cathery added, 'Her dead husband was involved in dealing. Story is, she's about to do the same. So when you're shagging this woman, with our permission and approval this time, try to find out if she's heard anything about this bloody manuscript . . . or about Anwar Zahiri.'

Chapter Four

1

Arnold had been proved correct in his assumptions: his new job as acting head of department demanded that he spend more time on office work than he found congenial. He was able to alleviate matters somewhat, however, because of the fact that his new assistant, Karl Spedding, was a stranger to the hills of Northumberland. It meant Arnold had good reason to accompany him on his field work, to show him around some of the archaeological sites with which he was to be involved.

Accordingly there were opportunities to drive with Spedding into the Northumberland countryside. They visited the joint university/department project at Ogle, and from there made their way into the uplands towards the Cheviot. Arnold explained what was happening at the Roman wall site, and what artefacts had already been discovered there, and was gratified at the enthusiasm – and depth of knowledge – Spedding displayed when they discussed the cache of thousand-year-old private letters that had been unearthed, priceless accounts of the daily lives of the wives of garrison officers stationed on Hadrian's Wall, the social functions they arranged and attended, the minutiae of their relationships, the details of their personal purchases and anxieties and preoccupations.

There were other calls to make: a Romano-Celtic dig at the coast which was progressing well, the development of the wrecked *Vendela* exhibition site where Portia Tyrell had faced the destruction of a cherished relationship which had led to her recent resignation, the projected investigations into grave sites at Berwick, tumuli on the hills beyond Alnmouth, and historical documents unearthed at the ruined pele house near Warkworth Castle.

The wanderings, and a shared enthusiasm for the work, should have given the two men the opportunity to reach a closer understanding of each other, and led to a development of their relationship, but somehow this failed to occur. Arnold was unable to put his finger on what exactly was the problem. He was forced to admit to himself that he was not the easiest of men to get on with on account of his obsessional preoccupations, but that should not have been a problem in view of Spedding's own interests, so close to Arnold's. The two men travelled in one car, lunched together several times in isolated taverns on the coast headlands and in the hills, and they discussed professional matters, but there seemed to be no relaxation in Spedding's behaviour: he remained stiff, aloof, uncommunicative when not talking of the work, seemingly incapable of establishing any kind of warmth with the man to whom he now reported as head of department. Arnold wondered whether that was the problem, basically: perhaps Spedding resented the fact that, highly qualified as he was, he was yet forced to report to a man who lacked a university education, and whom, possibly, he regarded as his professional inferior. And yet it was more than that, Arnold concluded.

Rather, he gained the impression that for much of the time Spedding seemed intellectually detached, his mind fixated on other things. His discussions and observations were occasionally mechanical, his thoughts seemed to be drifting elsewhere. Arnold wondered whether he was concealing some kind of personal mission, some undisclosed reason for taking up this inferior position, and the initial distrust he had felt when he had first met Karl Spedding was not alleviated as he spent more time in the man's company.

At least Arnold was able to satisfy himself that the fault did not lie with him. He made efforts to be friendly, but they were largely ignored. And he noted that when they were both interviewed, first separately, and then together by Detective Inspector Farnsby, Karl Spedding was as unforthcoming and taciturn with the police officer as he had been with Arnold. It was as though he was prepared to say only the absolute minimum to Farnsby, explain himself briefly even when challenged.

And an irritated DI Farnsby seemed to regard it much like drawing blood from the proverbial stone.

'Not a talkative man,' he opined to Arnold as they waited for Spedding to join them in Arnold's office.

'Maybe it's because he feels he has nothing pertinent to tell you,' Arnold suggested defensively, prepared to stand up for his colleague in spite of his own experience with him. 'I really have the same feeling myself. I'm not at all sure just what this is all about. We were each interviewed by the French police –'

'That was in France,' Farnsby observed sententiously.

'The questions have been largely the same,' Arnold contended, 'and they related to murders committed in La Rochelle. I'm not at all clear just why the Northumberland police are questioning us.'

For the moment, Farnsby ignored the implied query. He consulted the notes in the pad he held on his knees. Arnold watched the man: he was lean in appearance and manner, saturnine, his mouth dissatisfied as though nursing some kind of resentment, hugging to himself a feeling of being wronged by the world. Arnold had known his previous DCI: perhaps Farnsby had expected, and desired, to replace Culpeper, and had been disappointed when a man from outside had been appointed. Ambition thwarted, Arnold mused. Farnsby raised his narrow head. He evaded the question Arnold had raised. 'I've already talked with Miss Stannard and I see no reason to bother her further. She's a busy woman. And you all three seem to be telling the same story.'

'So why do you want to talk again with me and Spedding?' Arnold asked.

Farnsby sniffed. 'Miss Stannard's duties have, I understand, now changed. She is no longer involved in archaeological matters, having been promoted. Whereas you, and Mr Spedding –'

'So you think the killings in La Rochelle were linked to the trade in archaeological artefacts? How do you think we are involved up here?'

There was a light tap on the door. Farnsby turned his head. The door opened and Karl Spedding stood there. His tone was cool. 'I'm sorry I'm a little late, Inspector. I had some urgent files to deal with.'

Farnsby clearly felt that the word *urgent* was not something that could be attributed to files held by the Department of Museums and Antiquities. He said nothing, however, as Spedding took a chair beside Arnold's desk and faced him, seated stiffly, arms folded over his narrow chest.

They went over ground already dealt with in individual interviews. Each confirmed the events of the evening in La Rochelle; neither was able to add anything to accounts already given of the heated words exchanged with the American dealer Adam Shearbright on the night he had died; and Arnold was able to reiterate that he had been present on that occasion as little more than an observer.

'But I gather that you didn't like Mr Shearbright?' Farnsby asked Spedding, with a slight sneer.

Spedding's tone was constrained, his glance indifferent. 'I had no feelings about the man. I knew of him, but I had never met him before that evening in the bar of the Hôtel de la Monnaie. Though I will admit I had strong feelings about the *business* he was in.' His glance was now glacially steady, holding Farnsby's in a firm challenge. 'I came across the results of his predations in my former employment. I disapproved of what he – and others – have been doing. The destruction of heritage; the damaging of archaeological environment; the greedy grabbing of ancient artefacts for selfish, personal gain. Apart from that,' he shrugged, 'I was indifferent to the man.'

Arnold suddenly understood why they were being questioned. He leaned forward. 'This isn't really about the killings as such,' he observed.

Farnsby stared at him, one eyebrow raised. 'What are you trying to suggest, Mr Landon?'

'You think – maybe the French police think – that the smuggling trade in antiquities has links up here in the north-east.' The thought allowed him to take another mental step. 'But you can hardly believe that *our* presence in La Rochelle is somehow tied up with Shearbright's business and . . .'

As Arnold's voice died away in disbelief, Farnsby permitted himself a thin smile. 'My beliefs are not in issue, Mr Landon. But since you raise the matter, I see no reason why I should not explain matters to you a little further. You, and Mr Spedding here, you were among the last people to see Mr Shearbright before he died, he was involved in illicit trade currently being investigated throughout Europe, and if your presence was coincidental . . . well, it doesn't prevent us from assuming you might have some information, locally, that might cast light upon the events that occurred in France. Shearbright died while you, Landon, were enjoying your own company at . . . a café, I understand. And while you, Mr Spedding, were apparently wandering the medieval streets of La Rochelle, alone . . .'

Neither Arnold nor Spedding seemed to feel it necessary to explain further. Farnsby waited for a few moments, and then asked, 'The French police seem to regard you as not strong suspects, but as to the background to the enquiry, are you gentlemen aware of any links up here in the north, links with international smuggling operations?'

'That's almost laughable!' Arnold snapped.

Spedding seemed less surprised. He frowned. 'The scope and extent of such operations are widespread. But I'm not personally aware of any such problem emanating from the north-east – even though there are many important investigatory digs taking place in the area. On the other hand, since I am newly employed in my present capacity –'

'Surprisingly so,' Farnsby muttered. When Spedding made no response and barely twitched a muscle in his face, Farnsby turned to Arnold.

'You'll be much more familiar with what goes on in this area.'

'In archaeological terms, yes.'

'Have you information you may share about possible smuggling activities, or the sale of looted artefacts, or the collecting of unprovenanced items?'

Arnold grimaced, and shrugged. 'Of course, over the years we've had examples of items being stolen, looted, sold at auction, and our services in the department have been called on to give advice on artefacts of doubtful provenance. Occasionally, I've been called upon myself to give evidence of provenance in the courtroom. But to suggest from the isolated events that I've come across that there might be an organized trade established up here, well, that's another matter.' He hesitated as a sudden thought crossed his mind. Gordon Portland had been a collector and dealer ... He discarded the thought almost immediately, shrugged it aside. But Farnsby brought him back to it.

'So the meeting with Shearbright was nothing more than coincidence,' Farnsby nodded sagely. 'But you attend auctions, you give advice, you investigate sites, you supply provenance of items for the museums in the county ... Do you have any information about the deceased Gordon Portland?'

'He's dead,' Arnold replied stupidly, thrown by the sudden shift in the conversation, and alarmed at the manner in which Farnsby almost seemed to have read his mind.

'A year ago, yes, that's why I described him as deceased,' Farnsby said mockingly. 'But Portland was a collector, was he not?'

'That is so.'

'Were you familiar with his activities?'

'No.'

131

'The records show that Portland made his money in the construction business, but indulged a passion for collecting paintings, sculptures, pottery, rare books, medieval weapons. Used an item from his collection to kill himself, in fact. You probably wouldn't have been aware of the detailed nature of his acquisitions, but you must be aware that his widow recently sold items from that collection.'

'I am.'

Karl Spedding had shed his indifference: he was leaning forward slightly, listening intently to what DI Farnsby was saying.

'You might also be aware that she seems recently to have registered a new limited company, the objects of which include the trading of antiquities.'

'You're well informed, Detective Inspector.'

'And you, somewhat tight-lipped.'

Farnsby's tone irritated Arnold. It was true he could have been more informative about the planned activities of Isabella Portland, her recent discoveries at the apartment in Edinburgh, and her business intentions in partnership with Angela Fenchurch, but annoyed as he was he felt disinclined to offer anything to Farnsby that he was not forced into.

There was more verbal fencing during the next ten minutes as the Detective Inspector pursued Arnold regarding his knowledge of the trade in antiques in the north-east. Spedding now sat quietly, uninvolved, as Farnsby questioned Arnold further about his understanding of the local market for antiquities, the operation of the auction houses, and the declared provenance of items held by museums under his own departmental control. Even so Arnold thought he detected a certain tension in his colleague's attitude, as though he was as interested in Arnold's answers as was Farnsby. As for the questions themselves, Arnold answered them almost mechanically, but still vaguely puzzled: he felt constantly that Farnsby was in some manner skirting around an issue, asking questions that were peripheral, seeking to disclose nothing he himself did not wish to: he suspected there was a hidden agenda behind Farnsby's inquisition, and Arnold was unable to decipher it.

Eventually, the flow of questions began to dry up, and Arnold glanced at his watch. 'You'll forgive me, I'm sure, DI Farnsby, but I have an appointment to keep.'

'Of considerable consequence, I'm sure,' Farnsby replied sarcastically. 'Well, I guess that'll be enough for now. All I will add is that if you and Mr Spedding here think of anything further that might help us in our enquiries, we'd be grateful if you would communicate with us.' He smiled unpleasantly. 'So you go ahead and keep your appointment, Mr Landon, and we'll continue with our investigation. Perhaps our paths will cross again.'

Not if I can help it, Arnold thought to himself. He glanced at Karl Spedding: he suspected his assistant would be of the same mind. Nevertheless, after Farnsby had left the room, Spedding lingered. He shuffled somewhat awkwardly. 'This collection the DI was talking about . . .'

'Gordon Portland's?'

Spedding nodded. 'Was it an important collection? I mean, did it contain many items of value . . . historical value, that is?'

Arnold scratched his ear thoughtfully. 'It wasn't a big auction, as I recall. Some paintings. A few sculptures. Various items of militaria. A few of which were actually confiscated by the police after the suicide . . . But I believe there were a number of private sales made, of which we know nothing, and since then . . . I didn't mention it to Farnsby, but Isabella Portland, the widow, she's come into possession of a larger collection since her husband's suicide. She'll be putting the collection on the market, once the items have been catalogued. Going to set up in business, it seems.'

'Are you involved in all this?' Spedding asked. There was a strange huskiness in his tone.

'Not particularly. Karen Stannard has introduced me to Isabella Portland, asked me to help her deal with questions of provenance of certain items.' He glanced at his watch again. 'But I've really got to move. I'm meeting someone at the airport.'

As he brushed past Karl Spedding he gained the impression the former museum curator would have liked to learn more about the collection inherited by the widowed Isabella Portland.

The roads were clear on his drive from Morpeth to Newcastle Airport. He left his car in the short-term car park and hurried into the reception area. He checked the arrivals board and saw that the flight he was expecting had already landed. He had to wait for only a few minutes before chattering passengers began to stream through the arrivals gate. He spotted Carmela Cacciatore immediately.

She travelled light. She wore an open jacket that exposed the formidable spread of her chest: the only luggage she carried was contained in a back pack, the strap of which parted her considerable breasts, emphasizing their magnificence. The worn jeans were moulded tightly to her muscular thighs, and the boots she wore were tough brown leather, designed for working rather than travelling. She came rushing forward when she caught sight of him, threw her arms around his neck, crushed him against her bosom enthusiastically. 'Arnold! It is good to hold you again! You remember how we wriggled together, that dangerous night in Berwick?'

He remembered indeed. Laughing, he extricated himself from her embrace with difficulty, kissed her on each cheek, stepped back, looked her over and said, 'You look ready for work in the field.'

'This is a compliment?' she beamed. 'I will take it as so.' She linked her arm into his affectionately as they turned and walked out towards the car park. 'As I have explained to you on the telephone, this is to be a quick visit only, because there is much to do back at the Piazza Sant' Ignazio. So much new evidence is coming in to us from

Switzerland, since we have followed the *cordata* trail. But it is important that I came to meet you. Both to see you again,' she grinned at him with a flirtatious twinkle in her eyes, 'and also to have a discussion with you. You have a hotel booked for me? Or do I stay with you at your apartment?'

'Hotel,' Arnold replied firmly. 'But this evening, we'll go to dinner in town, when we can talk about why you thought it necessary to come to the north-east to see me.'

Arnold drove her to the small private hotel in Gosforth and waited downstairs as Carmela unpacked, showered, and changed her clothing. She eventually joined Arnold in the hotel bar. He was surprised to note that the back pack must have been more capacious than he had suspected, or maybe he had underestimated the ability of women to pack significant items into small spaces. However it may be, he felt Carmela looked wonderful and he told her so. She smoothed the cream-coloured, clinging dress she wore with pleasure, and Arnold studiously avoided the display of cleavage the straining top afforded.

She ordered a Campari while he settled for a whisky and soda. He explained he had ordered a taxi to take them into the city to an Italian restaurant he knew well. She looked down at her bosom. 'So you think I will improve with even more pasta?' she asked, grinning at him.

They relaxed for a while, sipping their drinks and talking about the progress of Carmela's investigation into the smuggling rings in Europe, and the links with Swiss-based organizations, until Arnold's curiosity finally got the better of him. 'I suppose your visit has something to do with the photographs I sent to you?'

She nodded vigorously, her blonde hair falling across her eyes. She brushed away a stray lock. 'Yes, that is so. We will talk in detail about these, but first of all, in your covering letter you have not told me who will be trying to sell these items in the market.'

'Her name is Isabella Portland. She's starting up a new business, with the collection left by her deceased husband. You will like her, I think. She is from your country.'

'She is Italian?'

'From Tuscany, I believe,' Arnold asserted. 'I understand she was born in Lucca –'

'Ah, *que citta!*'

'– but she was brought up and educated in England, though she still has family in Tuscany, I believe. She speaks fluent Italian, of course. Her husband was a builder, with an interest in ancient artefacts. The photographs are of certain items I wasn't sure about. I thought maybe you could provide me with some assistance.'

Carmela nodded thoughtfully. 'I picked them up at the Piazza after I got away from the . . . unpleasant business at La Rochelle.'

'Has anything further happened about those killings?' Arnold asked.

Carmela sipped her Campari. Doubtfully, she replied, 'I am not kept fully in touch with matters, you understand. It is the business for the French police. But before I returned to Rome I was informed by Inspector Leconte that there has been another murder, which they believe to be connected with the killings of Shearbright and Carpentier.'

'Another dealer? Sounds like it's getting to be a dangerous business.'

She shook her head vigorously. 'No, no, not a dealer. But some person who is connected. They did not give me details but I believe they are . . . how do you say . . . winding down their investigation in regard to the links with my own enquiries.'

'Into the illicit trade in antiquities? I thought it was all part of the same thing.'

She contemplated the red liquor in her glass. 'They found a corpse in a river, some miles north of Fontenay-le-Comte. It had been there for some days. I don't know whether it was the fish, or the battering the man took to the face, but I understand from Inspector Jean-Pierre Leconte that they think this man had something to do with what happened in La Rochelle, even though they have difficulty in establishing his identity.' She grimaced. 'The fish . . . it is not a pleasant thought.' She finished her drink in a gulp. 'Tonight, I think I will forgo the *loup de mer* and eat *pollo matriciana.*'

She smiled at him. 'I shall have chicken, Montepulciano, and *dolce gabbiata*. And we can talk about the photographs, and you will tell me more about this Italian lady.'

In the darkness of the hotel room the perspiration dried slowly on O'Connor's body. He lay on his back, staring blindly at the ceiling. Their love-making had been frenzied, as it almost always had been in their previous meetings; locked almost fiercely together they had reached a climax in a mindless whirl of sensual passion. He had been obsessed with Isabella Portland since their first encounter, when she had offered him a lift outside the railway station at Newcastle. There had been an immediate, mutual attraction; their affair had begun like a whirlwind, and the shuddering passion had continued, perhaps exacerbated by the circumstances that had surrounded them – her loveless marriage, the jealousy of her husband, and the shattering event that had occurred at Belton Hall.

And yet now, subtly enough, for him this evening it had been different.

He doubted that she had been aware of the turmoil in his mind. The fact that their liaison was known about at Ponteland headquarters, that he was under instructions to use their relationship for purposes connected with a criminal investigation, had inevitably raised resentment in his mind. He felt he was no longer in control of his own life; whereas his affair with Isabella had previously been edged with danger, and this had perhaps sharpened their sexual appetite for each other, now it was scarred with guilt, anger and self-disgust. He had long ago lost his equilibrium as far as Isabella was concerned: now he was completely unbalanced, unable to collect his thoughts, fearful that she might discover, inadvertently, what was gnawing at his conscience.

She stirred beside him in the bed, moaning lightly in the warm darkness. She turned, reached out for him, took his hand and placed it upon her breast. It was soft, warm, yielding. She moved closer to him, one thigh moving smoothly across his, her groin pressing against his, her lips whispering in his ear. 'You think it is more sexy, here in a hotel room? We would have more freedom in my own home. It could be your home, too.'

Previously, he had resisted her out of a conviction that it would be safer to find isolated country hotels to continue their liaison. Now, it was because, with his new motivation, he had the feeling it would be an even greater betrayal if he were to sleep with her in her own bed, in her own home.

He lay still, almost rigid, unable to relax. Her hand began to caress him, lightly, the butterfly touch of her fingers moving across his body, teasing, tempting. He took a deep breath, turned a little towards her.

'So how is your new venture progressing?' he asked her softly, but unable to keep an edge of bitterness out of his voice.

'You want to talk about my business?' she queried dreamily, 'at a moment like this?'

'I've always wanted to know everything about you,' he muttered evasively. 'And this new venture, you know so little about it. I mean, who do you expect to be dealing with? What contacts have you made? You've no experience in the trade, it was your husband who was the collector. Have you been able to discover who his contacts were? And if you have, are you sure they won't con you, give you bad advice? If you tell me who they are, maybe I could run a check on them for you.'

Isabella nestled closer, wriggled against him. 'How could I ever be conned with a great big copper to help me if I got into trouble?' Her lips were close to his. 'Big, and bigger and bigger. . .'

Her light, lascivious fingers were doing their work with a practised efficiency. He was unable to resist, cling to the insistence of the men back at headquarters, and he tried to thrust to the back of his mind the agonies churning his conscience. But when he drew her closer, slipped into her

with a familiar ease, his mind was still clouded, and it was
as though their love-making was something that was happening to someone else, to two other people, and he was
unable to avoid the consequences of his actions, even as his
climax sent the thundering blood into his head . . .

Carmela was astonished by the elderly butler with the immobile features. 'Is he *real*?' she whispered to Arnold as they were led through the hall into the library.

'Did you not ever see the film of *Il Leopardo*?' he teased.

As they traversed the hallway itself, she exclaimed in delight at the sight of the long curving staircase. In the library her Italian exuberance bubbled over at the magnificence of the grand stone fireplace, the neo-classical splendour of the decor, the elegant furniture and the heavy gold and purple drapes at the tall windows overlooking the terrace and lawns. She ran her hand appreciatively along the smooth surface of the long oak table, and admired various items in the antique collection on show in several glass-topped display cases. Some were empty: clearly, Isabella Portland had sold off most of the original collection housed in this room.

'Mr Portland must have been very wealthy,' Carmela commented, as she moved along the book-lined walls, noting with approval some of the leather-bound titles.

'He had various business interests, as far as I recall, mainly in timber. Apart from collecting, it would seem he also did some dealing in the antiques market,' Arnold suggested. 'I also read some time ago that there was an insurance claim made by him regarding the shipping of some Italian marble sculptures: a fourth-century triptych, a Greek Orthodox icon ... I understand the matter went to court.'

Carmela turned to look at him, her brow wrinkled in curiosity. 'What was the reason?'

'I don't know the full story. According to what I read in the newspapers at the time, apart from his construction business he was also involved in distribution of commercial materials, timber, electrical goods. And included occasionally in the shipments, there were artefacts being shipped to the States and sometimes Asia.'

Carmela grimaced thoughtfully, and wrinkled her nose. 'And when they went missing he claimed on insurance?'

'It seems so.'

'These contacts he had in America and Asia, were they . . . how do you say . . . suspect?'

Arnold could guess what she was thinking. He shrugged. 'I wouldn't know. I simply recall reading reports at the time. The insurance company paid out anyway, after protest, so I suppose there was no real case of fraud against him.'

'He committed suicide.'

'That's right.' Arnold hesitated. He had heard of the reasons for the man's death, his jealousy, the possessiveness that had led to murder, but it seemed irrelevant to talk of it now. 'And at the time, his collection – and his dealing in antiquities – was thought to be fairly limited. But since his death, it seems that his widow has discovered a considerable number of other items, stashed away in a flat in Edinburgh. That's how she comes to be starting up a business, and that's why my department's become involved, and the photographs I sent you –'

'Yes, the photographs –' Carmela interrupted him, but then was herself interrupted as the library door swung open and Isabella Portland entered.

She came forward in an easy, self-confident stride, her glossy, red-gold hair framing the perfect oval of her face, her welcoming smile displaying the flash of white, perfect teeth that contrasted with the natural darkness of her flawless skin. She was above average height, her waist was slim, her full bosom taut under the light blue sweater, and when she uttered her welcome her voice was low, slightly husky, melodious. Facing her, Carmela seemed short, even dumpy, a peasant before an aristocrat. Arnold began to make introductions.

'Mrs Portland, Carmela Cacciatore –'

He was drowned out, ignored, as the two women suddenly burst into a torrent of Italian, immediately holding hands, conversing rapidly and excitedly as though they had known each other for years, the meeting of old friends in a strange environment. Both women were smiling, laughing; Arnold caught names – Lucca, Verdi, Volturno,

Montepulciano, Garda, Verona – but otherwise was lost in the warm, enthusiastic chattering of two women delighted to have the opportunity to converse in their own language, far from a common homeland. It was Isabella Portland who was first to remember there was an Italian non-speaker in their presence. She turned, held out an elegant hand to Arnold.

'Ha, Mr Landon, forgive us. It is so pleasant to meet someone who knows Tuscany so well . . . and it is rarely that I have the opportunity to converse in my native language.'

Carmela also was apologetic. 'I am sorry, Arnold. But you did not tell me Isabella was so beautiful, and so welcoming.'

'A bottle of wine is called for,' Isabella Portland insisted and turned on her heel to leave the room and make the necessary arrangements. During her absence Carmela prowled around the library, again inspecting the book-lined walls, her eyes glowing with enthusiasm. 'I like Mrs Portland,' she remarked over her shoulder to Arnold. 'Such *style* . . .'

The wine turned out to be a perfectly chilled Chianti; Isabella served it herself in tall frosted glasses, and they sat at the end of the long polished oak table. Arnold was forced to wait a while again as the two women chattered together like excited birds. It was several minutes before the conversation slowed, and took a more serious turn. Isabella hesitated, smiled at Arnold. 'You must think us extremely rude. But we have been talking of Lucca, and the years gone by and . . . well, you will know how these things can get out of hand.'

'It's not a problem.'

'But Arnold and I are really here on business, so we should now talk in English,' Carmela admitted, suddenly frowning. 'You will be aware, Isabella, that Arnold has consulted me, and that I work for the Carabinieri Art Squad in Rome.'

'I gathered as much.' Isabella Portland hesitated, glanced at Arnold. 'I'm not sure why he felt you should be involved, but I had asked for his assistance ... And it is most gracious of you to take the trouble to come all this way, Carmela ...' Her voice died away suddenly, as though she began to realize that Carmela's presence was perhaps more serious than she had anticipated. Her glance locked with Arnold's. 'I take it this is to do with the photographs that you took away?'

Arnold nodded, and turned to Carmela. She picked up the black leather briefcase she had brought with her, unlocked it. She drew out some sheets of plastic: Arnold realized that the photographs he had sent her for perusal had now been placed individually in slots in three plastic sheets. She unfolded them, staring at them. 'I presume you did not take these photographs yourself, Isabella?'

Isabella Portland shook her head; a lock of red-gold hair fell across her eyes. 'No. When I learned about the apartment in Edinburgh and visited it, I found a considerable number of artefacts there, and a folder containing photographs which largely linked to the stored items. I showed them to Mr Landon; he extracted a certain number for further consideration.'

'And I sent the selection to you,' Arnold confirmed.

'So these photographs would have been taken by your husband?' Carmela asked.

'I would imagine so,' Isabella replied. 'Perhaps they were taken as a record of what he was holding, or maybe to interest buyers. But I can't be sure. I mean, I didn't even know he was so deeply involved in this kind of business.'

Carmela was silent for a few moments. Then she grimaced. 'I am not suggesting ... His name ... it does not appear in the list of dealers known to us.'

'Known to you?' Isabella Portland frowned. 'I don't understand ...'

Carmela sighed. 'We have recently come into possession of a list of men who are involved in the *cordata* ... dealers in the illicit trade, smuggling looted artefacts on an international basis.' She hesitated, and murmured reluctantly, 'I understand your husband had various business dealings with contacts in the USA and Asia.'

Isabella had paled. 'I believe so, but I understood it was all legitimate business ... indeed, it wasn't about antiquities, but other matters, electrical goods, other commercial products ...'

'With, it now seems, a lucrative sideline in looted artefacts,' Carmela added drily.

There was a tap on the door; Arnold glanced up and saw Angela Fenchurch coming in to join them. She was dressed in a light sweater and jeans but the casual nature of her attire detracted little from her attractiveness; she was still affected by the loss of her grandmother, however, Arnold concluded, for she had dark hollows under her eyes, and she seemed somewhat withdrawn, listless in her manner.

'Sorry I'm late,' she murmured, then shook hands with Carmela after Isabella Portland introduced them. She glanced almost indifferently at the sheet of photographs that Carmela was holding.

'We were just about to discuss them,' Isabella explained. Then she turned to Carmela. 'You said *looted* artefacts!'

Carmela nodded. 'I've separated then into two groups. These present no problems as far as I am able to ascertain ...'

Isabella accepted the plastic packet and glanced briefly at the photographs it contained. She nodded, then handed the plastic sheet to Angela Fenchurch. 'These include some of the items of jewellery that you put into the collection.'

Angela grimaced. 'I might have to withdraw them, in fact, in view of what James Detorius has explained to me about my grandmother's estate.'

Carmela seemed puzzled; Arnold glanced at her and shook his head slightly. The matter was irrelevant. Carmela returned her attention to the remainder of the photographs. 'These, on the other hand, do present certain problems. Isabella, how much do you really know of your late husband's business dealings ... as far as the antiquities trade was concerned?'

Isabella Portland shrugged, shook her head. 'I've explained. Next to nothing. I knew about his collection here at the Hall, and there was the court case over that insurance matter ... but apart from that, the items he'd been holding at Edinburgh were a complete surprise to me.' She hesitated. 'I have the feeling you are about to give me bad news.'

Carmela chewed at her lip, nodded soberly. 'I am afraid so. From what I observe in these photographs, it is my belief that your late husband was a serious dealer in looted antiquities. When Arnold sent me these I could not deal with them immediately for reasons he is aware of. When I got back to my headquarters in Rome I was able to inspect them, discuss them with some of my colleagues, undertake some research and then ... well, in view of my friendship with Arnold I thought it best to come to England to see him. He did not tell me from whom he had received these photographs.'

'But you're convinced they come from looted tombs?' Arnold asked.

Carmela nodded again, glanced at Isabella anxiously. 'You do not know where your husband obtained these items?'

Isabella shook her head. Her eyes were clouded. 'I've no idea. I presume he bought them from other dealers, but I've come across no records of purchase or sale. He kept his business interests well away from me.' Her chin came up in a certain bitter, defiant recollection. 'In reality, he treated me as merely another acquisition. It would never have occurred to him to discuss such matters with me.'

There was an embarrassed silence for a little while. Carmela looked down at the photographs, shrugged. Quietly, she said, 'I suspect we might never find out who sold them to your husband. As to whom he was selling them to, that is another matter. I could give you a list of museums ...'

'But how can you be so sure of these items?' Isabella asked.

Carmela leaned forward, pointing to some of the displayed photographs. 'These acrolytes here –'

'Acrolytes?' Isabella queried in a puzzled tone.

145

'The marble hands, or feet in this case, that are added to a statue. These, along with this *dinos* – this deep bowl of silver – this broken Laconian kylix, and this *oinochoe*, they all come from the same hoard.'

'And you can identify it?' Arnold asked.

Carmela nodded. 'Some years ago the Metropolitan Museum in New York acquired from a New York dealer a treasure of gold, silver, bronze and earthenware objects. The dealer claimed to have obtained the items from ignorant itinerant traders in Europe, on separate occasions. But it was not long before archaeologists were able to identify the treasure as coming from ancient Lydia – the western part of modern Turkey, the kingdom of Croesus.'

'As in as rich as Croesus,' Isabella murmured.

Carmela nodded. 'It was concluded that the hoard came from four entire tombs that had been looted near Sardis. The Turks knew that tumuli in the Usak region of west central Anatolia had been broken into and looted by villagers: some objects were recovered, and these were clearly linked to the items acquired by the Metropolitan Museum. But of course, many other items from the same tombs escaped the net.'

'And you think these come from the Lydian hoard,' Arnold murmured.

'Exactly.'

There was a long silence, as they all sat staring at the scattered photographs. Arnold glanced at Angela: her head was down, a worried frown on her features, her fingers linked together in her lap. He had the feeling, nevertheless, she was not concentrating on the matter in hand, as the others were.

After a while, Isabella stirred, and sighed. 'So, where do we go from here?'

Carmela was reluctant to speak, and was clearly embarrassed at her disclosures. 'I suppose there are two options open to you, Isabella. Neither may be an easy route for you.'

'Tell me.'

146

Carmela flashed a worried glance at Arnold, then went on. 'In some ways, I am sorry that these photographs came to my attention. But it has been done, so that is the end of it. The first option, Isabella, is to place the items on the market as you had intended. I am certain that there would be many dealers and private collectors who would be very interested in some of these objects. But if you follow this course, it is my duty to warn you that there will be consequences.'

'How do you mean?'

'Some sales could no doubt be conducted in secret, but in due course, particularly if you were to sell to museums, where you would probably get the best prices, questions would inevitably arise as to the provenance of the items. And I would be duty-bound to give my own opinion on the matter of the sale. Indeed, I would probably have to take action on the matter, officially. I regret this, but now that I am aware . . .'

Isabella noted the regret in Carmela's tone, smiled faintly and inclined her head. 'You said I had two options.'

'That is correct.' Carmela hesitated, clearly reluctant. 'The other way to deal with the matter – and I think the proper way to act – is to return the items to the Turkish authorities. It is possible they would provide you with some . . . compensation, but I cannot be sure about that. They would claim the objects were stolen in the first instance. If you follow this course, the artefacts can then be placed in museums in Turkey and be made available for further investigation by Turkish and other scholars and archaeologists. I am aware that it had been your intention to use these items as part of your new business, but . . .'

Her voice died away. Isabella Portland sat gazing at the photographs. She glanced briefly at Angela Fenchurch and then she shook her head. 'I don't really think I have any choice. I'm sure you're right in your assessment – you're the expert, after all – and I'm grateful that you've taken the trouble to come over to explain this to me. Clearly, the way forward is for me to hand over these objects to the appropriate authorities.'

'I can be of assistance in this matter, of course,' Carmela murmured in a gentle voice. 'I hope that this does not mean your plans for a business will be destroyed. I believe these artefacts from the Lydian hoard are only some of the items that have come into your possession.' She glanced at Arnold. 'The others come with a satisfactory provenance, I imagine.'

Arnold nodded. 'As far as I can make out. There should be enough to –'

Isabella held up her hand, shook her head. Her eyes were sad. 'No. I don't think I would want to go on with the idea of the business now. Finding the cache at Edinburgh was a surprise, and with such a windfall I thought it would be interesting to start a business, but these revelations have knocked me sideways. I don't feel I want to go on: it's bad enough discovering that my husband was probably involved in illicit trading of this kind – apart from the rest of the whole bad business leading to his death – but I certainly would not wish to enter into this kind of world . . . tomb looting, illegal sales . . . No, I think I would wish to do as you suggest, Carmela, make the items available to the proper authorities. After all, I don't need the money. My villain of a husband,' she added bitterly, 'left me well provided for.'

'I think this is the best decision,' Carmela said sympathetically. 'And the Portland name, it could appear on any bequest you make, as a collection. There need be no publicity regarding the provenance of the objects. We need make no statement as to how they came into the possession of your husband.' She glanced at Arnold. 'Apart from the items from the Lydian hoard, I am sure there will be interest expressed from local museums.'

'We at the department would be happy to talk to you further about it,' Arnold offered.

Isabella nodded, raised her head and with sudden decision said, 'Right. That's what we'll do. If Carmela can make the necessary contacts the Lydian items can be returned to Turkey through the appropriate channels; the others, well, I'd be happy to accept your help, Arnold.'

It was almost by way of a guilty afterthought that she turned to direct her gaze at the silent woman seated beside her. 'Angela, I'm sorry, I've not even given you the opportunity –'

'Isabella, please, don't worry. Those objects are yours anyway, not mine.'

'Yes, but we were going to make a start together . . .'

Angela Fenchurch shook her head vigorously. 'No, it's of no consequence, Isabella. As things stand, it's doubtful if I could have fulfilled my side of the agreement anyway. I was pledged to provide the jewellery items from my grandmother, and work in the business, but it was all a pipe dream, really. I have to draw back the jewellery, in view of what my lawyer, James Detorius, now tells me.'

'But surely –'

'My grandmother was mortgaged up to the hilt. Everything will have to go to pay off creditors. She'd been living on borrowed money for years . . . and using the money largely to support me in my life and aspirations.'

Isabella Portland reached out and took the younger woman's hand in her own. 'You can't blame yourself. It was her choice. And you weren't even aware –'

'And now to top it all,' Angela interrupted gloomily, 'there's been a break-in at the castle apartment.'

The other three were silent. Arnold stared at the young woman. He had earlier thought she was distracted, barely listening to the conversation between Carmela and Isabella Portland. Now he could understand why. He leaned forward across the table. 'When did this happen?'

'Two nights ago. I've been staying in Newcastle with some friends: I haven't been too happy staying alone in the apartment at Stanhope since my grandmother's death, and my friends thought they could cheer me up: we went to a concert at The Sage in Gateshead, and then I stayed over. Then, when I got back to Stanhope –'

'You poor thing! Was there much damage?' Isabella asked.

Angela Fenchurch frowned and shook her head. 'No, nothing really. In fact, I don't think it looked like the work

149

of the kind of young thugs you hear about. A window had been forced, but not a great deal had been disturbed.' She frowned. 'I mean, there was no mess. It was all, well, kind of professional.'

Carmela Cacciatore was puzzled. 'The intruder took nothing of value?'

Angela's eyes were wide. 'As far as I can tell, he took nothing at all! I was aware as soon as I walked in that something was wrong; things were out of place, slight disturbances . . . but drawers had been carefully opened and closed again; wardrobes, similarly; a desk had been forced open but although financial papers inside had been disarranged nothing was taken, at least as far as I can see. But it leaves you feeling sort of unclean, going back into a place that's been entered in that way.'

'I suppose someone will have heard of your grandmother's death, realized you were not there at the flat, and broke in hoping to find something of value,' Isabella suggested soberly.

'What a dreadful experience!' Carmela muttered.

'And a puzzling one.' Angela brushed back her hair from her eyes, shook herself as though containing her emotions, pulling herself together. 'Still, as I've already said, there was nothing there of any value to take anyway. My grandmother and I – we were on our beam ends.'

'At least the jewellery wasn't there,' Isabella countered.

Angela nodded. 'You're right. The thief would almost certainly have been unable to resist it if he had come across it. Anyway, the whole lot will have to go to the bank now. The debts are quite crippling, it seems. James Detorius is handling everything, dealing with the bank, talking to creditors, and he's looking into the matter of the cottage up at Elsdon as well. It will have to be sold, of course. ' She sighed. 'It's all such a mess. If only I'd known . . .'

'You've informed the police about the break-in, of course,' Arnold said.

Angela nodded. 'I rang them immediately I was sure a stranger had entered the apartment. But, well, they didn't seem to be particularly interested. Since nothing was taken, I don't expect to hear any more about it.'

Isabella Portland squeezed her hand gently. 'Leave it to me, Angela. The police can't just walk away, ignore the whole matter. I'll see what I can do about it.' She hesitated, glanced uncertainly at Arnold. 'There's someone I can have a word with. Just leave it to me.'

The junction of the rivers Mer and Vent had been trawled extensively for several days by police divers but nothing more of consequence had been discovered. Inspector Jean-Pierre Leconte sat in the sunshine on the café terrace overlooking the bend of the river, fingering his light moustache, admiring the sharp blue of the sky, and below him the thick green spread of the ancient former royal forest of Mervent-Vouvant. As he sipped his black coffee his thoughts drifted to the medieval myths and legends surrounding the fairy Melusine, the fey princess reputed to have inhabited these woods along with wolves and deer and bears, and pilgrims visiting the Grotto of Père Montfort; now it was walkers and campers who flooded into the area during the summer months, using canoes and kayaks to explore the twin rivers, back-packing their way along the winding tracks of the shady, signposted hiking routes.

It had been one of those casual visitors who had first caught sight of the half-submerged, heavy, rolling body of the dead man face down in the water.

Jean-Pierre Leconte sniffed fastidiously and gave his neat moustache a final caress. Whoever had killed the big man and dumped him in the river had acted hurriedly: the body had been stripped, the face battered beyond recognition, the teeth smashed, possibly with a bar of iron, a tyre jack or something similar, but the corpse had not been long in the river. The fish had begun their work, nibbling at the soft, raw exposed tissue, and the task of identification would be difficult, but the forensic team were giving it a degree of priority now that much of the work on the two corpses in La Rochelle was done and reported upon. Fingerprints had already been despatched to Europol for checking against their database.

The thought of La Rochelle turned his mind towards Carmela Cacciatore. Before she had left for England on some mission of her own he had informed her of this new discovery, and of his suspicions after conducting interviews in Mervent and Vouvant. There was nothing concrete that he could rely upon; it was little more than gut instinct, and the small piece of information that an old man seated in the garden of the Château de la Citardière had given him, concerning a brief conversation about antiquities with a stranger. But Jean-Pierre had confided in Carmela, suggesting that he was of the view there was a link between the dead man at Mervent and the two bodies in the antiquities warehouse in La Rochelle.

What that link might be, he was uncertain. But it would be something to do with the man described by the CIA agent, Richard Gonzalez.

The killer, Anwar Zahiri.

Jean-Pierre Leconte heaved a sigh, finished his coffee, rose, walked to the fenced-off edge of the escarpment and leaned on it, staring down the long drop to the curling river and the scattered kayaks busy on its surface. Perhaps the forensic team would come up with something to go on. Meanwhile, he had promised to return the phone call of the boorish English policeman, Assistant Chief Constable Cathery. He had never met the man, but he had disliked the harsh tone of his voice during the brief discussion they had earlier had over the phone.

Overbearing, arrogant, distrustful ... Jean-Pierre Leconte had a mental picture of the English police officer which he guessed would not be far from reality. The charging of a bull in the ring. He himself believed in a more measured, less aggressive approach to police work. He touched his moustache again, thoughtfully: careful, patient, even plodding attitudes brought better results in his experience. It was foolish to jump to conclusions before the evidence was laid out before him. Particularly when, as at the moment, Jean-Pierre Leconte had so much on his plate – the murder in Mervent, the earlier killings in La Rochelle, the spreading investigation of the *cordata*, and the liaison work involved in the searching out of French dealers linked into the illicit antiquities trade, balanced with confusing information from Interpol and Europol.

And then there would be the preparation for trials later, he sighed despondently. So much work ... but at least there would be the pleasure of working again with Carmela Cacciatore. The consideration brightened his mood. His relationship with Carmela had been based, like all his work, on patience and slow progression, but he had high hopes of reaching his objective. What a woman!

For a brief moment the image of his wife flashed up in his mind, her small, rosebud-tipped bosom, her wide hips and short legs, but the picture of Carmela Cacciatore interceded, smiling, in his imagination holding out her arms. A light moan of anticipation escaped his lips as he thought of his face buried between her magnificent breasts.

He clucked his tongue, angry with himself. Better to think, at this moment, of his phone call to Assistant Chief Constable Cathery. That way no madness lay.

DCI O'Connor had already reached his decision before he prowled around the apartment in Stanhope.

When Isabella Portland had told him about the break-in at the castle apartment, complained about the lackadaisical attitude of the local police, and had asked him to do something about it, he had agreed to look into the matter, but with reluctance. He had decided to discuss it with ACC Cathery.

'I don't want to be treading on the toes of the local coppers. And a break-in like this, it's such a minor matter –'

'The Portland woman's asked you to check it out, hasn't she? And the Fenchurch girl ... isn't she getting involved in the antiquity business with Mrs Portland? Go along with it, O'Connor. This will help you ingratiate yourself even further with your girlfriend, get yourself drawn deeper into the antiquities business.'

Sourly, O'Connor had countered, 'I keep telling you, Isabella Portland isn't really in the antiquities business. In fact, it now looks as though she won't be going ahead with her plans after all. She didn't explain the reasons to me in detail: just said some problems had arisen.'

Cathery's mouth twisted into an unpleasant smile. 'Then you'd better find out just why she's backing out. Maybe she suspects you of pumping her – if you'll forgive the expression.'

'I –'

'Or maybe she's always been involved deeper in the trade than you believe – after all, it looks as though her old man was in it up to his neck, before he topped himself.' Cathery leered at him. 'We never did get the full story on that, did we? You were there that day at Belton Hall when he blew his head off. The story you gave us at the time was that he topped himself when he knew he was going to be charged with murder . . . but now I wonder whether there was more to it than that. Like what was going on between you and his wandering wife.'

Grimly, O'Connor said, 'I don't see the point of this investigation. I want to be relieved of it.'

'You know my answer to that, DCI O'Connor. You got a job to do! Just get on with it.'

'I'm not convinced that my dealing with Isabella Portland will bring about any results.'

'Don't be so bloody squeamish, man. Besides, think of the perks the job offers!'

Resentful of the licentious tone in the senior officer's voice, O'Connor burned his bridges. 'I'm walking away from this, Cathery!'

Assistant Chief Constable Sid Cathery was not accustomed to defiance: he stood up, empurpling, displaying the furious bulk that twenty years earlier had caused rugby front row scrums to buckle. His nostrils flared, his cauliflower ears reddened, his eyes bulged with sudden fury. 'Who the hell do you think you're talking to? You're walking straight into a suspension, O'Connor!'

'So be it,' O'Connor snapped, and stalked out of the room.

He explained the whole situation to Isabella that same evening, including the fact that he had been working to instructions.

155

She had been pleased to agree to the unexpected assignation, with warmth, but she quickly fell silent and remained so for a long time after he explained things to her, told her of the directive he had received from Cathery. The fact he was telling her now had not removed the shocked stoniness from her beautiful features: he knew what she would be thinking. The times they had lain together in the passionate darkness, the subtly phrased, careful questions he had asked her recently while they lay side by side. He could not be sure whether she understood the sacrifice he was now making: running the possibility of giving up his career in the force because of the guilt he felt in his behaviour to her.

'So all the time, recently,' she murmured, 'when we were making love, it was known to your superiors . . . you were in fact acting on their instructions?'

The disgust in her tone tore at his conscience.

'It wasn't as simple as that,' he defended himself awkwardly. 'Our relationship . . .'

The words dried up. He was suddenly unable to describe just what their relationship amounted to; unable to explain what it had meant to him. It had changed since the early days, but he could not find words to identify the manner in which it had moved on. They sat silently in the lounge bar where they had arranged to meet, as usual, at an isolated public house in the country. But he felt now that such tactics were no longer necessary. He had made the decision to defy Cathery: he could come into the open about his relationship with Isabella. On the other hand, as he saw the cold anger in her face he could not be certain that there would be any further meetings at all.

'This suspension,' she murmured at last, almost reflectively. 'What does it mean? I suppose you won't need to see me, use me again. So is this an end to our relationship?'

O'Connor hesitated. 'An end to our *recent* relationship,' he confirmed. 'I'm off the case entirely. It will probably end with my dismissal from the police. As to what it means to us . . . I think that must be for you to decide.'

She had stared at him for a long time, but he was unable to guess what was going through her mind. At last, she suggested in a quiet voice, 'I must think about this. I've told you, often, that there could be a future between us, if you were to leave your job. We could stop the hole in corner business, we could make our relationship an open one. But now, after what you admit to me, the background to our recent love-making, the fact you were *instructed* to sleep with me . . .'

The silence had grown around them like a bitter vacuum in which nothing could be resolved or decided upon. At last she had heaved a deep sigh and said, 'I promised Angela I'd ask you if you'd look into the matter of the break-in. That is all I can decide upon for this moment.'

It seemed the one positive thing he could do in the wreck of their relationship and the likely end of his career.

At the Stanhope apartment Angela Fenchurch had opened the door to him; behind her stood a man she introduced as her lawyer, James Detorius. O'Connor disliked him immediately. He was unable to explain why the man in the pinstripe suit set his nerves on edge: he was too obsequious, too unctuous in his behaviour towards the young woman, but there was something else in addition. O'Connor distrusted men who sweated, and James Detorius was certainly of the sweating kind. He was nervous, quick and edgy in his movements, and although he insisted he was there to offer whatever assistance he could, O'Connor was left with the strange feeling that the man was in reality covering up, avoiding direct answers, even in subtle ways hindering the progress of O'Connor's inspection of the premises.

He was quick enough to show O'Connor the forced window through which he suggested the burglar had entered. O'Connor took nothing on trust: he wandered through the apartment with an open and enquiring mind. When he asked what had been taken, Detorius butted in hastily. 'Nothing! That's the strange thing. Possessions were disturbed, furniture was turned over, but it doesn't look as if anything was actually taken away.'

Angela Fenchurch seemed to be about to say something, then bit her lip. O'Connor glanced at her curiously. She had said very little; she was clearly upset still, grieving since the death of her grandmother, and the funeral the previous day. He moved on, checking the state of the rooms, listening to an account of what had probably happened from James Detorius. O'Connor spent some time closely inspecting the front door, and the lock that held it.

At last he took a seat in the sitting room and accepted the offer of a glass of whisky from the lawyer: it interested him that it was Detorius who seemed most at ease in the apartment.

'You knew the old lady very well,' he observed.

'I was her lawyer for a long time.' Detorius glanced at Angela, seated quietly to one side, and smiled faintly. 'Angela has asked me to sort out the estate now, because of my long involvement.'

'Do you think this burglary was an opportunistic one, or maybe in some way linked to the old lady's death?'

'Oh, opportunistic, certainly. After all, nothing was taken.'

'Because there was really nothing of value here?' O'Connor queried.

'That's my guess.'

O'Connor frowned. 'But everything was left rather tidy; the place was searched but not damaged, nothing destroyed –'

'And nothing taken,' Detorius reasserted.

O'Connor glanced at Angela Fenchurch. She hesitated, then nervously murmured, 'Well, I think there is one thing that's missing.'

Detorius seemed irritated. 'I don't think you're right, Angela. It's been misplaced somewhere –'

'What is it?' O'Connor queried.

She shook her head doubtfully. 'It's nothing of great consequence, really. Sentimental value only. It's a leather-bound photograph album.'

Puzzled, O'Connor glanced at Detorius. The lawyer averted his eyes, shook his head slightly in silent disagreement. O'Connor turned back to Angela. 'So what was in this album?'

'Nothing of importance. Photographs of the family – my grandmother as a young woman, several of me as a child, some taken at the big house, one or two at the cottage up near Elsdon – and there were two of me as a baby, with my mother. She was very beautiful.' Her tone saddened. 'My father also was in one of them. I never knew either of them, really. But to lose the album . . . I regret it, it's like losing my past.'

'I'm sure it will turn up,' James Detorius said dismissively. 'It's simply been mislaid –'

'When was the last time you saw it?' O'Connor asked.

Angela shrugged. 'I can't be certain. The thing is, my grandmother treasured those photographs – cracked and faded though they might have been – and she kept them close to her. I'm certain that the last time I saw the album it was in the desk in the other room. I'd taken it out when I extracted some other photographs I'd slipped into the album; the ones I gave to Mr Landon and Miss Stannard. I put the album back in the desk afterwards. During the break-in the desk had been forced – the drawer was locked – and the papers in there had been disarranged. I looked through them, nothing seemed to have been taken, but it's only later that I recalled, it was in that drawer that Grandmother kept the album. It was slim, leather-bound . . .'

'I can't say I ever saw it,' Detorius remarked roughly. 'And the papers in the drawer were mainly financial documents, bank statements, copies of the mortgage and loan agreements –'

'It's seems an odd thing to take,' O'Connor mused. 'Little intrinsic value.'

'If it was taken at all,' Detorius snapped. His tone was dismissive. 'Now, is there anything else you want to see, Chief Inspector? Is there any other way in which we can help you?'

He seemed eager to see the back of the policeman. It was as though he considered O'Connor's visit a complete waste of time.

Karen Stannard was brimming with confidence and it seemed even to enhance her usual stunning appearance: her eyes were bright, her hair recently cut and fashionably arranged, her skin tones perfect, and she smiled more than was her previous custom. She was not only handling her new job with notable competence, she appeared to be enjoying it hugely. The gossip in the Department of Museums and Antiquities was that the councillors were already in awe of her: she had introduced a number of minor administrative reforms which had speeded up the decision-making process considerably, she had obtained council agreement to change the committee structure and she had managed to persuade four people at senior level to take early retirement.

The contrast between her performance and that of her predecessor Powell-Frinton had been much commented upon and was openly admired in the council corridors of political power; there were some elected members who compared her to a whirlwind; she was gaining a reputation as a no-nonsense administrator, and she had already been nominated to become a delegate from the county to a prestigious political committee in central government.

'And I hope you'll appreciate the rise I've managed to negotiate for all senior officers,' she commented to Arnold and Karl Spedding as they sat in her office.

As well as for herself, Arnold thought. It mattered little to him: he felt that he was well enough paid already for a job he enjoyed.

They were seated facing her in Karen's new office. The discussion had amounted to a final loosening of the departmental reins by Karen. Carefully, she went through the dossier placed in front of her, on the immaculately neat desk. One by one she dealt with the individual projects that Arnold's department was working on; she ticked off each listed archaeological site and the progress report on the work done there before passing the relevant file to Arnold, or to Karl Spedding, as the responsibilities fell. As the sheets in the dossier grew fewer she seemed to work faster, slipping through each item with the fervour of someone who was getting rid of an irrelevant burden. She had fallen into her new role with enthusiasm: she was a Chief Executive and the past could now be left to others, to her minions.

'So that's it,' she announced with a triumphant sigh, and leaned back in her leather chair to smile at the two men facing her. 'Arnold, if you go across to that cabinet over there you'll find some glasses, and a bottle. Let's relax and have a chat for a while.'

Arnold was taken aback. It was an unprecedented suggestion: in the past Karen had always maintained a certain distance in their official meetings, conscious of her status, but she was clearly now feeling in complete control, and unassailable. She had risen above petty squabbles. It remained to be seen whether it was an attitude that would continue.

As Arnold opened the cabinet and carefully measured out three glasses of whisky Karen addressed herself to Karl Spedding. He tone was light, and airy. 'Well, then, Karl, I imagine you will have settled by now.'

As Spedding murmured the expected positive reply Arnold glanced at him. He could not deny that Spedding had fitted well into the department, professionally speaking: his background, his extensive experience at digs in various countries, his wide knowledge of the world of museums and antiquities meant that in many ways he could be regarded as a positive asset to the department. Moreover, he did not throw his weight around: as far as Arnold was concerned the man rarely offered an opinion before he was asked for one, and he seemed to maintain a quietly loyal attitude to the newly appointed head of department. Yet he did not seem to have made any friends among the staff. He was a loner, that was obvious: he did not seek company and Arnold had no idea how he spent his spare time. Arnold did not even know where Spedding lived, or even whether he drove a car: it was rumoured the ex-curator was renting a flat in Alnwick and coming in to work by public transport. But apart from that Arnold could not warm to the man. It was not merely Spedding's reserve and self-containment: there was something odd about him, a restrained, coiled anger that had been exposed only once, in the Hôtel de la Monnaie, and then there was the suspect reason for his being here in the department, his reluctance to offer any information other than the absolutely necessary regarding his previous professional existence.

And for no specific reason that Arnold could identify, he did not trust the ex-curator of the Pradak Museum.

He sat and listened as Karen cheerily discussed with Spedding some of the sites he had been given responsibility for, demonstrating her own intelligent analysis of some of the recent finds. Spedding remained reserved in his comments, offering little other than confirmation of Karen's suggestions.

At last she turned to Arnold, seated silently beside her. 'I don't need to ask about you, of course, because I've been keeping an eye on you myself. And anyway, you know the work of the department better than I do – old fixture that you are.'

Arnold wasn't certain he enjoyed what was probably meant as a compliment.

'And you've come to terms with a more desk-bound existence, I warrant,' Karen continued. 'I'm sure you'll still manage forays into the hills, and there's always distant conferences to attend. Talking of which,' she added, a slight frown appearing on her brow, 'the police haven't been back to me after the one interview regarding our time in La Rochelle. What about you two?'

'The enquiry into the murders?' Arnold shrugged. 'DI Farnsby interviewed us both, separately and together, but I can't imagine what he was after. I mean, the French police spoke to us, took statements, and we've heard no more from that end. I'm still not clear why the local fuzz up here

162

has got involved anyway, in the killings. I mean, the three murders were in France, not here.'

'Three?'

The surprise in Karen's voice startled Arnold. He realized she had been in London for a few days and wouldn't be up to date with developments. He was aware of Karl Spedding's watchful eyes upon him as he explained, 'You wouldn't have heard about it. It seems there's been a third killing. A body found in the rivers north of La Rochelle, up near Fontenay-le-Comte. The French police are linking it to the murders of the dealers. I've no idea who the dead man might be, or what the link is, and as for the reason why Farnsby –'

'Did you get this information from DI Farnsby?' Karen asked, frowning.

'No.' Arnold hesitated. 'Carmela Cacciatore.'

Karen raised an eyebrow and her lips thinned. 'Your Italian girlfriend.' There was a short silence as she regarded him steadily. There had always been a certain ambivalence in her attitude towards Arnold's relationship with the woman from the Carabinieri Art Squad. In an obscure way she seemed to regard Carmela as some kind of rival, even though Arnold had no relationship of an intimate nature with either of them. 'So she's been on the phone to you?'

Arnold shook his head. Reluctantly, he replied, 'No, she came over to see me. She's staying in Gosforth. In fact, I'll be picking her up this evening to take her back to the airport.'

Karen's eyes were wide and innocent but there was an edge to her tone. 'Carmela came to England to tell you about this third murder?'

'No, no,' Arnold replied hastily. 'That was just by the way. She'd come over to talk to me and Isabella Portland. You remember you asked me to assist Mrs Portland. I was worried about some of the artefacts. I sent photographs of those that concerned me to Carmela for her view.'

Karen smiled but there was a hint of sarcasm in her voice. 'And she felt it necessary to come over to see you about them?'

163

Arnold took a deep breath. 'She thinks some of the antiquities collected by Gordon Portland before he died, kept in the Edinburgh flat and shown in the photographs, had probably once formed part of the looted Lydian hoard.'

'I haven't been told about this!'

The sudden outburst from Karl Spedding startled both Arnold and Karen. They looked at the ex-curator. His head was up, his eyes angry, and Arnold was aware of a trembling in the man's hands. It was as though he felt they had been hiding something from him, and his indignation was boiling over. Arnold sent a puzzled glance in Karen's direction and then explained in a soothing tone. 'Identifying these objects, it was something we were asked to do. The request pre-dated your appointment. Strictly speaking, it's nothing to do with the department, not directly, though in fact we may well profit from it in the long run, with some items coming to our museums.'

'Not from the Lydian hoard,' Spedding snapped. A light foam seemed to have appeared on his lips. He rubbed his mouth with the back of his hand; he was clearly annoyed, greatly disturbed and Karen recognized it.

She turned to Arnold. 'You'd better fill us in. *Both* of us.'

Somewhat irritated by Spedding's clear fury, which to Arnold seemed ill based, and by Karen's coldness, Arnold brought them up to date with the events: Carmela's views on the antiquities, Isabella Portland's decision to return the items in question to the Turkish government, the end of her plans to enter into business with Angela Fenchurch. Karen heard him out, her brow dark. She made no secret of her annoyance that Arnold had not told her of this earlier.

Karl Spedding had subsided. He was in control of himself again, and listened to Arnold's account without speaking. But Arnold gained the impression the man was holding himself in with difficulty. Something inside him was raging, but he had no desire to expose it to either Karen or Arnold.

When he had finished, Karen asked coldly, 'Where does all this leave Angela Fenchurch?'

Arnold shrugged. 'As it happens, it seems she couldn't have gone on with the business proposal anyway, linking up with Isabella Portland. Her grandmother incurred large debts: the items of jewellery that Angela was putting into the business pot will have to be withdrawn from the projected business, sold to meet financial obligations.'

After a short silence, Karen leaned back in her chair, clearly irritated. She sniffed, then said stiffly, 'Well, if you'll drink up and leave me now . . . I have work to do.'

Her tone was peremptory. The brief period of relaxation had come to a swift end. But that evening, after Arnold had seen Carmela off on the flight from Newcastle Airport, it was not Karen's attitude that remained in his mind. She had been offended, returning to her former ways, needing to feel she was in control, having to know all that her subordinate officers knew.

But Karl Spedding was a different matter. Arnold was puzzled: he could find no reason for Spedding's rage, the controlled fury that had seized him, and the firm grip he had later held on his emotions. There was something about Karl Spedding that was not quite right.

And the thought made Arnold unhappy.

Chapter Five

1

The auction had been arranged to take place in a former Baptist chapel in Alnwick. The sales catalogue listed some twelve properties for sale by auction, repossessed by the bank, and as a consequence the ground floor of the chapel was almost full with interested potential purchasers. Arnold looked up, glanced around him: the vaulted gallery above his head was richly carved for a chapel and he wondered what purpose the building had served prior to its Victorian use for religious purposes. No one sat in the gallery now: the buzz of conversation was confined to the crowd seated among the pews. There was a dampness in the air, the smell of wet clothing – people would have been caught in the brief but fierce downpour that had swept through the town before the opening of the auction.

Standing near the back of the room he browsed idly through the catalogue. It included a number of terraced houses in Alnwick itself, a former hunting lodge near Warkworth, and some cottages described optimistically as 'investment opportunities'. Recent credit squeezes and financial constraints in the mortgage field had led to a rash of second homes coming on to the market, over-extended buyers being forced to resell when they realized they could no longer afford to maintain the payments to which they had rashly committed themselves.

On the sixth page of the brochure he saw the photograph of the cottage that had belonged to Angela Fenchurch's grandmother. The photographer had taken the point of best advantage: the cottage was located on a steep hillside, above a small brook that meandered down from the fell. Its isolated position, protected at the back by a copse of trees, was attractive but the cottage itself showed signs of considerable dilapidation: the roof of the lean-to at the side of the cottage had fallen in, much of the whitewash had peeled from the façade and the small front garden was much overgrown. He read the printed details: two up, three down, a utility room . . . in need of renovation . . . former sty at the rear . . . outlook over the valley . . . outstanding opportunity to acquire a country holiday home . . .

Arnold sighed, looked about him vaguely. He was not sure why he had decided to attend the auction. It had been his original intention to spend the weekend up near Berwick and Lindisfarne, enjoying the sharp sea air, perhaps taking a boat trip out to the Farne Islands to see the seals, behave like a visiting tourist, getting away from the office and even the archaeological sites in the hills that he so much enjoyed.

Perhaps it had been the weather forecast that had caused him to change his mind. Saturday morning was predicted to be wet and stormy, followed by mild, cloudy weather for the rest of the weekend. Or maybe it had been the thought of Angela Fenchurch, still grieving over her grandmother, beset by financial problems. Her plans for the establishment of a business with Isabella Portland had crashed, and it seemed she would now have to consider carefully what she was to do in the future.

Near the front of the room he caught sight of the figure of Angela's lawyer, James Detorius: he had probably turned up in his capacity as administrator of the old lady's estate. He would be looking out for Angela's interests. Arnold's glance wandered around and he was surprised to see that Angela herself was seated a few rows behind Detorius, and that beside her was Isabella Portland. But an even greater surprise emerged: seated at the end of the row behind the two women was another person he knew. As Arnold stared at him wondering why he would have come to the auction, the man turned his head, caught sight of Arnold and their eyes locked.

A few seconds later the man rose from his seat and made his way to the back of the room. He was heading to join Arnold.

'DCI O'Connor,' Arnold said as the detective stood beside him. 'I'm surprised to see you here. You thinking of entering the property market?'

O'Connor did not reply immediately. His eyes were restless, his glance flicking around the room, and he seemed edgy. Then suddenly he turned to Arnold. 'Do you think we could have a word in private? Perhaps we could step outside.'

The auctioneer had stepped up to the rostrum, was opening the first page of the catalogue, preparing to begin the morning's proceedings. Arnold shrugged. 'If you wish.'

They left the room, crossed the small hallway and stood in the doorway of the building, shielded from the gusty, driving wind that sent occasional sheets of rain slashing down the length of the street. The sky was dark above their heads, but a sliver of promising blue could be seen, beyond the town, sliding towards the castle towers, perhaps presaging the better weather the forecasters had promised for the afternoon.

DCI O'Connor stood silently beside him, shoulders hunched, hands in his trouser pockets, seemingly reluctant to begin the conversation he himself had requested. As Arnold waited, O'Connor took out a pack of cigarettes, removed one and lit it with a battered lighter. 'Haven't used this for three years,' he muttered. 'Never thought I'd get back on the fags.'

'Stress of the job?' Arnold queried.

O'Connor snorted. 'Hardly that.' He hesitated, turning his thoughts inward, perhaps contemplating the past. 'My old man died last month, you know? Cancer. He'd had Alzheimer's for years. Didn't know me, when I visited him in York. Seemed pointless going to see him, but I did, regularly. I could have started back on the fags then, but I didn't. So why now?' It was a rhetorical question, Arnold

168

knew. He waited, silently, as the gusty curtains of rain swept down the empty street.

'Life can be a bastard,' O'Connor muttered. Arnold made no reply.

'You and Karen Stannard,' O'Connor said abruptly, 'when you were at La Rochelle you were attending a conference. That right?'

'That's right.'

'And your assistant, Spedding?'

'He'd accepted an invitation prior to applying for the job in the department. He was presenting a paper at the conference.'

'So what was James Detorius doing there?'

There was a short pause. Arnold shrugged. 'Haven't you asked him? Hasn't he been interviewed?'

O'Connor drew thoughtfully on his cigarette. He grimaced in distaste, as though he was not enjoying his fall from grace. 'He was interviewed briefly by DI Farnsby, but we've not given much priority to him. He said he was attending the conference as a matter of interest.'

'But why are you concerned in that business?' Arnold queried in a puzzled tone. 'And Farnsby too. It all happened outside your jurisdiction.'

'Farnsby!' O'Connor almost spat the name, but when he continued he ignored the question. 'And there's the fact that Detorius wasn't one of the group that had the confrontation with Adam Shearbright.'

Arnold hesitated. 'He saw it, though.'

O'Connor turned his head. His eyes gave nothing away; the glance was cold and professional. 'How do you mean?'

'We'd arranged to dine together: Karen, Spedding, me and Detorius. He was doubtful about making it at first, but he managed to get away from his meeting earlier than expected and arrived at the hotel while we were at the bar. I got the impression he didn't join us when he saw that we were in the middle of something that was heading towards an altercation – and I don't blame him for that. So he didn't enter the bar; he saw what was going on, turned away, and waited for us in the reception area.'

O'Connor frowned, mulling things over in his mind. 'You said Detorius told you he had a meeting. What kind of meeting?'

'Ask him. He didn't give us any details.'

O'Connor hunched his shoulders, peered out at the driving rain. 'You know much about Detorius? About his practice?'

'I know him only through his connection with Angela Fenchurch. What about his practice?'

'I've been making enquiries. It was never a big firm, just him and a senior partner who died some years ago. I asked some contacts I have in the Law Society. They seem surprised Detorius is still in business. Not much of a clientele. And there's a whisper that he's a bit of a gambler. It's even been suggested to me that the old lady, Mrs Fenchurch, she was just about his only client. But maybe he's got private means . . .'

Arnold frowned. 'I don't understand what you're getting at. What's this all about?'

O'Connor threw away the barely smoked cigarette. It fell into the gutter, swirled away in the rush of water. As Arnold waited, O'Connor seemed to be considering something. In a few moments the decision was made. He shrugged aside Arnold's question. Instead, he reached into the inside pocket of his jacket. He took out a leather wallet, extracted a folded photograph. He stared at it thoughtfully for a few seconds then proffered it to Arnold. 'Did you happen to see this man, in your wanderings in La Rochelle?'

Arnold took the photograph, inspected it carefully. The features were lean, strong, bearded and unfamiliar. He shook his head. 'Who is it?'

'I'm told his name is Anwar Zahiri. A religious fanatic, formerly a member of the secret police in Iran. A dangerous man, it seems. Not to be approached.'

'Why?'

'He's suspected of committing the murders in La Rochelle.'

170

Arnold recalled his conversations with Carmela Cacciatore. 'The two men – Shearbright and Carpentier – they were connected with the illicit trade in looted antiquities.'

'So it seems. Which brings us back to Detorius. He was in La Rochelle. He was attending the conference. He also had some kind of business meeting. And he's been acting as legal adviser to the old lady who died at Stanhope Castle.'

'And administrator to her estate, now,' Arnold added. He frowned. 'You don't like Detorius, do you?'

O'Connor did not reply immediately. 'Let's say I don't like men who sweat for no apparent reason. And there's something about Detorius that leaves me uneasy. He's not central to what's been going on, it seems – and yet he's always around or nearby. Like in the scene at the hotel bar in La Rochelle. There's something odd about it.'

'If that's what the police think, why don't you –'

'I'm off the case,' O'Connor interrupted abruptly. 'I'm here in an unofficial capacity, you might say.'

'Why?' Arnold was puzzled. 'If you're not involved in the investigation any longer, what are you doing here?'

There was a short, awkward silence. 'Personal reasons,' O'Connor ground out at last. He glanced at Arnold. 'And you? What's this auction got to do with you?' He threw Arnold's own remark back at him, sarcastically. 'Are you thinking of bidding for something?'

Arnold reddened. It was a question he had already asked himself, without reaching an answer. He scratched his cheek. 'Nothing better to do on a wet Saturday morning, I suppose. And ... well, I feel sorry for Angela Fenchurch. She seems to have had a rough deal recently. She's lucky, at least, to have the continuing support of Isabella Portland.'

O'Connor twitched. He seemed discomfited. He thought for a moment, staring at the leaden sky. 'You feel concerned about Angela. Did you know about the break-in at the castle apartment?'

Arnold nodded. 'Nothing was taken, apparently.'

171

'Not correct. A photograph album is missing. One that you've probably seen, in fact.'

Arnold stared at him, uncomprehending. Then he nodded in recollection. 'I have indeed. Angela kept the photographs of the artefacts in it, I seem to recall. But they were removed; I caught a glimpse of the other photographs in the album, just family shots.' He frowned. 'So what's this all about?'

O'Connor shook his head. 'I don't know. But since you're here . . . and concerned about things, are you prepared to help?'

Arnold shrugged. 'To do what?'

O'Connor took a deep breath. 'I have a gut feeling that there's a link between what's been going on, and what's about to happen today. I'm here to keep a close eye on the auction. Unofficially. But as a matter of interest, I want to know just who will be bidding for the cottage up near Elsdon.' He glanced at Arnold. 'Two pairs of eyes and ears would be better than one. Are you up for it?'

Arnold was still unable to comprehend the reason for O'Connor's presence but he nodded. He was interested himself, in any case, in finding out what price the cottage might achieve, the extent to which it might assist Angela Fenchurch in her trouble. As the two men walked back into the auction room O'Connor stepped aside for a moment, threw the rest of the pack of cigarettes into a litter bin placed by the entrance. Somehow it seemed to be a decisive gesture.

They separated inside the main room. The sale had already started: as far as Arnold could make out two properties had already come under the hammer, so the auctioneer was wasting no time. Arnold took up position near the back of the room, leaning against one of the dozen or so pillars that supported the gallery. O'Connor moved away from him, further down the hall, and found an empty seat at the end of a row. He moved the wooden chair slightly to give himself a clearer view of the front rows ahead of him.

The dark-suited auctioneer wound up the sale of a third terrace house and moved on, raising his spectacles to look carefully at the catalogue and his notes before dropping them again on the bridge of his long nose, to gaze around his audience. He called out the catalogue number, recited the details from memory, almost word perfect, and bidding commenced. It was soon over: the property was not expensive to begin with, it was in a state of disrepair, the bank had set a low price and the bidding was desultory. The house was knocked down to a middle-aged, florid woman with orange hair. She seemed unexcited at her purchase. It reflected a general attitude in the room.

Arnold looked around at the people to his left and in front of him. He could pick out Angela Fenchurch and Isabella Portland easily enough; James Detorius had changed his place for some reason and was now seated at the end of a row a little further back in the hall. Some individuals were hidden from Arnold behind the pillars along the side of the room. The auction proceeded swiftly.

Fifteen minutes later the Elsdon cottage came up for bids. Almost involuntarily, Arnold straightened his stance.

The auctioneer read out the details, briefly describing the location, mentioning the cottage's general state of disrepair, and inviting bids. There was a quick response from the woman with orange hair, raising a fluttered catalogue. Arnold grimaced; she clearly intended to get into the business of property development. Equally obvious was the fact that she was after a bargain only: when two other bidders came in and the price rose by some ten thousand pounds she shook her head, dropped out of the contest.

For a few minutes the bidding developed into a competition between two burly farmer types: bald-headed, craggy-featured, stocky in build. Arnold guessed that they knew each other, and gained the impression there was a certain antagonistic rivalry between the two men.

The impetus of the auction slowed, the competitive bids narrowing in range to hundreds rather than thousands. Arnold glanced towards O'Connor: his face was immobile, but his eyes darted glances around the room. He was ignoring the two bidders, as though he considered them unworthy of interest. A few moments later, his attitude changed. The auctioneer was about to wind up the auction, and then stopped as a new bidder was identified.

Arnold leaned forward slightly. The bidder was a heavy-shouldered, dark-haired man of swarthy appearance. He was leaning forward in his seat: there was an element of urgency in his stance. Arnold caught only a glimpse of his profile. O'Connor fixed his glance on him as the auctioneer paused, looked towards the previous bidders. One of them shook his head; the other, with an almost triumphant air of having outlasted his competitor, raised the newcomer's bid by a thousand pounds. The auctioneer managed a smile, straightened, lifted his gavel and pointed it towards the swarthy man. 'The bid is against you, sir.'

The response was a positive one. Another five hundred was added to the offer and the auctioneer looked back to the other competitor. But the remaining farmer type had made his point; he had outlasted his rival and enough was enough. He shook his head. For a second time the auctioneer was about to call a halt, had raised his gavel, when yet another bidder entered the challenge. A voice called out, making a higher offer, and the auctioneer stopped in mid-sentence.

There was something familiar about the voice. Arnold was unable to see the person bidding; the man was hidden behind one of the pillars across the other side of the room. He glanced towards O'Connor: the policeman was staring fixedly at the bidder. He glanced briefly toward Arnold, but there was nothing to be read in his eyes.

The rate of bidding increased, the responses of the two men interested in Angela Fenchurch's cottage were swifter and Arnold caught a movement at the corner of his eye: James Detorius had risen from his seat. He was now standing against the wall, looking towards the pillar that shielded one of the bidders from Arnold. He seemed oddly agitated, arms folded tightly across his chest, flashing glances at the swarthy, foreign-looking man along the row from him, and glaring at the competitor behind the pillar.

The auctioneer himself was displaying pleasure: no doubt his commission from the bank would be affected.

As the price offered for the cottage increased Arnold frowned. He knew the area where the cottage was located; its isolation would be attractive to some but narrow access to the valley, the size of the building and its state of disrepair would detract from its desirability for many purchasers. The auctioneer himself was clearly of the view that the price had already risen significantly above what he deemed to be its appropriate market value and there was a new, preening briskness in his manner as he encouraged the two men to fight on in their bidding.

Detorius could hardly keep still. He had begun to prowl along the aisle, hands behind his back, a portly, disempowered tiger in his cage. The bidding had slowed. There was a further raising of a hand, an additional five thousand from the man behind the pillar, and the swarthy competitor seemed agitated as he swivelled around as though to seek out the man standing against him. The auctioneer called out for a further five hundred; there was a hesitation, a protracted silence, and then the swarthy man nodded.

The auctioneer beamed towards the man behind the pillar. 'Over to you, sir. Another five hundred?'

There was a long pause. Detorius was standing rigidly, glaring at the man hidden from Arnold's sight as though willing him to respond urgently. The swarthy man was sitting stiffly, staring straight ahead. Angela Fenchurch was leaning close to Isabella Portland, murmuring in her ear. Arnold moved slightly, attempting to obtain a better view of the proceedings.

And then, almost anticlimactically, there must have been a shake of the head. The auctioneer looked back to his general audience. 'If there are no further bids?'

Moments later the gavel snapped down in favour of the swarthy man, the auctioneer was turning to the catalogue for the next property as his assistant approached the successful bidder for details, and James Detorius slumped against the wall. Several people took the opportunity to leave their seats; one of them was the defeated bidder but as he moved from the hall someone stood up in front of Arnold and he was still unable to make out who the mystery bidder had been.

Isabella Portland and Angela Fenchurch had also risen, clearly having no further interest in the auction. Angela caught sight of Arnold as they moved from their seats, and waved. He nodded, felt she would be expecting him to wait, have a word with her. DCI O'Connor had left his position and was making his way along the cross-aisle. He paused as he reached Arnold. 'I'll give you a ring later,' he muttered.

O'Connor moved away, stayed near the entrance until Isabella Portland reached him. They had a quick word together and then she left. O'Connor was still standing near the exit as Angela Fenchurch laid her hand on Arnold's arm. She smiled at him, relieved. 'Well, the place raised a better price that I'd expected. The auctioneer certainly undervalued it. Of course, I would have liked to retain it, for old times' sake, but with the debts . . . Now, at least I'll be spared some financial embarrassment, anyway.' She sighed, shook her head. 'I need a drink. Would you like to join me?'

He was happy to do so, but hesitated. 'What about Mrs Portland? Didn't you come with her to the auction?'

Angela shook her head. 'No, I arrived with James Detorius. No doubt he'll be pleased at the outcome. It'll help with the winding-up of the estate. He's already left, as far as I can see, and Isabella's gone also, so it'll be just you and me to celebrate the end of an era. My childhood gone – just like that,' she added, with a snap of her fingers.

It was near lunchtime and they found the lounge bar in the Royal Hotel virtually deserted. Arnold bought the drinks and carried them across to the window seat where Angela was waiting. He thought she looked quite beautiful: her regular features seemed more relaxed, it was as though the sale of the cottage, while distressing to her, had nevertheless removed a burden of anxiety from her shoulders. She raised her glass, silently toasting the future.

After some desultory conversation, Arnold turned to the matter of the auction. 'Did you know the buyer who made the successful bid?'

Angela shook her head. 'I've no idea who he was. I looked around and saw him, but he was a stranger to me.'

'What about the unsuccessful bidder?'

'No idea. Didn't look at him really. He was behind me, near the pillars.'

Arnold frowned. 'His voice was familiar. Still . . .' He sipped his drink. 'Anything more on the burglary at the apartment?'

'The mysterious loss of a worthless photograph album?' She shook her head.

'It was worth something to you,' Arnold reminded her.

Angela nodded. 'That's true. And if it came up in a car boot sale tomorrow I'd probably buy it and no questions asked! But why on earth anyone should want to steal a bunch of old family photographs is beyond me. Isabella was kind enough to ask DCI O'Connor to come to the apartment, and I showed him around, but I was a bit embarrassed – I mean, such a trivial matter, and to involve a senior policeman in investigating such an affair . . .' She hesitated, glanced at Arnold. There was a certain query in her tone. 'He seems very friendly with Isabella. I saw them having a word together before she left.'

Arnold had his own suspicions about the relationship, but it was none of his business. 'Well, they left separately. But as for the break-in, I don't suppose O'Connor found out anything new about it?'

Angela shook her head. 'Not really, though he seemed to feel it was a professional break-in, and he doubted that the burglar came through the window, as we thought. He's of the view the man came through the front door – picked the lock. The window thing, it was just to make it look like a casual break-in. But if that's the case, why was it all left so neat, and why steal only a moth-eaten old album?'

She made a dismissive gesture with her left hand as though waving away any further speculation and they spent the next half-hour chatting, mainly about her memories of her childhood, life in the big house before her grandmother had been forced to sell it, the general silence from the old lady when Angela had asked questions about her parents. 'You know, like all kids do, I wanted to know what my mother was like, whether Grandmother had known my father and what happened to him, that sort of thing . . . It usually came up when we had looked at the old photographs, but she always used to end the conversation at that point.' Somewhat wistfully, she added, 'I regret that, really . . . and now it's too late. There are so many questions I should have put to her, so many answers I wanted her to give me. A common regret, is it not? You want to ask questions when it's too late . . .'

They finished their drinks and left the hotel. The skies had cleared and a watery sun picked out the towers of the castle as Arnold walked Angela back to her car. She kissed him lightly on the cheek in goodbye, and as she drove out of the car park he watched her go with mixed feelings. He was sorry for her, he admired her, but they were a generation apart . . .

He walked back down through the high street in Alnwick, made his way through the narrow town gateway and climbed the hill to the park where he had left his own car. He had just reached it when his mobile phone rang.

'Landon? O'Connor here. I think we should meet. Are you still in Alnwick?'

'I was just about to leave.'

'We need to talk. The guy who was successful in the bid for the cottage . . . he wasn't bidding on his own behalf.'

'I don't understand.'

'He works for an estate agent. I followed him, had a conversation with him, and when he realized I was a copper he set aside what he called his professional obligations. He also told me the keys to the cottage have already been handed over to his principal.'

'So who was he acting for?'

There was a grim note in O'Connor's voice. 'None other than the lawyer who's supposed to be acting on Angela Fenchurch's behalf.'

'James Detorius?' Arnold asked in surprise.

'The man himself. Now why would the lawyer acting for Angela Fenchurch make a bid for the cottage through a third party?'

'Keeping his personal position secret.'

'Exactly so.'

'Is that what you want to talk about?'

'That . . . and one more thing. I suppose you recognized the man making the late bids for the cottage – the buyer who failed.'

'I didn't. He was concealed behind a pillar. But I thought I'd recognized his voice, when he called out at the beginning.'

'You should have done. He's a colleague of yours.'

'A colleague?' For a moment, Arnold was puzzled, then enlightenment came to him. 'It was Karl Spedding.'

'That's right.' There was a short pause. 'Both of the men bidding for the Fenchurch cottage were in La Rochelle. I'm of the opinion there might be a connection.'

Arnold's mind was in a whirl. He liked neither man, Detorius nor Spedding, but he was unable to fathom what O'Connor might be driving at. After a short silence, during which various suspicions chased through Arnold's mind, he nodded. 'Yes. I think you're right. I agree . . . we need to meet.'

2

The valley below them was silent. Dusk was gathering about the copse of trees that sheltered them: across the hill the faint glow of lights from the village of Elsdon stained the sky. They had left the car on the outskirts of the village: Arnold knew the area fairly well and O'Connor had decided it would be better if they made their approach to the cottage unseen. Accordingly, after leaving the car parked in a narrow lane near a screening hedge, Arnold had led the way across the fields towards the low hill overlooking the cottage Angela Fenchurch had known so well in her childhood, and which had just been purchased, surreptitiously, by James Detorius.

Arnold had discussed the matter with DCI O'Connor as they drove to Elsdon. 'Why didn't Detorius simply buy the cottage directly from Angela and pay off the mortgage?'

'Maybe because as the lawyer supposedly acting in her interests he could be seen as taking advantage of his position.'

'You mean using undue influence to get a good price?' Arnold stared at O'Connor doubtfully: he had the curious feeling that O'Connor was not convinced by the suggestion. 'You don't think it's as simple as that.'

'No. I don't.' O'Connor hesitated, chewing something over. 'As you know, I'm on suspension, not strictly involved, but I'm acting on a hunch, sort of a gut feeling, that all this is about something quite different.'

'Connected with what happened in La Rochelle? I don't understand. What can Detorius buying the cottage have to do with illicit dealing in looted antiquities, and two – or three – murders in France?'

DCI O'Connor was slow in responding. At last he grimaced, shook his head. 'It's the fact there's been a joker in the pack.'

'I don't follow.'

'Detorius. His presence in La Rochelle. The burglary at Stanhope. His purchase of the cottage. A missing photograph album.' O'Connor shook his head, gritted his teeth.

'You won't know the full story, but the fact is the killings in France arose out of ... well, the offer for sale of an important artefact. International dealers were involved; so was a hired assassin; and so is the CIA.'

'The *what*?'

O'Connor hesitated. 'That's why we've been involved locally here with what went on in France. The hunt for the assassin Anwar Zahiri, the man who killed the dealers in La Rochelle, has moved to the UK. There's a CIA agent, Gonzalez, who briefed us: he's convinced that Zahiri has followed the trail here to the north-east. That means some-one from the north-east was offering the artefact for sale in La Rochelle. That person had arranged to meet Adam Shearbright, but perhaps the meeting never came off because Shearbright got involved in an argument in the hotel bar. And the artefact – or at least, the man offering it for sale – returned to the north-east after the two dealers were killed by Zahiri.'

'But why were they killed?'

O'Connor shrugged. 'Maybe because Zahiri thought they had the artefact, maybe it was all a bad mistake ...'

'You're being very mysterious about this so-called arte-fact,' Arnold complained.

O'Connor hesitated. 'It's an ancient religious manu script. Apparently, Zahiri wants it to return it to Iran.'

There was a short silence as Arnold thought the matter over. Finally, he muttered, 'You suspect that maybe Detorius was involved.'

'Maybe. But then again, what the hell is Karl Spedding doing here in the north-east? And he was bidding for this cottage – why is he so interested?' He stared at Arnold, frowning. 'Detorius and Spedding, rival bidders for the cottage. What's so special about that building?'

'I can't imagine.'

'And why was a photograph album stolen from the apartment in Stanhope?'

Arnold shook his head. 'I can't see why you're linking these events together. And I still don't understand why you're personally involved in all this, when you're suspended from the investigation.'

O'Connor's eyes were flinty. 'I was set up to find out if Isabella Portland was involved in any way. I resent that.'

'The items she obtained from her dead husband's Edinburgh hoard ... the photographs that I sent to Carmela Cacciatore ...' Arnold glowered. 'So many questions, no clear links –'

'That's why I think we should try to find out what's going on,' O'Connor muttered fiercely.

Now, under the cover of the copse overlooking the cottage, Arnold was still in something of a daze, and even uncertain why he was there with the suspended detective. Various wild possibilities swirled in his mind, but he was unable to believe that either Isabella Portland or Angela Fenchurch could possibly be involved in the sale of an ancient manuscript, and the likely roles of both Spedding and Detorius remained obscure. Moreover, he was of the opinion that O'Connor himself was only vaguely aware of possible links – he was driven by a suppressed anger, a desire to dig, tease out the truth, irrespective of what his superior officers or his peers might be making of the matter.

'There are two cars down there,' O'Connor muttered.

Arnold could see them in the gathering dusk. The first car was parked just to one side of the dilapidated cottage; the second car was in the grass-covered entrance driveway, slewed slightly as though deliberately blocking egress from the cottage. A faint light gleamed through the front window of the cottage; it was moving about. The electricity supply would not have been turned on: the light would be from the beam of a torch.

'You recognize either of those cars?' O'Connor demanded gruffly.

Arnold narrowed his eyes, squinting at the vehicles. They were some distance away, on the floor of the narrow valley. 'I couldn't be sure. It may be I've seen the first one at Stanhope.'

'Detorius?'

'I can't be sure.'

'The other vehicle. Do you know what Spedding drives?'

Arnold grimaced. 'I know next to nothing about Karl Spedding. He keeps very much to himself. I don't know where he lives; I don't know what he drives, if anything; I don't know why he's really come to the north-east. The man's an enigma. You think that second car belongs to Spedding?'

O'Connor was silent for a little while. His breathing was light, but tension was betrayed in his voice when he spoke at last. 'Spedding ... maybe. But more likely, Anwar Zahiri.'

It was as though something cold had touched the back of Arnold's neck.

'What do we do now?'

O'Connor shifted awkwardly, rubbed his shoulder. 'Staying here isn't really an option. If these characters leave, there's no way we can follow them – we'd lose them while getting back to our own transport. I need to go down there, find out exactly what's going on. And if it's Zahiri there ... You have a mobile phone?'

Arnold nodded, took his phone from his jacket pocket. 'Yes, I Blast it. The charge has run down.'

O'Connor grimaced, then shrugged. 'No matter. I was going to suggest you stayed here, while I went down, and we could keep in touch by phone. But maybe it's better if we stay together.'

Arnold knew what was at the back of O'Connor's mind. He had described Anwar Zahiri as a trained assassin. It was more sensible to act together, going down to the cottage ...

They made their way carefully out of the shadowing trees and picked a trail down the hillside. The grass was still wet from the morning rain. As the sky darkened even further they stumbled down the hillocky slope and Arnold became aware of dampness seeping into his shoes. At the foot of the hill was a small stream: they managed to scramble across it on scattered exposed stones and found themselves in the lane, some twenty yards from the car blocking egress from the cottage. O'Connor walked forward, inspected the vehicle, made a mental note of the registration. Then he nodded to Arnold and side by side they walked towards the small garden in front of the cottage.

The light had gone from the windows. O'Connor paused at the open gate, glanced at Arnold, then walked purposefully towards the front door of the cottage. When he reached it he hesitated, then stretched out his hand, pushed at the wooden door. It swung open. Arnold was close behind him as he entered the narrow, dim passageway. Arnold made out on his right the staircase leading to the floor above: ahead of them seemed to be the kitchen area, and to the left was a door which presumably led to a sitting room. O'Connor pushed the door open and as they stood in the entrance the beam of a flashlight flicked on, outlined them, moving from O'Connor to Arnold, and then it was lowered, switched off. In the following dimness Arnold could make out the burly figure of a man, seated beside a table. Arnold's heart thundered in his chest. In the brief glimpse he had had of the thickset man he realized it was neither Karl Spedding nor James Detorius.

In a low, controlled tone O'Connor said quietly, 'I didn't expect to find you here.'

'Nor I, you,' the man replied.

The accent was American. O'Connor half turned, to glance at Arnold. 'Meet Richard Gonzalez,' he muttered. 'The man from the Central Intelligence Agency. The hunter of Anwar Zahiri.'

Gonzalez held the flashlight in his left hand, his right elbow placed casually on a parcel on the table. He leaned sideways, placed the flashlight on end so that the beam was directed to the ceiling. It allowed their view of the room to extend, in a dimly reflected glow, and Arnold became aware of the chaos of scattered, upturned furniture. Seated at the table, Gonzalez seemed tired, despondent, his head lowered, shoulders sagging. The package on the table, under his elbow, was covered in what seemed to be waxed paper.

O'Connor stepped forward uncertainly. 'You found it?' he asked, gesturing towards the package.

Gonzalez nodded, sighed, and rubbed his free hand across his eyes. 'The manuscript? Yeah, I got it.'

'Where did —'

'It had been kept here, at the cottage. For years, I guess. Hidden, though not particularly cleverly.'

'By whom?'

Gonzalez shrugged, almost indifferently. 'By old Mrs Fenchurch, it seems.'

'And Detorius?' O'Connor asked after a short silence.

'The guy who put the manuscript up for sale?' Gonzalez nodded again, despondently. 'Yeah, it was Detorius. He was acting for the old lady. That's why he was in La Rochelle. He was supposed to meet Adam Shearbright, to discuss terms. The meeting never took place. And Anwar Zahiri got misdirected. When Shearbright met the French dealer, Carpentier, Zahiri thought the Frenchman was the seller. When he realized, too late, he was wrong, he killed both men in a fury.'

'And set out to England, on the trail of Detorius?'

'That's about right.'

'What's that smell?' Arnold demanded suddenly. He had been aware of the sickly-sweet odour, but had been distracted by O'Connor's questions of the CIA man.

'Petrol,' Gonzalez said wearily. 'Once Zahiri got what

he wanted, I guess he was going to fire the place to cover his tracks.'

There was a short, puzzled silence. O'Connor sighed, then asked, 'So where is he now? Where's Detorius? What the hell's gone on here?'

Gonzalez raised his head, and in a dispirited tone replied, 'You can see for yourself. In there.' He pointed across the room to a dark doorway. 'It wasn't what I'd expected, but it was all over before I even got here. Detorius, and Anwar Zahiri ...' He picked up the flashlight, offered it to O'Connor. 'Go see for yourself.'

O'Connor accepted the flashlight and the beam danced around the room. He turned, about to walk towards the door Gonzalez had pointed out, then stopped as Gonzalez said, 'I need to talk to Cathery. Your Assistant Chief Constable. You got his office number?'

O'Connor hesitated, turned back, fumbled in his jacket for his mobile phone. He flicked it open, checked his call list. He pressed the call button. 'Here it is. You can use my phone to call him.'

Gonzalez grunted his thanks, took the phone, held it to his ear as O'Connor directed the flashlight beam towards the door and walked forward. Arnold followed him, curious, even more conscious now of the strong odour of spilled petrol. Dark stains marked the wooden floor, and it looked as though the liquid had been thrown on the wall and some of the furniture also. Two petrol cans stood near the doorway, a third lying on its side.

The door was old, heavy and opened outwards into the sitting room. O'Connor hesitated, glanced at Arnold then pulled at the door and stepped into the dark room beyond. Arnold followed close behind.

As far as he could make out the long, narrow room was windowless, a suspicion confirmed as the beam of the flashlight traversed the walls. The room had clearly been used for storage and was piled with items of ancient furniture, some trunks, a narrow oak table heaped with rubbish. Dust hung in the air, drifting in the flashlight beam which wavered, hesitated, then stopped to focus on the stone fireplace in the corner of the room. It had been partly demolished, loose bricks thrown down carelessly to the littered floor. Presumably it was where the package had been hidden. O'Connor turned, slowly moved the beam around the room; it danced, then paused, moved on and finally stopped on the shapeless, twisted form that lay against the back wall furthest from the door, half hidden by a splintered chair. O'Connor moved forward, stood over the recumbent, unmoving huddle.

Arnold stood just behind him, staring at the body. 'Detorius!'

O'Connor half crouched, inspected the corpse. The flashlight beam lingered on the man's head. Detorius had been beaten badly, but it was not the beating that had killed him. Death had come from the savage slicing of his jugular vein: his life had ebbed away in a steady, pumping flow of blood.

O'Connor straightened, flashed the beam around the storeroom. In a bitter tone he muttered, 'So where's this bastard Zahiri?'

A moment later, almost by way of an answer there was a grinding sound behind them, followed by a thud. O'Connor turned, and Arnold saw the light flash over to the door. There was a second grating sound, rusting iron grinding against iron, then the clanging, slamming sound of a bolt being thrust home.

There was a momentary, shocked silence when neither man moved.

'Gonzalez!' O'Connor yelled and rushed towards the door. He shoved his shoulder against it, but it was solid and unyielding. 'Gonzalez!' he yelled again. 'What the hell do you think you're doing?'

It was only too clear to Arnold. 'He's locked us in.'

O'Connor swore and shouldered the door again, uselessly. Then he stood silent, listening. After a moment Arnold heard the movement also, beyond the door. A faint splashing sound, furniture being moved. Then silence until, finally, a sudden *whoosh*.

187

The smell of petrol, a rush of sibilant sound, and almost immediately the hint of smoke in the air.

Quite calmly, but with an edge of bitter disbelief in his voice, DCI O'Connor muttered, 'The bastard's firing the cottage!'

Both men stood rooted to the spot for several seconds. Arnold was the first to move: he ran his hands over the door, inspecting it. There was no inside handle: it had always been closed with iron bolts on the sitting-room side. He tried to collect his thoughts: no window, probably no trapdoor, a ceiling and roof that might have weakened over the years but would probably withstand even their most determined efforts to break through. He could smell the smoke more strongly now as the fire in the sitting room spread rapidly, sucking up the spilled petrol: he could even hear a dull roaring sound as the blaze took hold.

Gonzalez would have hurried out as soon as the fire took hold; the front door would have been left open to increase the draught, and he could visualize the man O'Connor had introduced as a CIA agent hurrying down the lane to his car. O'Connor grabbed his shoulder. 'That bastard took my phone! You got yours?'

Arnold shook his head. 'I told you – the battery's drained! In any case, this cottage is so isolated there's no chance of the fire services getting here in time. And there's only one way out of here – through that door!' The smoke had begun to seep under the door, there was an acrid smell in the air and there was a roughness at the back of Arnold's throat. O'Connor began to cough. He dropped to his knees, dragging Arnold down beside him. He flashed the beam around the narrow room again, frantically, searching. The noise of the fire taking hold had now grown, a steady roaring sound from the sitting room.

The two men stood side by side, irresolute. O'Connor cursed desperately, flashed the torchlight beam around the room again and then exclaimed, the light concentrating on the long oak table. 'Use it as a ram. The door opens outwards from us – it's our only chance!'

Arnold knew it. He grabbed one end of the table: it was heavier than he had anticipated. The two men lifted it, carried it towards the locked door. They knew from the sounds they had heard as Gonzalez had locked them in that the door was secured by two bolts, but it was likely they were old, weakened by rust and age.

'Ready?'

In unison the trapped men swung the end of the table, hammering it violently against the door. The shuddering crash sent a tremor up through Arnold's arm to his shoulder, and he adjusted his grip. O'Connor yelled again, and once more they slammed the table end into the locked exit. Something cracked like a pistol shot, but Arnold was unsure whether it was the door or the table itself: the smoke was thicker now and he felt pain in his chest as he began to cough. Beside him, O'Connor was retching. He had thrown the flashlight aside in order to use both hands on their makeshift battering ram and in the dim, reflected light Arnold could make out the coil of choking smoke that rose, drifting around them, oily, pungent.

They pounded at the door again and again, frantically, and the shuddering thuds sent pain shooting up Arnold's arms, but he was aware that O'Connor would be in the same situation, and they had no time to stop, regather their strength. O'Connor lurched, gasping and coughing, but doggedly the two men swung again, hammering the table end until Arnold felt it split. The old wood of the table was breaking apart, heavy as it was, but it was the only thing available to them. They charged forward once more, desperately, and were rewarded with the sound of splitting timbers, followed by a further gust of oily smoke. O'Connor relinquished his grip on the table, stepped back a pace and with a roar of frustrated fury threw himself at the weakened door, crashing into it violently with his shoulder.

The bolts screamed and gave way and then they could hear only the mounting roar of the fire in the sitting room beyond. The door was now outlined clearly, its timbers split at the top, and O'Connor stepped back and kicked hard. The barrier gave way drunkenly and the two men were faced with a wall of fire that leapt towards them, licking hungrily into the storeroom. They were forced back momentarily, and then O'Connor shouted something unintelligible to Arnold, struggled out of his jacket and covered his head. Arnold followed his example. They stood there for a moment, staring at each other, and then O'Connor's mouth opened, yelled above the roar of the fire: 'Let's get out of here!'

The room was an inferno. The open doorway was to their right, but a solid wall of flame blocked their way. O'Connor had no hesitation. He turned left in the choking smoke, and Arnold followed him towards the far end of the sitting room, to the window at the back. The panes had already shattered under the heat and as O'Connor hurled himself through, crashing against the frame, shards of glass flew outwards into the small garden at the rear of the cottage. Arnold felt the heat all about him as he followed O'Connor, stumbling, charging with muffled head down to dive through the window space.

Next moment he was falling, rolling painfully over the rough concrete of a narrow yard, colliding with O'Connor as he lay prostrate, half stunned, coughing and retching violently. The heat from the burning cottage hammered at them, flickering flames out into the yard, and Arnold groaned, staggered upright, grabbed O'Connor's shoulder and half dragged him away from the walls which would surely soon collapse. O'Connor cried out, then struggled to his knees as Arnold continued to pull at him. Then moments later they were both staggering deeper into the long narrow strip of land at the back of the house, to the dry stone wall where they leaned for a few moments, chests heaving, eyes burning, lungs straining as they coughed and retched.

O'Connor was trying to say something as he dragged at the smouldering jacket still partly wound around his head and shoulders but Arnold could not make out the words. But no explanation was needed. He threw aside his own jacket and painfully reached to the top of the wall, dragged himself up on to the harsh, jagged stones and put out a hand to O'Connor as the policeman followed him. They fell into the six-foot drop beyond, carelessly, eager to escape the heat that came from the rumbling cottage. There was cool tussocky grass under their hands and they lay there for a little while, gasping, then finally rose, staggered upright and half ran, half fell down the slope to the stream that flowed at the bottom of the slope.

They threw themselves down at the stream's edge, thrusting their burning faces into the rippling water. They cooled their hands and arms, soaked their smouldering shirts, and Arnold finally lay back, exhausted, looked upwards to the night sky. The moon was rising; stars flickered vaguely beyond the hazy cloud, and a light breeze touched his skin, caressed his singed hair and eyebrows.

'Bastard,' DCI O'Connor muttered savagely, between clenched lips. He threw his head back, glared at the sky.

'Bastard!'

The burns Arnold had received were not as serious as he had feared, and by the end of the week, after treatment at the hospital as an outpatient, he was able to return to work. His bandaged hands made it difficult for him to handle files so he used the impediment as an excuse to visit some of the sites under his control, calling upon one of the office staff to act as his driver. The air of the Cheviots invigorated him; the sea breezes off the rocky headlands beyond Seahouses cleared his head, and by the time he returned to the office he was able to get rid of the more violent images that had remained in his mind and disturbed his sleep patterns during the previous week.

But inevitably there was the need to expose himself to the impatient curiosity of the Chief Executive. Karen Stannard called him to her office; he sat there, flanked by his second-in-command Karl Spedding.

'I think, Arnold,' she announced freezingly, 'you need to tell us what the hell has been going on!'

Arnold had already been in touch with Carmela Cacciatore by telephone. In a long conversation they reckoned they had been able to piece together part of the story. And then there had been the meeting with DCI O'Connor in the pub, where they had commiserated with each other over the extent of their burns and agreed they had been lucky to escape alive. They were pleased that Gonzalez had not succeeded in his objective: he had been arrested by Customs and Excise security officers at Portsmouth, trying to leave the UK with the artefact he had seized from James Detorius.

'It was a priceless eleventh-century manuscript that had come into the possession of Angela Fenchurch's grandmother. Angela's father, a man called Mohamed Mehti, had stolen it from the Baghdad Museum, given it to Angela's mother, who had sent it for safekeeping to the old lady. Mrs Fenchurch had been given the task of raising her granddaughter after Angela's mother died, it had proved expensive, she had lost the financial support Angela's mother had provided, and the money that came for a while from Mehti, and at the end, when Angela decided to enter into business with Isabella Portland, the old lady had asked her lawyer, James Detorius, to put the manuscript on the market.'

Karl Spedding frowned. 'As a lawyer, he must have realized such dealing would be illegal?'

Arnold shrugged. 'Maybe he did – but there's no knowing now. Anyway, the old lady didn't actually hand him the manuscript. She gave him a description, asked him to find a buyer, and he finally made contact with an American dealer and arranged to meet him in La Rochelle. But his trip was abortive. The man he was supposed to deal with, Adam Shearbright, well ... Detorius failed to meet him because Shearbright got incensed about Karl Spedding's lecture, confronted him, and missed his meeting with Detorius. Then the American went on to meet a dealer, and was murdered. Shaken, Detorius came back to the UK, but now realizing how valuable the manuscript probably was. Then his client died.'

'And he decided to grab the manuscript for himself?' Karen guessed.

Arnold nodded. 'He was a one-man firm, the practice was failing. It seems he was a bit of a gambler and he thought he could solve his own problems if he could find the manuscript, sell it for himself, say nothing to Angela. But where had the old lady hidden the artefact? He'd searched the apartment, unsuccessfully, ostensibly acting for Angela as administrator of the estate, and then Angela told him about the Elsdon cottage. He guessed it might be there ...'

'And that's when he made the bid to buy the cottage?'

Arnold shrugged. 'It seems so. The trouble was, he didn't want to expose himself to a charge of fraud. He must have thought that by purchasing the cottage through an intermediary – the estate agent who bid on his behalf – he'd be able to go to the cottage, have plenty of time to rummage through the place, and then later, surreptitiously, make another attempt to sell the manuscript, this time for his own benefit.'

'Bloody lawyers,' Karen muttered contemptuously.

'As far as we can make out, Detorius found the manuscript fairly quickly. It had been wrapped in oilskin, hidden behind a loose brick in the chimney breast –'

He heard the brisk intake of breath from Karl Spedding. 'Hardly a sensible place to hide a priceless manuscript!'

Arnold shrugged. 'The owner was old. And the cottage hadn't been used for years. Anyway, Detorius found it, but it looks as though he was unable to enjoy possession for long. He'd been followed to the cottage.'

'By the man who killed him, and then tried to fire the building,' Karl Spedding muttered, unable to avoid glancing at Arnold's singed hair and eyebrows.

Karen Stannard leaned forward. 'Just who was this character?'

Arnold thought back to the conversation he'd had with DCI O'Connor . . .

'I knew from the beginning there was something wrong about the bastard,' Assistant Chief Constable Cathery had boasted at the debriefing.

'So why didn't you warn the rest of us?' O'Connor snapped angrily. 'When you called us all together to be briefed, you gave us the impression you wanted co-operation from us, not questions!'

Cathery stopped his excited pacing and put his hands on his hips. He stood there glaring at O'Connor, a stocky, pugnacious man proud of himself when he had no cause for pride. His contemptuous glance roamed over O'Connor's bandaged hands, the reddened skin of his face, the singed hair on his head. 'You look like the bloody Mummy . . . Co-operation,' he snarled, 'didn't mean you had licence to go up to that bloody cottage looking for Detorius. Particularly when you were on effing suspension.'

'If I hadn't –'

'If you hadn't, we'd have got Gonzalez anyway!' Cathery almost shouted. 'In the first instance I was acting under orders from above to co-operate with this so-called CIA agent, and Gonzalez's accreditation seemed to be okay, but when I had time to check his CIA history, and was able to consult with that bloody frog Inspector Leconte, it was clear Gonzalez was running a scam on us! We'd have got to him in a couple of days!'

'Was he really CIA?'

'Ex-CIA,' Cathery corrected sneeringly. 'He resigned from the service almost a year ago, but kept hold of his accreditations.'

'And Anwar Zahiri?' DI Farnsby asked, seated beside O'Connor.

Cathery shifted his attention from O'Connor, and some of his ire disappeared. He bared his teeth in a savage grimace. 'The SAVAK hitman. Ha, yes. Well, you know what these spooks of the CIA are like – same as our own in MI5. They're always cloak and dagger; dealers in half-truths and evasions; raising bogeymen, shades of their own creation. Shadowmakers, if you know what I mean.'

'You mean Zahiri didn't exist? He was just a shadow created by Gonzalez?' O'Connor asked incredulously.

'No, no.' Cathery waved blunt pudgy fists in denial. 'He existed all right. And he was ex-SAVAK. But he wasn't the terrorist Gonzalez made out. He was out for himself, not the regime he'd left. In fact, he and Gonzalez were working together, ever since their paths first crossed eighteen months ago in an official capacity. Gonzalez had been hunting him, but when they finally met, and Gonzalez learned from Zahiri about the manuscript, they made a deal: they went into partnership, Gonzalez retired from the service though still using his CIA contacts to follow the trail, Zahiri in the wings as the hitman, ready to take the necessary steps when the time came.'

'So what happened to Zahiri?' DI Farnsby asked.

'According to Inspector Jean-Pierre Leconte, he was dragged out of the water at some place called Mervent. It took them some time to identify him, because his face had

195

been battered in to prevent early recognition, but once Europol were given his prints it didn't take long to produce his files. It looks as though Gonzalez picked up on Shearbright's desire to purchase the manuscript when it came on the market, they followed the trail to La Rochelle but Zahiri got sidetracked. He was watching Shearbright; he didn't realize the manuscript seller, Detorius, had failed to make contact with Shearbright, and when the American dealer met up with the French dealer Carpentier Zahiri muscled in. But then he discovered he'd got it wrong, and he didn't have the manuscript. Zahiri must have gone berserk. He killed both men.'

O'Connor shuffled uncertainly. 'So why did Gonzalez kill Zahiri?'

Cathery shrugged his indifference. 'Didn't need him any longer. Before he died, Shearbright must have told Zahiri the seller was Detorius. Maybe Gonzalez realized he could do without his muscle man; maybe they quarrelled. Who cares? The SAVAK agent got his face smashed in, was dumped in the water, and Gonzalez set out alone for England.'

'Where he conned you into lending support,' O'Connor muttered.

Cathery reddened, but decided to ignore the comment. 'He needed cover to explain his presence in the area. Anyway, after he arrived up here he watched Detorius, checked on his movements, realized there was a connection with Stanhope and broke into the flat. He found the album. He still had the thing with him when he was picked up by immigration officers, trying to board the ferry to St Malo.'

'What about the album?' DI Farnsby asked, glancing in puzzlement at O'Connor.

Cathery grinned broadly, and his piggy eyes creased in malicious amusement. 'The album he found in the Stanhope apartment? Gonzalez knew Detorius could probably lead him to the manuscript but didn't know how the lawyer had become involved with it. He took a look around the apartment Detorius was paying so much attention to. When he came across the album the photographs inside confirmed his suspicions – gave him the link he needed. The photographs in the album, they contained one of Angela Fenchurch's mother, and one of her father as well.'

'I don't see –'

'Angela Fenchurch's father was the guy Gonzalez told us about, the ex-aide to the Shah, the man who lifted the manuscript finally from the Baghdad Museum. Mohamed Mehti. He gave it to Angela's mother for safekeeping. She sent it to Mrs Fenchurch. As for Angela's mother . . .'

He paused, for effect, his unpleasant grin broadening further. 'Well, she'd serviced the Shah of Persia himself. She'd worked out of Paris: her professional name was Christine. Angela Fenchurch's mother had, in fact, been nothing more than a high-class whore!'

Karen Stannard was silent. She stared at her desk, her green eyes clouded with thought. Beside Arnold, Karl Spedding sat stiffly, saying nothing. At last, Karen asked, 'Does Angela know all this?'

Arnold shook his head. 'I don't know. I don't feel it's really my place . . .'

Surprisingly, after a few moments, Karen sighed, and said, 'No. Maybe I should have a word with her. It'll be a shock . . .'

She placed her hands flat on the desk in front of her; her fingernails were long, but unvarnished. She looked up. 'I think that's all for now. Arnold, you sure you'll be okay now?'

He nodded. 'I'll survive.'

Karen was unable to deny herself a little dig. 'Well, when you get in touch with her again, give my regards to your girlfriend Carmela Cacciatore.'

In the corridor outside Karen's office Karl Spedding paused, turned to Arnold. 'What's about to happen to the manuscript now?'

Arnold pursed his lips. 'I don't know. According to Carmela there's likely to be an enquiry, which will take some time to resolve, to determine just where the artefact will go. Probably back to the Baghdad Museum, now that security has been re-established there. Maybe Angela will get some compensation, which will help resolve her financial difficulties.' He paused, shuffled, eyeing Spedding uncertainly. 'By the way, I owe you an apology.'

Spedding's eyes were hooded, his features without expression. 'For what reason?'

Arnold struggled to find the right words. 'I had thought that perhaps you were . . . well, involved in the hunt for the manuscript.'

Spedding raised his head. His eyes were cold. He faced Arnold, head raised in challenge. 'Now what was leading you to that supposition?'

Arnold scratched his chin awkwardly. 'Well, you were at the auction in Alnwick. You made a bid for the cottage . . .'

His voice died away under Spedding's cold gaze. At last Spedding said, 'I'm living in a small, cramped flat. I've been unable to bring my possessions with me since leaving the Pradak Museum. I enjoy solitude, my own company . . . When I made a bid for that cottage, I was merely looking for a *home*, Mr Landon.'

Arnold's mouth was dry. He began to mumble. 'I'm sorry . . . But there was this whole business of you joining us as well. I mean, to be curator at the Pradak and then come here . . .'

'I'd better make things absolutely clear to you,' Spedding said icily, 'since you seem unable to take matters at face value, or accept what I said at interview. Curator at the Pradak . . . You know what that really meant?' His lips curved into an unpleasant grimace. 'Do you know I was threatened with dismissal on at least three occasions? It was claimed I was unable to get on with my colleagues . . . a suggestion you might be prepared to countenance.'

'I –'

'But in fact the objections of the directors had more to do with my involvement in museum politics, my outspokenness against the museum's power structure. But more than

198

that, there was the matter of the four occasions on which I had sent written memoranda to the museum administration, calling for a change to its acquisitions policy in regard to antiquities. They did not like my drawing their attention to the fact that they were acquiring plundered and smuggled ancient artefacts.' He smiled thinly. 'In the end, when I three times succeeded in appealing successfully against my dismissals – I hired good lawyers – they discussed matters with me and we decided, mutually, that it would be better if they paid me off and I took a job elsewhere. Without a stain on my character, of course. Though leaving doubts, perhaps, in the minds of ungenerous persons . . .'

He began to move away. As he walked down the corridor towards the room which had once been Arnold's he said, over his shoulder, 'You see, Mr Landon, there are people other than your friend Signorina Carmela Cacciatore who are concerned about the illicit trade in looted artefacts from the ancient world . . .'

As Arnold stumped back to his new office as Head of the Department of Museums and Antiquities, he took a deep, dissatisfied breath. He had misunderstood Spedding, jumped to the wrong conclusions, been unjust in his suspicions. But he still couldn't warm to the man.

Grumpily, Arnold considered he was more than ever certain he was not going to enjoy the job that Karen Stannard had bequeathed to him.